MAGIC WAKING

LEGENDS REBORN SERIES #1

EVA CHASE

To the readers who keep the magic alive

I

The day I found my king started with a stomachache.

I stretched on my bed amid the tangle of blanket and sheet, still waking up. The warmth of the sunlight streaming through the narrow window soaked into my skin, but the knot in my stomach didn't loosen. I knew what it meant. My heart thumped.

Today, after twenty years, four months, and six days of searching and waiting—not that I'd been counting or anything—I was going to set eyes on *him* again.

I rolled over and caught sight of a creature I was much less enthusiastic about.

A gloom was lurking under my computer desk. No one else would have been able to distinguish that patch of thicker darkness within the regular shadow, but my magic-touched sight could make out even those mindless scraps of dark intent. I grimaced.

The gloom crept along the wall. When I breathed in deep, its presence prickled at the back of my mouth. Just one couldn't do much damage—and wouldn't bother trying to damage any ordinary human being—but set a whole crowd on the attack and no one would laugh. I'd witnessed swarms like that more times than I cared to remember.

They were the vermin of the dark fae, so I dealt with them the way I'd deal with a cockroach or a rat—extermination.

I sat up in the bed and snapped a twig off the weeping fig in its pot beside the window. A whisper of the living energy nestled inside the wood tingled against my fingers. It would fade by the end of the day, but in the meantime, it held power.

I raised my hand and pointed it at the gloom. My fingers clenched around the twig. "*Darkness begone,*" I murmured in the archaic English of my first existence.

A spark lit within the patch of shadow and spread across its body. In less than a second, it ate away my unwelcome visitor.

The twig had gone dry and dead against my palm. I tossed it into the base of the pot. Technically, I didn't have to be up for another hour, but there was no way I could relax now.

I paced the room and grabbed a pair of jeans and a sweater from a basket of folded laundry. My hair resisted the ponytail I finger-combed it into. Several brown strands slipped free to drift across my face as I ducked to retrieve my sneakers from under the bed.

So what? I was going to see my king today.

No, I wasn't as ready as I wanted to be. I still hadn't figured out how to fix this mess I'd gotten us into—this repeated cycle of lives lived and cut short. I wasn't even sure I could avoid my past mistakes, escape what had happened last time—

My throat constricted. Catching that thought before it could blossom, I balled it up and tossed it away. I'd never been completely ready. But we *were* both still living. At least I'd accomplished that much.

I knelt to pluck several more twigs off the fig's outer branches, stuffed the handfuls into my pockets, and opened my closet.

My wands waited in a shoebox I'd stuffed under winter boots and a spare blanket. I ran my fingers over the smooth sticks. The magic I'd worked on them had sealed their life inside—if I'd left them out in the sun, they'd have started sprouting leaves. I tucked the birch one into my backpack.

To find a pair of gloves, I had to dig through my remaining moving boxes. But it wasn't just glooms and other dark rabble my king would need protection from.

It was also me.

I jammed a thin cotton pair into my back pocket and stepped out of my bedroom, my pulse still jittering.

Priya, my roommate, stood in the kitchen. She was spreading jam on a piece of toast. Her head of sleep-rumpled black hair bobbed up at the sound of my door, and a smile leapt to her face.

"Good morning, Emmaline!" She waved the knife at me with her usual frenetic grace. "Want eggs? I was just thinking I'd fry some up to go with my toast."

No one else called me "Emmaline" except my mom—I always told acquaintances and teachers to stick to "Emma." But Priya had seen my given name when we'd been filling out the lease and declared it one of the most beautiful names she'd ever heard. Somehow I hadn't had the heart to tell her I found it incredibly stuffy. In her cheery voice, it did sound kind of pretty.

I was already smiling back at her despite the twist of impatience inside me. Priya's boundless enthusiasm made it difficult to be irritated at her, which was probably why we were tentatively becoming friends. I hadn't been in the habit of making many of those—in this life or those prior.

"Thanks, but I think I'll stick to toast," I said. "Leave the jam out?" Food derived from animals didn't always sit well in my stomach. No need to add to my supernatural indigestion.

Priya chattered about an article she'd read for her politics course and her theories about the latest episode of a TV show we'd been watching while I gulped down my quick breakfast. Normally, I'd have contributed more. As I swallowed my last bite, Priya tilted her head.

"Something's bothering you," she said. "What's up?"

I might not have been perfect at hiding my emotions, but I had centuries of practice at lying. After all, there weren't many situations in which I *could* be truthful about being the reincarnation of a legendary sorcerer. People tended to get twitchy about even one part of that equation.

Downplaying worked better than flat-out denial. "It's nothing major," I said with a shrug. "Lab report due for a prof who seems like a tough one."

Priya nodded, accepting my explanation unquestioningly. No amount of practice stopped the little jab of guilt I felt at seeing that.

"I'm sure you've got it in the bag. You work *too* hard."

"New school, new expectations," I said. "I'll worry less once I'm into the swing of things."

I tugged on my gloves as soon as I stepped out onto the street. Thank the light the October weather was just nippy enough that wearing them didn't look totally bizarre. My gaze flitted over the streets the whole way to campus, my skin prickling at every shift in the breeze. I couldn't be sure of anything about *him* except he'd be the same age as me. He might not even be a *he* in this incarnation. Unlike me, with my regular flipping back and forth, he usually arrived male, but I could never be sure.

When my eyes hit him, I'd know him, no matter what.

At the edge of campus, a broad lawn stretched toward the sprawl of three- and four-story buildings, the older old-fashioned brick ones skirted by modern concrete additions. The view sent a jolt through my chest, even though I'd seen it dozens of times now.

It was the same image that had swam into my head and prompted me to transfer here for junior year—after skimming through page after page of internet search results before figuring out where my capricious psychic ability was pointing me.

My nerves jumped every time someone new walked by me, but I went through classes, lunch, and more classes without any revelations. I ducked into the change room to prepare for fencing practice with more than a little relief. Feinting and parrying would burn off some of my tension.

"Advanced learners, split off into pairs to spar," Coach ordered after the warm-up exercises. I nodded to the guy standing next to me. We stepped to the side and began a conversation between our training blades. With each tap and dodge, a grin crept farther across my face behind the dark mesh of my protective mask.

Once upon a time, I could have been called clumsy, especially when asked to handle a weapon. That was exactly why I'd decided to take up fencing when I had the chance. After many lives worth of drills, the moves were starting to come naturally to me. I was stronger and more coordinated than I'd ever been.

Which didn't mean I was infallible. My partner lunged, I swung to block his strike, and a low, rolling laugh carried from the doorway several feet behind me. The sound smacked into me, knocking the breath from my lungs. My arm wavered, and my opponent's saber caught my hand. My fingers twitched apart as I yanked them out of the way. My own saber flipped through the air and nearly speared the guy standing in the doorway.

He stepped back without a flinch. My weapon clattered to the floor. The guy raised his eyes. They were a blue so striking I could identify it even at a distance, so deep it was almost indigo. He gave me a cocky smile and ran his hand over his sun-streaked blond hair. The muscles in his arm flexed against the sleeve of his fitted raglan shirt.

Every muscle in *my* body had frozen. Recognition sang through my every cell on a level beneath thought, beneath memory.

A level the guy in front of me clearly wasn't aware of yet. No hint of shock crossed his face. I looked no different to him than any of the other fencers in our training gear. While *I* was born knowing who we were, my spell kept my king's memories locked inside his mind… for now.

"I hope you're normally more coordinated than that." He nudged the saber back toward me with his foot. "I don't want to have to worry about being impaled every time I come into the room."

An echo of his voice from our first lives rang through my head. *Gods, you're more likely to impale* me *than the enemy.* Those words had been spoken in affectionate jest, not this guy's distant cool. The quiver of excitement that had been racing through me dimmed.

This incarnation of my king was a jackass.

The difference was so jarring I couldn't help bristling. "My coordination is infinitely improved when people aren't making sudden loud sounds in the training area," I said. "And you could simply not come in."

He hesitated, blinking at me. Before I'd spoken I bet he hadn't even realized he was talking to a girl. I took advantage of his silence to stride over and retrieve my saber.

Two other figures were peering into the room beside the new guy—the friends he'd been laughing with. A lanky black guy, who had a couple inches on my critic's already-formidable height, elbowed him with a rakish grin. A willowy girl with pale auburn tresses stood at Mr. Blond's other side, hugging her cardigan over her gauzy maxi dress. She squeezed his forearm in apparent reassurance, and something wrenched in my chest.

She was his girlfriend, no doubt. Well, why *wouldn't* he have a girlfriend with those looks? That was a good thing. His off-putting attitude was a good thing. Every reminder I could get to keep my distance, emotionally and physically, was a gift.

I existed to be his mage, to get him out of the snarl I'd created with my magic. Anything more risked us both, as I'd had ample opportunity to discover before.

That pinching in my chest was not jealousy. Not even a little bit.

"Have fun, Darton," the rakish friend said with a playful salute. "Return to us with all your parts intact." The girlfriend shook her head at him, and they headed off. The new guy—my king who didn't yet know he was my king—strode in to talk to Coach. I studied his shadow to confirm no glooms were tailing him and rejoined my sparring partner after Coach ambled over.

Darton. Funny how in every life something of our essence wove even into the names each set of parents granted us. A sound or a syllable carried from our origins.

At least by all appearances, he hadn't started to wake up on his own. As long as I could keep it that way, I had time to finally set things right.

My blade rapped against my opponent's, and Coach's voice traveled to my ears. "You're here to become a better quarterback?" His tone was skeptical and amused.

"I want to up my game," Darton said. "Coach Michner says my weakest area is dexterity. Fencing sounded like an enjoyable way to work on that. Is that a problem?"

"No," Coach said. "We don't have any requirement that you're devoted to the art. I *will* expect you to respect it—and to show up for practices on time."

A smile curled my lips behind my mask. Darton sounded a tad chastened in his reply.

"Right. Of course."

Coach believed in fencers staying fully suited up for practice so we were as comfortable as possible with the equipment we'd wear in competition, so they walked off to get Darton prepared. I felt his movements through the room with a faint tickling over my skin. My sparring partner disarmed me twice. I'd just paused to take a breath and regroup when Coach headed back our way, Darton in tow.

"Emma is one of our most experienced members,"

Coach was saying. "Since you two have already 'met,' I'll have her lead you through the basic warm-up."

My back stiffened. He often asked senior members to teach the junior ones, but it hadn't occurred to me he'd come to me, now, with this. Sodding hell. Darton was already eyeing me. If I acted cagey for no obvious reason, I'd draw his attention even more.

If I was careful, the risk of skin-to-skin physical contact was minimal. The other risks, which had to do with the heart pounding away in my chest, I'd just have to deal with.

I drew myself up straighter and tucked my one bare hand deeper into my sleeve. "Sure, I can take him through the paces."

Darton raised his eyebrow at me. "Don't worry. I'll keep up."

He did, which was a relief because it meant I didn't need to get close to adjust his position. It was also an annoyance, because I could hear him getting smugger with each comment he tossed out. He'd been a master with a broadsword way back when. It wasn't surprising he'd pick up fencing quickly. But that didn't mean I had to like how this unaware incarnation talked about it.

"So why do people get into this as a hobby anyway?" he asked when we paused after the first set of exercises.

"You mean if they're not just using it to make them better at some other sport?" I said. "Fencing is a sport too, FYI."

He'd pulled his mask up, so I saw the disbelieving face he made. "You can't say it's the *same*. And it's not as if you're likely to end up in a sword fight outside this room."

I restrained myself from asking how often he got into

tackling fights with people off the football field and motioned for him to turn so we could start a two-person drill. "Some of us find the practice enjoyable regardless of how 'useful' it is. If you commit, you'll find it's intensive training for the body and the mind. You're not going to feel the full effect if you come at it like a tourist."

To give the guy credit, he took that critique in stride. He followed my instructions through several parrying sequences in silent concentration.

"Maybe I will get more into the training for its own sake," he remarked. "Now that we're on to the actual fighting, I can see the fun factor."

He chuckled and picked up his pace. Did he really think ten minutes of practice was enough to justify pushing a senior student's limits? My king might have always been talented, but he'd also had some humility.

I matched Darton beat for beat. Back and forth, back and forth—

He broke the pattern. His saber swiped at my padded shoulder.

My pulse stuttered, but I kept my footing as I sidestepped. I whipped my blade around his and flicked it up. His saber slipped from his grasp. It clanged to the floor at his feet much as mine had half an hour ago.

"Hey," he protested. I lowered my blade, leaving my mask on. Coach was already sending some of the other members off to the change room. We were done here.

"You *never* start sparring without getting your training partner's okay first," I said. "And if you don't want to make a fool of yourself, get the basics down before you start escalating."

I stalked away before Darton could say anything in

response. My legs had gone shaky.

How was I going to keep enough distance with him hanging around fencing practice three days a week? I'd found my king all right, and he was already proving more trouble than glooms and visions combined.

2

"Since when are you into football anyway?" Priya asked. She leaned back against the bleachers with a knowing smile. We were sitting near the top where I figured the players on the field would be less likely to notice us. The October wind tugged at the jacket I'd pulled on over today's sweater. For a "windbreaker," it wasn't living up to its name.

I hunched my shoulders against the early morning chill. "I enjoy sports." That was true, in moderation. "I just thought it might be fun to try something new."

"Like freezing our asses off watching our home team face off against itself?" Priya's smile widened. The cool weather didn't seem to faze her at all.

"I heard they're pretty good." Also true, from my hasty research last night where I'd dug up whatever I could find out about Darton's schedule. "I figured I'd check them out before I commit to watching a whole game."

"Mmm," Priya said. "Now I think we're getting somewhere. *Check them out*, huh? I don't suppose there's any one particular hunk of manhood down there you're focusing on?"

I wrinkled my nose at her. "No. They're all the same

to me."

Technically, I wasn't here to *check out* Darton on the field. I was just… keeping an eye on him. As long as the soul inside him stayed dormant, the glooms and various other lesser creatures of darkness wouldn't be drawn to him. But I needed to figure out what his normal looked like and be around often enough to notice when he *did* start to awaken. If he woke up and the glooms caught on first—

I swallowed hard. It was not going to happen that way this time.

Football practice had crappy timing, but it was one of the few places I'd be able to observe Darton without sticking out like a sore thumb. And without catching his attention. I'd already done that far too well in fencing practice yesterday. Thank the light for masks.

Here, at least fifty other spectators were scattered throughout the stands—mostly friends and girlfriends of the players, I guessed. The rakish guy and the willowy girl who'd followed Darton to fencing club were sitting on the lowest tier with a few other guys who must have been part of Darton's larger entourage.

On the field, Darton broke from a skirmish to dash across the goal line. "All right," the willowy girl shouted with a clap of her hands. "Nice one, Art!"

My head twitched at the nickname. She called him *Art*, did she? I wouldn't be surprised if all his friends did. That was almost funny. And yet, it made my gloved hands clench. I tucked them deeper into my pockets.

I had no claim on him, not the kind she might. I couldn't let myself *want* that kind of claim. Even when I got that wish fulfilled, it only ever made our lives fall apart faster.

Priya tossed her dark hair back from her face. "*I* had a crush on one of the wide receivers for a couple months last year. I went to a bunch of games so I could... *appreciate* his performance. It's nothing to be ashamed about. We're only human after all. If there is a guy down there you think you might like to know more about, you can always pick my brain."

I considered her offer as the players rearranged themselves into a new formation. Maybe Priya did know something useful. She'd been at this school two years longer than I had, after all. I'd just throw her off the scent a bit.

"What's the story with the guy with the bad leg?" I nodded to the running back who'd started limping about fifteen minutes into practice and was now on the bench massaging his calf.

"Marco Castaneda," Priya said. "Sophomore. Everyone thought he was on track to making quarterback until he got twisted up bad in a tackle halfway through last season. He was out for the rest of the year. I guess he got the okay to give it another shot. Either way, he'll be fine. I've heard his real passion is computers, and he's already got a gig lined up with Google."

I laughed at her speedy recitation. "You really do have the deets. Okay. How about linebacker number fifty-one?" The large, dark-skinned guy appeared to be the most boisterous on the team, bouncing off the ground and bellowing a victory cheer whenever his side in the practice exercises "won."

Priya cocked her head. "That's Tommy Franklin. He's a senior but only joined the team last year. The guys were kind of standoffish with him until he started hosting parties at his apartment, but now he's everyone's fave."

"Are you sure you were just 'checking out' and not actively stalking these guys?" I nudged her teasingly, and she bumped her shoulder back against mine in retaliation. The moment felt so blissfully normal—like I really was just a college junior joking around with a friend I wasn't keeping any deep dark secrets from—that the next question rolled off my tongue without any hesitation at all.

"What about the quarterback, then?"

I didn't think I'd let my voice or my expression change, but Priya's eyes immediately sharpened. She glanced at the field and then back at me. "Oh, is *that* who you're hung up on?"

I gave her my best bewildered look. "Why are you fixating on him? You didn't think I was head over heels for Marco or Tommy."

"It's a sixth sense." Priya waggled a finger at me. "I'd ask why *you're* fixating on him, but it's really not that hard a question to answer. Darton Rowe, star quarterback and all-around golden boy. He's good looking, rich, dean's list worthy, and a respected athlete—what's not to like?"

With a resume like that, no wonder he was cocky. "Maybe he's the one *you* have a crush on," I muttered.

"Had," Priya said. "And nope. My guy graduated, more's the pity. But I can still applaud your excellent taste in men. I'm pretty sure Darton is single right now, you know. He's got a rep for being a bit, ah, picky, but I bet you could turn his head if you tried."

She contemplated my face with an intentness that made me squirm. "I'm not interested in turning his head," I insisted, although the "single" remark had grabbed my attention. I couldn't see how to ask about the girl cheering him on from the stands without giving away my interest.

It shouldn't matter anyway.

Priya arched her eyebrows at me. I waved her skepticism away and swiveled back toward the field.

Practice was wrapping up. The coach had called a huddle, but several of the guys were already taking off their helmets. Darton's hair caught the sunlight even damp with sweat, flaxen strands glinting amid the darker gold. It was almost the same shade in this incarnation as it'd been when I'd first met my king, all those centuries ago. My mouth went dry.

The coach finished talking, and the guys jogged to the edge of the field. The spectators around us started getting up. Darton's friends gathered around him as he gulped from a bottle of water.

I pushed to my feet, swung my backpack over my shoulder, and turned to head to the opposite end of the bleachers, where I could climb down without risking crossing paths with him. The less he saw me without a fencing mask on, the better.

Priya grabbed my arm. "Where are you going?" she said, her voice low. Her eyes gleamed. "You should go down and say hi! Look, he's coming right this way."

Darton and his entourage were ambling along with the apparent intention of skirting our side of the bleachers. I shook my head. "I don't want to say hi, Pri. I'm not into him. Really."

She gave me a light tug. "Oh, come on. Don't chicken out on me. I can tell you're at least curious. He won't bite."

I wasn't so sure about that, given he'd come at me

with a blade yesterday. And it was beside the point.

"I've got to get to class. Maybe another time." I made a mental note *not* to let Priya invite herself along next time.

"Emmaline," Priya pleaded. At the same moment, a guy a few rows below us dropped his phone with a clatter. He swore loudly. Darton, who was just coming around the stands with his friends, glanced up. My pulse stuttered. One flick to the right and his gaze would hit me.

I spun around and jerked against Priya's grasp—just as she let me go of her own accord. "All right, all right, have it your way."

The unnecessary force I'd put into breaking free propelled me backward. I stumbled, and my back slammed into the rusty guardrail. It must have weakened over the years after holding up however many drunken sports fans, because it didn't hold *me* up. With a squeal, the bar popped out of its frame. I tumbled past it over the edge.

The twenty-foot drop to the ground didn't give me a whole lot of time to think, so it was a good thing I'd had centuries to hone my instincts. My heart lurched, but my lips spat out a few quick words. One of the twigs in my pocket disintegrated.

The pillow of air I'd called into being caught me. I still hit the ground, but the impact jarred my body without breaking any bones. If I'd cushioned myself any more, it would have been obvious to anyone observing that something unnatural had happened.

My breath had jolted out of me. My head spun. I blinked at the grass beside my face as my awareness caught up with my instinctive reactions.

Well, that was one way to make a quick exit.

Someone was yelling. Multiple people, actually. I

pushed into a sitting position, and a rush of dizziness washed over me. Before I could find my bearings to stand, the one guy I'd been trying my best to avoid leaned over me.

"Are you all right?" Darton asked. From the flush on his face, he must have run over. His friends and a few other players were coming up behind him.

I groped for my inner poise. "Um. Yeah."

He offered his hand to help me up, but I was already scrambling to my feet. My legs wobbled. Damn it.

Darton caught my arm to steady me, and I had to stiffen to keep from flailing away like a maniac. Heat washed through my body. Only two layers of fabric lay between his bare hand and my skin. Two thin shields holding off disaster.

I stepped backward, and Darton let go. He was eyeing me with concern. I met those intense blue eyes for as little time as I felt I could get away with while appearing convincingly stable. "I'm okay." I was reaching for an excuse to hightail it out of there when Priya dashed over from the stands. She'd taken the longer, safer route down.

"Thank God!" She came to a stop beside me and looked me up and down. "I was terrified. The school needs to do better maintenance on those bleachers."

"No kidding." I rubbed the elbow that had taken a sizable portion of the impact. My hip was aching.

Priya's attention shifted to the guy in front of me. An unnerving spark lit in her eyes.

"Thank you for racing over so quickly to help," she said to Darton in her most chipper voice. "I'm Priya."

"Darton." He gave her a brief nod, but his gaze slid right back to me. Expectantly. Oh, swine crud and cattle sod. I *really* shouldn't have let Priya come with me.

I could have admitted we'd already met. But maybe he'd never figure that out. If he found out now, it was only going to fix my face more firmly in his memory.

"Emmaline," I said quickly, hoping he wouldn't make the connection to the "Emma" Coach had directed him to yesterday. "And yeah. Thank you. I, ah—I've got a class to get to—"

"Then you'll want this." Darton's rakish friend scooped up my backpack, which had rolled a few feet away, and handed it to me with a sly grin. "I'm Keevan. Kudos on the impressive fall. You took it like a champ."

I wasn't entirely sure that was a compliment. "Thanks."

Darton frowned. "Are you *sure* you're okay? If you need a hand getting to the campus medical center…"

I couldn't help being touched by his refusal to let the situation go, as inconvenient as it was. The guy wasn't a total ass. Nevertheless, I didn't want his hands anywhere near my vicinity. That kind of touching was severely inadvisable.

"One-hundred-percent injury free." I took a step to the side to show off my now-steady feet. "Guess I was lucky."

"Really lucky," Darton's maybe-girlfriend murmured.

Darton's frown turned puzzled. The back of my neck prickled.

My voice. The fencing mask would have muffled it a little, but that didn't mean he *couldn't* notice the similarity. I had to get out of there before he put two and two together.

"Well, ah, hopefully we won't meet this way again." I

offered a brisk wave of my hand and took off.

I'd only made it two steps before Priya caught up with me. She leaned in conspiratorially. "At least you did get to talk to him. He knows who you are now. That was a pretty memorable entrance."

"Yeah." That was the problem. Even if Darton didn't connect the girl who'd fallen from the bleachers to his sharp-tongued fencing partner, he'd recognize me now. My responsibilities had gotten ten times harder in the space of a second.

3

The crushed Himalayan salt rattled into the glass bowl. I opened the baggy of dried ague root and poured it over the rough crystals. The faintly tart odor tickled my nose. I kneaded the powder and salt together. The damp afternoon breeze drifted over me, but the hedge at the edge of the campus grounds held the worst of the wind away from my spell-making.

The pages in the leather-bound book spread open beside me fluttered. They were crisp and yellowed, knowledge recorded more than a hundred years ago in some other life I only retained a few hazy memories of. I'd retrieved it from my storage locker an hour ago. My recollection of my lives after the first might be hazy, but the magical beacons I'd set in place each time always led me back to my stash of scribblings.

Looking at those stacks of supplies and journals, the oldest of them long since crumbled, always left me cranky. They made a thorough record of my failures. All the lives cut so short because I'd slipped up somewhere. All the lifetimes in which I hadn't been able to untangle the spell that was drawing the dark rabble to us and keeping us locked in this cycle.

Not again. This time, I'd do everything right.

I pulled a wand from my bag and pointed it at the mixture in the bowl. The words in the old tongue rolled from my throat. "*When fae darkness crosses, witness and tremble.*"

A shiver ran through the wand and up my arm. The tingle of life in the stick dulled. Soon, this wand would be nothing more than dead wood, which was why I'd brought backups.

I straightened up and scanned the grounds. I'd picked a spot secluded enough that no one would have seen or heard the details of my preparations, but a group of girls—freshmen, I'd bet, by their giddy nervous energy—was ambling down the drive toward the entrance. A couple of them shot me curious glances.

I had the entire property to circle. No way was I pulling that off without drawing some notice.

Normally, I'd have waited and cast magic like this on a Monday in the wee hours of the morning, after the weekend partiers were finally asleep and before the early birds were up for breakfast. But now that Darton was somewhat aware of my existence, I needed protective measures in place that *didn't* require having him in my line of sight. I was just lucky that it appeared he mostly studied, worked out, and slept on the college's grounds.

I was going to have to come up with other plans for his away games and for Thanksgiving, when I figured he'd probably make a trip home. If we survived that long.

For now, I just needed to avoid looking so sketchy that someone called campus security. I studied the traffic roaring along the road on the other side of the hedge, as if

I were waiting for a specific car, until the girls had passed me by. Then I gestured the wand toward myself and muttered a few words to deflect attention.

The wand's core shuddered and crumbled. The last of my words tugged right into my body. It was too late to reach for one of my spares. Sod it. I pushed the thump of my pulse and the light of life that flowed through my blood into the casting. A prickle raced over my skin, and the light around me rippled. I tossed away the dead wand.

No one would give me a second glance now. And if I'd put a day or two of this body's life into the casting, oh well. I wasn't likely to make it to old age anyway.

I grabbed one of the other two wands I had on me and palmed a handful of the herbed salt. "*When fae darkness crosses, witness and tremble,*" I murmured, sprinkling the mixture in a thin trail on the ground. I walked ten paces, sprinkled some more, and repeated the incantation. The wand twitched in my hand with each casting. It wasn't practical to lay the salt in a completely unbroken line, but if I kept the gaps small enough, any passing glooms—or more dangerous creatures of darkness—would trigger the warning.

My second wand died in my hand about halfway around campus. I'd expected to get more out of it—I must not have sealed that one well. I paused to catch my breath. Even when I used the energy in the wands to charge my magic, the focus necessary tired me out after a while. I might as well take a moment to check on a project of sorts I'd started before my encounter with Darton.

A gloom was squirming amid a clump of trees near the campus border, not far from the athletic department's track. "Hello, Carl," I said. Not that glooms had names, but it looked like a Carl to me. The clot of darkness roiled as it pushed against the magical binding I'd laid around it.

I brushed my hand over the sealing spell and frowned. The woven energy was starting to fray, worn down by the gloom's struggle to escape. It might take years, but the spell would eventually crumble and let this shred of darkness go free.

Balls. I'd hoped that new combination of words, herbs, and wood might create a permanent effect. Back to the drawing board. There had to be a way I could re-seal our true enemy that didn't rely on mine and my king's lives maintaining the balance.

There had better be, or I was never going to break this eternal cycle, not without freeing that enemy and bringing on my king's final death.

"I'm sorry, but I don't think we can stay friends any longer," I informed the gloom as I drew out my final wand.

"*Darkness begone*," I muttered, and Carl contracted into nothing. I turned away, my chest tight.

I'd captured the greatest dark fae of them all once. I'd kept her sealed away from humankind for fifteen hundred years. I *had* to be capable of doing it again, just a little differently.

Of course, it would have helped if I understood how I'd managed to create the first seal. I hadn't exactly been thinking clearly in the moment.

I charted a course past a couple making out against a maintenance shed, around the track and the bleachers where the railing that had broken off was now tied with yellow caution tape, and back to the hedge. Only a handful of salt remained when I reached the main entrance. I tipped that into a small silk bag and tied off the ribbon that closed it.

A tremble ran down my back as I raised the wand to lock the last bit of the incantation in place. I'd pushed myself to lay down the casting quickly, and I was paying for it now. But it was almost done. I'd handled far worse.

"*When fae darkness crosses, witness and tremble,*" I said one last time. The quiver of energy in the wand snuffed out. I shoved some of my own life's power after it. My nerves wrenched—and that was when the vision hit me.

They never came quietly. The world before me tore apart with a rush of spiraling darkness. My stomach lurched. The shapes before my mind's eye whirled as if I were falling... tumbling straight down toward a sprawl of forest.

Toward a small grove of trees surrounded by the patches of vibrant autumn reds and yellows. The vision slowed, and I stared. Blackened patches spread across the branches where the bark had disintegrated. The leaves that sprouted from them dangled brown and shriveled. The grass that was matted around the trees roots lay limp and gray. A chill permeated the air through the grove, so thick it penetrated the body my mind had left behind.

I shivered, and a fresh rush of darkness loomed like a fog rolling over me, icy cold as it spread down my throat and into my lungs—

I came to on my back on the campus lawn, gasping for breath. For a few seconds, the blue sky stretched above me struck me as impossibly bright, fake as plastic. I dragged in the cool, clear air and coughed.

My visions never offered much help, either. I had no idea where that cluster of trees was or when it would matter. I didn't even know what their existence signified. All I could say in the wake of the dread still crawling over my skin was that whatever had harmed them meant to do the same to me and all other things living.

* * *

When I was growing up—the first time, centuries ago—I'd only ever gotten brief flashes of feeling, barely even an image, there and then gone. So when my first *real* vision came, knocking me off my feet and flooding my mind, I couldn't ignore it. I saw a young man, fair and strong with the sun glowing off his face and the walls of his castle behind him, and I knew it was time to go.

My father wasn't so sure, even though he'd always said I was to volunteer my service to the king's son— eventually. "I thought we would wait until you were a little older," he told me. "The prince won't be king for some time yet. There's no good to come from rushing in."

"It's not rushing," I said. "I need to go, now." The vision had told me that as clearly as if it had spoken words. Whatever purpose I was to carry out, it was meant to begin, and I didn't have much patience for dithering. In that way, at least, I was completely my father's son.

In the end, Father nodded his pale head, squeezed my shoulder—we were never a hugging sort of family—and wished me luck as I packed a few possessions to bring with me.

I set out with total certainty, even though I knew sod-all about the current king and the son I intended to serve. My light fae community in the woods did not mingle much with humankind. Father had told me generalities—that the king was the most respected in generations, that nearly everyone considered him to be fair but firm, and that his son, though only a year older than me, had already started making a name for *him*self with his willingness to pitch in when ordinary folk were in need. That was the limit of my understanding.

My feet, seeming to know where to take me without any consultation needed, carried me to a town a few hours' ride from the castle. I came across a group of townspeople assembled in a courtyard on the outskirts. The prince's golden hair gleamed in their midst.

He was in the middle of explaining his plan to stop a gang of marauders who'd been thieving along the highways. His hands swept with passionate gestures mixed with the occasional joking remark, and his audience listened in obvious awe. I'd missed most of the explanation—he was just finishing.

The townspeople dispersed with enthusiasm. A few of the locals took note of me, the stranger in their midst, with wary glances. I hesitated at the edge of the courtyard. The prince walked apart from his guard to examine a cart that might have been part of his plan, so I pushed myself forward.

I strode up to him and dropped to one knee, bowing my head. "Your Highness," I said, "if I might speak with you."

The prince let out a sound somewhere between a cough and a laugh. "Of course, good fellow. Speak as much as you wish. But I'd rather you did it standing face to face with me."

His smile, small but warm, told me he meant that, so I got to my feet. "I've heard many remarkable things about you and your father," I told him with a directness that probably should have embarrassed *me*. "I admire the way you look out for your people and the good you've already done for them. I've traveled a long distance in the hopes that I can be of use to you. I'll take on whatever job you'll assign me, as long as it helps you with your work."

He blinked, and I had enough wits to realize my compliments had affected him, even as well as he'd kept his composure. I hadn't realized yet how rarely the over-awed ordinary folk spoke to him directly or how measured his father was with praise.

I hadn't quite decided during my journey there whether I should reveal my magic right away or slowly hint at it. I didn't have many skills that would be useful to a prince otherwise, but magic was the domain of my fae heritage, not my human side, and I'd heard enough stories to be aware that even the best people sometimes responded... poorly to what they didn't understand.

But the prince didn't ask for any proof of my skills. He clapped me on the back, grinned, and said, "With an attitude like that, I'm sure we can find plenty of ways for you to contribute. For a start, how about we carry these casks of wine to the inn? No one will think much of my generosity if I don't provide a drink to go with the meal I've arranged."

Was it the grin and the light it brought into his eyes? The way he went straight to *we* as if we were already allies? Or maybe the fact that he'd not only come to the town to deal with the marauders, but had also gifted them with a feast as well? All three combined, no doubt. In any case, I'd looked back at him with a grin of my own, and just like that, if I was being honest, I'd already prepared to follow my king-to-be to the ends of the Earth.

* * *

Fifteen hundred years later, I sat up on the grass beside the campus entrance and pressed my hands against my face. So many years had passed since that day, and yet I could still bring the taste of that wine and the tenor of his voice back in an instant.

I'd followed my liege so much farther than the ends of the Earth since then. I'd watched him die and followed him into death a hundred times. And still, the closest thing I had to answers were ominous visions that might as well have been blotches in a Rorschach test.

"It can't keep going like this, Arthur," I said to the ground, to the air, to the soul locked inside the unknowing young man sitting in a classroom right now. "We *have* to end it."

If only I had the slightest idea how.

4

My sparring partner lowered her foil. "Normally you'd never let me through like that. Where's your head at, Emma?"

I grimaced behind my mask. "Sorry. I'll try to stay more focused."

We resumed our stances. I stepped forward with a testing feint, but my mind still wasn't completely on the duel. A significant sliver of my attention stayed trained on the open doorway to the gymnasium—the one Darton hadn't yet walked through, even though practice was halfway over.

I'd managed to keep tabs on him here and there over the last week. There hadn't been any signs worthy of alarm. I'd watched him head into his Modern Social Theory course a few hours ago. So where in darkness was he? He'd shown up on time for the last three practices.

I might not have been so edgy if the chill of that creepy vision of the rotting trees hadn't still been hanging over me.

After a few quick back-and-forths, I found my rhythm enough to score the winning point. I lowered my saber and rolled my shoulders, sweat beading under my uniform.

"I'm going to grab a drink," I said, and my partner nodded.

In the hall, I pushed up my mask and gulped from the water fountain. I was just straightening up when a familiar baritone voice carried from around the corner. My heart leapt, and I tugged my fencing mask back on.

Whoever Darton had been talking to must have headed in a different direction, because he came around the corner alone. I should have ignored him and walked back into the gym. Unfortunately, my tongue had other ideas.

"Practice started forty minutes ago," I said.

A challenging glint leapt into his eyes, but his expression was otherwise regretful. "I know. I had to talk to a professor who has limited office hours, and the conversation went long…" His mouth curved at a teasing angle. "Were you hoping you'd seen the last of me?"

"It seemed like a possibility." I hadn't forgotten how uninvested he'd acted when I'd led him through the warm-up that first day.

He cocked his head. "Do you figure I'm the type to just give up on things?"

Was he goading me or bothered I might think that? His deep blue eyes fixed on mine even though he couldn't have made out more than the vague shape of them through my mask, and a memory flashed through my mind. A memory of a young man not that much older than the one in front of me adjusting a crown that hadn't yet sat easily on his head, but with eyes as intent and his jaw set firm as he'd prepared to speak to his people. My chest clenched.

"I'm reserving judgment for now," I said as tartly as I could manage. "It's Coach's opinion you should be worried about."

I headed to the far end of the gym on my own. Better that I stick to solitary practice for the rest of the hour in my current state of mind.

Even as I ran myself through a series of footwork drills, my gaze kept drifting to Darton. Maybe I'd been a touch harder on him than he'd deserved. Coach had obviously accepted his explanation with full grace—he was taking Darton through some of the paces. And the flexing of Darton's muscles, the careful attention with which he moved, told me he was putting every effort into following Coach's directions accurately. When he slipped up, he didn't laugh it off. He immediately tried again.

Something about his stance at certain moments looked off to me, though. I couldn't quite pinpoint the problem. A sort of stiffness when he turned at the waist? Or was I just making up excuses to study that well-built body even longer? I tugged my gaze away.

"All right, folks," Coach called out. "Great work today." He turned to Darton. "I can stay a little longer if you want to make up for your lost time."

"Thanks," Darton said with what sounded like honest gratitude. "I'd appreciate that."

I left my mask on until the last moment, hurrying into the change room as soon as I'd set it on the rack. I intended to leave surreptitiously as I had every practice before, but when I slipped into the hall a few minutes later, I nearly bumped into Darton's willowy, auburn-haired maybe-girlfriend. I caught myself just shy of colliding with her. She glanced over, and her face lit with recognition.

"Oh! You're—it was Emmaline, right?"

Swine crud. I pasted on my most agreeable smile. "Actually, I prefer Emma." I might as well set that much right.

"You're still okay after that fall?"

"Completely. I probably used up my luck for the year."

She chuckled, a heartier sound than the airy giggle I'd have expected. "I'm Izzy. You're in fencing club? I didn't realize you already knew Darton."

And straight into dangerous territory we went. "I didn't," I said quickly. "I mean, we hadn't really talked. He hasn't been around that long."

"Right, of course." She smiled back at me, so genuinely that guilt tweaked my gut. Not enough that I didn't wish this conversation was over, though.

Izzy looked toward the gym doorway, where she'd probably been headed. The sound of tapping blades drifted through it. "I thought practice would be over by now. Darton promised he'd look over a project of mine."

My gaze followed hers as I reached for an excuse. Coach was taking Darton through some of the footwork exercises I'd been doing earlier. I opened my mouth—and Darton hesitated with that stiffness at his waist again. The words I'd been going to say halted in my throat. There *was* something wrong. I edged a little closer, keeping enough distance that I didn't think he'd get much of a look at me if he happened to turn this way.

"He got here late, so he's just getting a little extra practice in," I said in answer to Izzy's last comment. My eyes stayed trained on Darton. Was that a bit of a wince as he stepped to the side?

Izzy ambled right up to the doorway. "It's more complicated than I realized. I mean, I thought fencing was mostly about what you did with the sword, not so much your feet and all that."

"Everything about your stance supports your weapon," I said automatically. I'd only heard that from Coach about a thousand times. "Anyway, you can't expect an opponent to stay still, so you have to know how to move after or away from them."

"Of course." At the corner of my vision, Izzy's pale cheeks pinkened. She was pretty in the gentle, doe-eyed manner my king had often been drawn to. A question I really had no business asking fell from my mouth.

"How long have you two been together?"

"Oh, we're not—I mean, we *were*, for a little while, but that was last year." Izzy rubbed her mouth. "We gave it a try, but it turned out we're better as friends."

I stifled the spark of relief that shot up inside me at that revelation. It didn't make any difference to what I had to do. And *she* still wanted more than that. The longing quivered off her as she gazed into the gym. She was waiting for her second chance.

"Sorry," I said. Suddenly, I really was. It was only a matter of time before Darton started waking up, and then he wouldn't be the guy she'd fallen for anymore. If I didn't get my act together and figure out how to get us out of this cursed spiral, she wouldn't have him as *anything* for much longer than that. "I just assumed."

"No, it's fine," she said with a little laugh, but then her brow knit. "It isn't at all *dangerous*, is it? The fencing? To be going at each other with swords and all…"

I had to laugh at that suggestion. "Not anywhere near as dangerous as football. Between the masks, the gloves, and the padding in the uniforms, we're well protected. And the training weapons aren't even sharp. It's not really *fighting*, just sport." Which maybe was why I could stomach it better than the swordplay of long ago.

"Well, that's a relief." Izzy shook her head. "Football is kind of scary, isn't it? Concussions and sprains. But there's no way he's ever giving *that* up. Boys!"

Coach had added the movements of the epée to the footwork exercise, and darkness take me if Darton wasn't picking it up like a pro. He moved with an elegant precision I wouldn't have anticipated from a football player, but then, he wasn't just that. Darton was a king at his core, even if he didn't know it yet. In that moment, it radiated from his every movement. Watching him made my breath catch.

Coach swung around to the right. Darton moved to copy him—and stumbled. He halted, his chest heaving, and my breath stopped altogether. Izzy leaned forward, the furrow on her brow deepening.

"What happened?" Coach said, his even voice bouncing off the high ceiling.

Darton made a face. "I don't know. I don't think it's because of the training. I've been feeling a bit—since this morning—"

He pressed his free hand to his abdomen, slightly to the left, just below where his rib cage would end. I swallowed hard. Icy fingers clamped around my heart. No. It couldn't be.

"I must have bruised a muscle or strained something without realizing it during yesterday's game," Darton was saying. I stepped backward. My legs wobbled, and Izzy's gaze darted to me. My expression must have given away a little of my horror, because hers softened with concern.

"Are you all right?"

"Yes," I choked out. "I just remembered something I need to take care of. I'll see you around."

I took off before anything else could tumble out of my mouth. The chill seeped through the rest of my body as I hurried toward the outer doors. In the back of my head, I was still seeing Darton standing there with his hand pressed to his side.

To the spot on his side where, hundreds of years ago, the Darkest One had driven her shadowy blade in to the hilt. The ring of her cackle as my king's body had slumped echoed through my memory. A red splotch had clawed across the fabric of the tunic beneath his split chainmail, dark and deadly, at the same time the color had leached from his face. And I'd hurled out the words, conjured the power, that had set everything since in motion.

That moment was where it all ended, and where it all began. But none of his past incarnations had shown a physical connection to that past injury. I'd have noted it somewhere in my stacks of decaying journals if he had. It didn't make sense.

Unless we were facing a greater threat this time around.

5

The pungent herbal scent of the incense filled my nose. Sitting cross-legged on the hardwood floor of my bedroom, I leaned over the smoldering sticks in their bowl and breathed deep. Energy whispered from the twigs I'd placed in a circle around me. I straightened up, set my hands in my lap, and closed my eyes.

"*The mind's eye*," I murmured in the old tongue. "*From here to there. Let me borrow, let me see.*"

I dragged in another breath and exhaled it long and slow. My awareness drifted upward with the air I expelled. Up and out, through the plastic and brick of the apartment wall, across the rising dawn—and into the head of a sparrow perched on the building's roof.

My sense of my human body faded. I was a bird standing on spindly legs, beady eyes giving me a panoramic view of the city. At my mental nudge, the sparrow spread its wings. With a few flaps, it was soaring on a cool air current toward the outskirts of the city. I urged it higher until I could make out the nearest patches of forest in the distance.

I knew what I was looking for—that cluster of death-touched trees that had chilled me in my vision. The image had clearly been a warning. I *didn't* know if it was connected to Darton's odd, echoing discomfort, but it seemed at least a reasonable guess. Something had affected him in a way I'd never seen before, which suggested a malicious power greater than any we'd encountered in our repeating lives. The sort of power that might leach the life from a grove of trees with its presence alone.

I really hoped they were connected. Because that was my only lead, and I had no bloody clue how I was going to help him if it didn't pan out.

The sparrow glided over the first stretch of trees. The autumn colors had swallowed up almost all the green. I guided the bird downward until it was skimming just a few feet over the canopy of leaves. Branches and shadows flickered beneath us as the wind warbled around the feathered body.

The grove should be easy to spot—a patch of gray amid the brighter leaves. It would stand out even more sharply with the sparrow's ultraviolent sensitivity. I swiveled its head, taking in the entire forest.

We soared over the field on the other side with no luck, so I nudged the sparrow to the west. This search was only going to work if the malicious presence was nearby. It ought to be—magic was difficult to sustain across a distance. I supposed if it were strong enough, it could be affecting Darton from halfway across the country.

As if glooms and the rest of the lower dark rabble weren't trouble enough. What in light's name did this thing want with Darton? How had it even latched on to him?

I needed those answers, but I suspected I wasn't going to like them.

The sparrow crossed highway, farmland, and another stretch of woods. Fatigue crept through its sinewy muscles along with a pinch of hunger. I didn't want my sight-riding to harm it. Time to find another mount.

I reached out again, and my mind caught on a crow balanced on an electric cable strung across a nearby field. A shiver of distaste ran through my awareness—scavengers and I didn't always get along—but its larger wingspan would get me farther, faster. I focused on it and leapt.

The crow had an itch under its left wing. I let it scratch at that with its beak, and then I tugged it into the air. We shot up toward the clouds so I could reassess my course.

Nothing below drew me with any urgency. I turned us north, because that was where the patches of forest looked the thickest. As the crow swooped toward them, the memory of the vision's chill crawled through me.

Yes, north *felt* right.

The crow had crossed one span of forest and just soared over another when an unpleasant prickling shot through its body and my mind. The bird veered closer to the treetops of its own accord. Its small heart raced in its chest.

It had sensed something I couldn't. We were being pursued. Something, somewhere, was tracking our movements and closing in.

The crow landed on a branch near the peak of an oak tree. It stood there, stock still, amid the shifting shadows of the leaves swaying in the breeze. I held there with it, waiting, watching.

A crow wasn't typical prey for any predator.

Whatever was out there… was it after the crow because of *me*?

A familiar, unnatural chill seeped over the crow's wings, numbing its muscles. *No.* I pushed it forward in a burst of feathers. Fly, fly, fly. Under branches and around trunks, now higher, now lower, left and then right. I didn't know how to dodge our pursuer when I had no idea where—or what—it even was, but I wasn't going to give it an easy chase.

The crow trembled as it flapped its wings, fear and the physical strain of our headlong flight sapping its strength. I could have let it go. Could have released it and let my awareness snap back into my body in my bedroom. If whatever was hunting us caught the bird with me in it, I couldn't be sure it wouldn't hurt me too.

But I wasn't ready to flee. The thing chasing us had the same horrible presence I'd felt in that grove of trees. I'd come here hunting for *it*. I needed to know more.

I couldn't ask the crow to give up its life to that cause, though. It dove between two pines, and I sensed a rabbit nibbling at a sapling's bark down below. With a bolt of thought, I jumped from the bird into that furry body.

The crow flapped away overhead. For the first several seconds, amid the jitter of my thoughts, I kept my consciousness balled tightly in the rabbit's head. The animal's eyes weren't much use to me, but its nose might be. No immediate impression of my pursuer came to me. Was it still fixated on the crow?

If it had found me here, maybe I was close to its lair.

I suggested to the rabbit that it needed to seek out a spot that smelled of rot. The bunny left off its nibbling and loped forward across the tree roots. It paused, and paused again, testing the air with a quiver of its nose. A tendril of something sour and decaying twined with the scents of dry soil and pine needles. *That way*, I told it. *Follow that trail.*

I kept it close to the tree trunks and the scattered bushes and ferns between them, to stay as sheltered as we could. But we hadn't stumbled on anything meaningful yet when the rabbit abruptly froze. Its nose twitched; its body went rigid. I couldn't tell what it had sensed, but it obviously wasn't anything good.

A branch creaked somewhere behind us. The rabbit bolted. Its feet thumped over the dry soil as fast as the patter of its heart. Before I could regain control, it had darted into a hollow beneath a granite bolder.

The rabbit spun around to brace its hindquarters against the back of the hollow. Nothing stirred outside. I watched the opening, my mind as still as my host's body.

I couldn't take on much of an enemy, not with only my mind and a rabbit's body. Fully casting without the ability to speak was impossible, and what magic I might be able to summon non-verbally was slight. But my pursuer's lair had to be close. I couldn't give up. Not when this thing might be hurting Darton even worse tomorrow.

I crouched there in the dark, sharing the rabbit's hope that if we laid low, our pursuer would back off—or at least wander far enough away that I could explore farther. The rattle of the animal's pulse and the tension wound through its body stirred a memory up from the depths of my history.

The bark of the tree trunk bit into my back through my thin tunic. I pressed against it harder. The tramp of footsteps carried through the forest, far too close for comfort. Especially because they

45

were the footsteps of men who very much wanted to kill me... and the prince braced against a different tree about ten feet away. My hands clenched tight at my sides.

It was my fault. I'd persuaded Arthur to take a little time for himself, just this once. Not that he'd done a very good job of it. He'd claimed we were going out for a ride, the king's son and his ever-present attendant, but within half an hour, that ride had turned into a series of village calls. I hadn't minded the excuse to get off the normally placid mare he'd stuck me on—horses never took well to me, and she'd gone entirely skittish—but I didn't see how asking after ill farmers and taking notes on grain stores was for himself.

And then, along the road between the third village and the fourth, six members of the marauding gang the king's soldiers had mostly managed to suppress earlier that year leapt out in an ambush. Just our luck.

I didn't remember exactly how we'd ended up in the woods, without our horses or our weapons but alive for the time being. Between the clang of swords and the rearing of my horse, the fall and my overall panic, I'd lost at least ten minutes in a blur. But now the four men Arthur hadn't managed to dispatch were prowling through the forest, intent on finishing the job they'd set out to do. Which I suspected involved our heads ending up on sticks.

I glanced over at Arthur where he stood braced and ready even without his sword, his gaze distant as he followed the sounds. He had to be thinking he never should have listened to me, that I'd pretty much gotten him killed with my well-meaning badgering. A pang filled my chest. In another minute or two, unless some miracle dropped out of the sky, I'd have to ensure he wasn't killed by using my magic, so blatantly he'd have to recognize it as a supernatural power.

I hadn't shown him even a hint of it yet. We'd never talked about the fae or otherworldly powers. I might save him only to have *him banish me from his sight, execute me, or...*

But there was no question which outcome, his death or mine, would be worse.

I curled my fingers around a slim branch low on the ash tree that hid me and looked at the king's son again. He met my gaze this time with a smile and a nod, small but confident. The pang deepened even as some other tension inside me released.

He didn't blame me for our predicament. Not even a little.

That knowledge gave me the courage to move. I snapped the branch and shouted into the air. A wind whipped through the forest. I stepped from behind my tree in time to see it pummel our attackers onto their backs. The gleam of Arthur's sword leapt into my mind. I reached out and called to it. The blade shot through the underbrush from wherever it had fallen to land at the prince's feet.

My pulse thudded in my ears. I turned toward Arthur. He was staring at me, his eyes wide. Then, before a new sort of panic could take hold of me, a grin stretched across his face.

I slipped out of the memory into an ache of homesickness. Gods, we'd come so far since then. I wished I could have smacked down my current pursuer with a surge of conjured wind.

It had been quiet out in the forest for a few minutes now. I directed the rabbit to edge a little closer to the opening.

It took one step, and the view of the forest outside caved in on us.

The boulder above us fractured and crumbled. A shudder of magical power hit the rabbit's skin with a rush of frigid air. The animal scrambled backward, and I threw myself out of its head. My awareness snagged on a robin gliding between the trees.

Not giving it a chance to adjust to the change in

management, I urged it onward, upward, fast. The air shrieked behind me. My pursuer had tracked my leap.

The robin swerved to the left, dipped, and dodged. I gathered myself again. An invisible force swept through the branches ahead of me, twigs snapping and leaves browning in its wake, and walloped the bird in the face with a cold fist of power.

My host spun, head over wings, and my mind jerked out of it.

I came to slumped on the floor of my bedroom. The incense was still smoking in its bowl. The twigs in their circle around me had disintegrated into dust—all except one. I raised a hand to my forehead, which was pounding. My stomach had twisted.

I hadn't found our enemy's lair, but I'd gotten enough of a taste of its power to know what we were dealing with. That hadn't been any lesser fae creature stalking me—oh, no. The clout of that strike—that had been pure fae magic. Only higher fae could wield the energies of the world with that much strength and precision.

And only one sort of fae did so with such a chill.

A full dark fae had come here, seeking my king. A dark fae who'd hurt him from miles away and been prepared for me to come searching for it. Everything I'd seen had the flavor of a mercenary.

I drew up my legs and rested my head on my knees. It couldn't know exactly where Darton was or it wouldn't be lurking around a forest on the other side of the state. I just had to keep it that way. The dark rabble I could handle, but we'd been lucky not to draw the attention of a full dark fae in any of our previous reincarnations. If this mercenary came calling directly, I might not have any hope of stopping him before he had taken what he wanted.

6

I opened my bedroom window to disperse the smoke from the incense, and a knock sounded behind me. "Emmaline?"

Priya's tone was so urgent that I dashed to the door. "What's up?" I said as I opened it.

Priya gave me a relieved smile, but she looked me up and down as if checking for injuries. "I called you, like, four times, and you didn't say anything."

Bat crap. "Sorry," I said, a lie automatically leaping to my tongue. "I had headphones on, music going. I didn't even hear you."

Priya tipped her head, her nostrils flaring. Could she smell the incense? But even if she could, there wasn't anything weird about incense.

This was why I preferred not to do any extended magic in the apartment. It was always a tricky trade-off, making sure I had a few direct connections to the modern world while maintaining a space for my stranger habits. Not for the first time and undoubtedly not the last, I wondered if I should have gone the roommate route after all.

The important thing was keeping up the illusion that

everything was normal. I shifted forward, and Priya stepped back to let me leave. I hadn't eaten anything that morning, since sight-riding came easier on an empty stomach, but now my stomach was asserting just how empty it was. It gurgled insistently despite my lingering dread.

Priya trailed behind me into the kitchen. "So everything is all right?"

"Sure." I walled off the memory of that cold, invisible presence in the back of my mind. *No, nothing is all right, not at all.* "Same as usual." *Other than the fact that for the first time in fifteen centuries, an actual dark fae has fixated on my king's supposedly hidden soul, and I haven't even been successful at saving him from glooms the last several dozen lives.*

Her mouth twitched into a frown. "You've just... Well, you've seemed kind of distant the last few days. Like your mind is always someplace else. I know we haven't been friends that long, but you know you can talk to me if something is bothering you, right?"

The genuine worry in her voice squeezed my heart. We might not have known each other long, but she was a good friend. One of the best I'd ever had since I'd started this repetitious cycle. Or at least she would have been, if I could have let her.

Instead, I had to keep lying.

"There's nothing. Really." My smile felt stiff, but I hoped she wouldn't notice. "Just, you know, the course load is picking up, lots of assignments to stay on top of. Nothing more serious than that."

She exhaled, still eyeing my face. "If there ever *is* more than that, I'm game. I can keep an open mind. Just try me."

Yeah, right. *Oh, well, in that case, let me tell you all about how I'm a hundred-times-reincarnated wizard, and I've got a king to save from an evil fairy creature.* Ha.

I was never going to be able to say anything like that to her. Or to anyone else—not my parents, not Coach, not the sort-of friends I'd left back home. I never could. This was how it always happened. I found my king, and the rest of my current existence fell to pieces.

I turned away to open the fridge. The pressure in my chest sharpened into an ache. But I had centuries of practice at holding my tongue.

"I'll keep that in mind. You know, there's nothing here I'm really in the mood for. And you're right that I haven't had much time to hang out. Do you want to go grab brunch at that place down the street that has the hash browns you're always raving about?"

Priya's face brightened. "That's an invite I'm never going to turn down!"

Her gaze lingered on me for a second longer, though, before she headed for the coat hooks to get her jacket. And I knew she didn't really believe I was all right, no matter what I said.

But then, could I blame her? I didn't believe it either.

* * *

"Come out, come out, wherever you are," I murmured under my breath. The campus green stretched out before me, and the gloom had to be around here somewhere. In my pocket, the salt in the pouch trembled again.

I skirted the fine arts department's small theater building, walking faster when the trembling intensified. Following the magical signal was like a game of Hot-and-Cold once I got in the general vicinity, but at least glooms moved at a leisurely pace. The other two I'd caught in the last week had barely drifted past the edge of school property before I'd found them.

I made for the parking lot up ahead, but before I was even halfway across the green, the trembling rose to an outright jitter. My gaze snagged on a hazy fragment of darkness rippling through the tiny interconnected shadows formed by the blades of grass. It jerked to a halt and then crawled onward in a slightly different direction.

Hmm. This one wasn't so leisurely. I hurried after it, finding I had to speed-walk to keep pace. Since my encounter with the dark fae mercenary this morning, I'd meant to try out a new containment spell on the next gloom I came across, but this might not be the best one for the job.

It looked almost... purposeful. Where was it heading? I could have cast it away right then, but getting the answer to that question felt more important.

The gloom continued in its swift, halting course across campus—back around the theater, between two of the residence buildings, darting from shadow to shadow. My fellow students wouldn't have been able to make it out, but they could see *me*. A few guys I passed shot me odd looks when I stopped abruptly as the gloom hesitated. Then it was off again.

We left behind the residence halls, passed the physical sciences building, and reached the edge of the college's central courtyard. An uneasy prickle crept over my skin. A memory stirred in the back of my head—and not one I wanted to return to. It was the last thing I'd seen in the life before this one—a young man's face twisted in pain and rigid with death as a swarm of glooms roiled around him.

One couldn't do much damage, but a bunch of them? Oh, yes. I didn't understand why the gloom was behaving so oddly, but I didn't like it. Maybe I was better off exterminating it before it got into any real trouble.

I palmed one of the twigs I'd stashed in my clothes this morning—and a jovial voice ran out from across the courtyard.

"Hey! It's Emmaline the Indestructible. She can give you some answers."

My head jerked up, and my eyes locked with the deep brown ones belonging to Darton's rakish friend Keevan. He grinned as he sauntered toward me. Izzy was right behind him. And there was Darton between them, laughing at something Izzy must have said. My pulse skittered.

The gloom had brought me straight to my king. It shouldn't have been drawn toward him at all, not when the soul inside him was still completely dormant.

My hand clenched around the twig. I couldn't start muttering and pointing at what would look to the three of them like empty air now that they were watching me. When I stepped forward to meet them, I moved in front of the gloom as I went. At the same time, I focused on the twig against my fingers and pictured an invisible wall sprouting from the ground around the gloom. My fingers tightened. The twig crumbled. My wordless spell shivered into place.

The magic wouldn't be very powerful, but it would keep the dark vermin contained—and away from Darton—for at least an hour or two. Way more than enough time for me to get out of this situation and deal with it properly.

"You seem to be keeping better balance today," Keevan said teasingly.

Izzy elbowed him. "Don't bug her about that. I bet Emma has better coordination than you with all that sword practice."

Darton's head snapped up at that, and my heart flipped for a completely different reason. "Sword?" he said.

"In fencing club." Izzy gave him a look that clearly said she thought he was being dim. She didn't know he hadn't made the connection yet. But that last bit of anonymity I'd held on to had just disintegrated. Darton's expression tightened as understanding followed by embarrassment and consternation shifted over it. His gaze held mine, more a glower than a glance now.

I offered a tiny shrug, and his mouth twisted. He wasn't going to admit he'd been unaware in front of his friends, of course. Too much pride for that. But I could tell I was going to be hearing about this at our next practice.

At least Izzy seemed pleased to see me. "We keep bumping into you," she said, smiling. "After two years of never meeting—it must be fate or something!"

Well, that was one way to look at it. "I wasn't here the last two years," I said, grateful I had a solid excuse that wasn't—*I just started stalking the bunch of you. Well, only one of you.* "I just transferred in."

"Oh, where from?"

That part was going to be trickier to explain. I briefly considered lying, but given my luck in the last ten minutes, I had the feeling I'd end up caught in it somehow. "Yale," I admitted.

Darton had stood still and silent through the exchange, but he couldn't keep his mouth shut at that. "*Yale?*" he repeated. "You got into Yale and decided to come here instead?"

I bit my tongue. *Yes, I did. For* you, *you arse.* "Are you only here because *you* didn't get into Yale, then?"

His glower returned. "It's family tradition." His tone implied he could have gone to Yale if he'd really wanted to. From what Priya had said about his grades, it might be true, so fair enough.

"Well, I didn't have any family tradition," I said. "It was a good school, sure, but something was… missing."

That wasn't even a lie.

"Which begs the question." Keevan waggled his thick eyebrows. "Did you find that something here?" He waved his arm at the sturdy but not especially impressive buildings around the courtyard.

My eyes twitched, but I managed not to glance at Darton. "I'm not sure yet."

Maybe something of that truth seeped into my voice. At the edge of my vision, Darton was still focused on me, but more considering than glowering now. As if he were contemplating how or why I might have ended up here, near him, at all.

I didn't want him wondering about that.

I turned to Keevan. "What answers were you talking about that you thought I could give?"

"Right!" He nudged Izzy. "Get her to do the survey, Iz. Maybe she'll have something more interesting to say than the bunch of us."

Izzy grimaced and pulled out the clipboard she'd tucked under her arm. "I'm supposed to ask people these questions for a presentation for one of my English classes," she explained. "You really don't have to."

"It's fine." Once we had that over with, maybe they would leave so I could finish taking care of the gloom. I resisted the urge to check behind me, where it should still be lurking beside the bench where I'd trapped it.

"Thanks." Izzy retrieved a purple pen she'd lodged behind her ear and poised it over the paper. "What's your major?"

"Double major, biology and chemistry," I said. Suddenly, all three of them were staring at me again. I'd gotten that a lot even at Yale. Apparently I didn't look the part of a scientist.

"That must be a lot of work," Izzy said. I suspected that remark wasn't part of the survey.

It wasn't, really, between the baseline sensitivity to living systems that my fae heritage had given me and the fact that I'd taken pretty much the same courses in every life since I'd survived long enough to make it to college, but I couldn't exactly tell her that. Better if they didn't think I was even weirder than I'd already come across. "Yeah, it is, but I manage."

"My older sister is doing her Ph.D. in physics here," Keevan put in. "The science department is hardcore. Kudos."

Izzy adjusted the clipboard. "I guess most of your assigned readings for school are nonfiction?" I nodded, and she checked something on the page. "How about recreationally? Do you read books or magazines that aren't for school?"

"Sure," I said. "Some."

A dark flutter of movement caught my eye. I swiveled

as if checking my backpack for something and glanced at the bench. My body tensed.

The gloom was edging closer to us. It was edging *over* the protective boundary I'd sent around it, toward the part of the bench's shadow that touched that of the nearest building.

My spell had been hasty and wordless, but it should have been strong enough to repel any regular gloom for more than a few minutes. Any *regular* gloom. This one had also made for Darton as if it'd been searching for him. If it pulled itself free of my trap completely, it could get to him in a matter of seconds. And if it touched him and recognized the magic twined through his spirit, we'd be totally screwed.

I turned back to Izzy to make an excuse and froze. She wasn't looking at me anymore. She was peering toward the gloom. Her brow had knit, as if something about the scene puzzled her. Her pale fingers clutched the clipboard. A shiver ran through me.

If she'd fully made out the gloom, recognized a patch of darkness was moving of its own accord through the shadows, she'd have looked terrified, not just confused. But she was seeing *something* when she shouldn't have noticed anything at all.

This was all wrong. Where had a gloom gotten enough power to overcome magical barriers and trigger human senses?

If Darton hadn't been standing right there, I might have tried to examine it further, to learn what I could about it. But he was, and my king came first, always. I couldn't risk him.

"You know what?" I said quickly, "I've actually got to

get to—to the library. I seem to have left my notebook there."

Before anyone could comment on that feeble excuse, I spun in the general direction of the library, grabbing a few twigs from my pocket as I did. At this point, I didn't trust just one to do the job.

With a dip of my shoulder, the strap of my backpack slipped off as if by accident. It thumped on the ground, and I swung my arm in a motion a little too broad to just be snatching after it, letting the noise of its fall swallow my murmur. *"Darkness begone."*

Light flared inside the gloom's filmy form. It blinked out of being. The anxious weight in my chest relaxed.

"You're not making a very good case for being coordinated." Darton hefted my backpack before I could reach for it properly and held it out. I accepted it from him, letting the dust of the twigs I'd sapped the energy from fall from my other hand. His gaze seemed to catch those fragments. Couldn't I catch a single break today?

"It's a good thing I'm not really concerned about proving anything to you, then," I retorted, and hurried away before I could blow my cover any more than I already had.

7

"Stop here," I said to the taxi driver. "This is good."

The cab pulled to a stop on the gravel shoulder of the narrow highway. The driver took in the sprawl of forest beside us and then looked back at me, his brow furrowed. "Here?"

"Yep." I checked the price on the dashboard console and handed him a wad of bills that covered it twice over. Having savings accounts that had been collecting interest for decades made certain parts of my repeated lives a lot smoother. "I'm meeting some friends for a camping trip. Thanks for getting me all the way out here."

The driver fanned the bills and gave a slightly sputtered laugh. "All right. Have fun!"

I couldn't blame him for his initial hesitation. According to the maps, the woodland I stepped out in front of stretched across hundreds of acres, most of them rarely disturbed. Because the forest's inhabitants made sure they weren't without humans even realizing they'd been magically persuaded.

I set off into the brush. My hiking boots crunched over the first fallen leaves of autumn. The fresh, dry scent of soil and wood should have been refreshing, but my stomach twisted. After the convoluted journey by large bus, then smaller bus, and finally the taxi that had gotten me here, it was almost lunchtime. I fished out the cheese and veggie sandwich I'd packed, but I'd only gulped down half before the twist turned into a knot.

It wasn't only hunger weighing on me. After all, this was no recreational hike. I stuffed the rest of the sandwich into my satchel and tramped on over the uneven earth.

The boundary tingled over me as I crossed it. The magic laced through it would have turned back any normal human with some unconscious sense that they needed to be elsewhere. I shook the itch off in an instant and kept walking, my head high and my feet steady.

They'd know who I was. They'd greet me when they took a mind to.

It only took a few minutes. Three luminescent figures shimmered into view ahead of me, as if out of the streaks of sunlight penetrating the canopy above us.

Light fae and dark fae were named by their natures and affinities, not by their appearance. Life energy glowed through the skin of the three fae who came forward to meet me, but that skin was pale gold on one, ebony on another, and bronze brown on the third, in the middle. He stepped ahead of the others. The faintest beam of sunlight set his coppery hair gleaming and shone in his hazel eyes.

The fae bowed slightly at his thin waist, which told me he was a hell of a lot younger than me. I might have several centuries on most of them in spirit, but only the newest fae recognized that seniority when it came packaged in my regularly changing human form.

"You are welcome here, Son and now Daughter of

Eóghan." His voice was so silvery I could almost see it shining. "What is it you seek?"

The fae only ever mentioned my father. My mother, the human woman who'd carried me for nine months and birthed me for the very first time, had never counted to anyone. Even to my father, she'd been more of a tool than a person. I wasn't even sure he'd bothered to find out her name. He'd been far more concerned about picking a mate with the appropriate physicality and brains. By the time it had occurred to me to ask, he'd already forgotten… if he'd ever known.

The way the fae raised their children, with each child belonging to the community at large, I hadn't even realized how strange that was until I'd entered Arthur's world.

The other two young fae flitted around me, their eyes wide. Had they ever even seen a human form up close? As the human world had expanded in population and power, the fae had withdrawn in turn. At least that had made it easier for me to avoid running into any dark fae who might be familiar with my history—until now.

"I need to talk to one of the elders," I said. "There's a dark fae active nearby, and I'm concerned."

The trio gathered together to murmur to each other. I crossed my arms over my chest as I waited. They might have been more comfortable if I'd used their overly formal way of speaking, but I didn't have the patience for it these days.

"I will return with guidance," the one who'd spoken to me before said. He glided away. The pale man darted away into the sunbeams like a leaping spark. The ebony woman hesitated, peering at me with nearly round eyes.

"I've heard so many stories about you," she said.

Light deliver me. "I doubt more than half were true," I muttered.

She shook her head. "Even if only that—I can't imagine, so many lives, in so many places. Not just on these lands, but across the ocean too. Is it very different there?"

My jaw tightened, but I resisted the impulse to tell her to leave me in peace. At least her childlike curiosity was a more enthusiastic welcome than I was likely to get from many others here.

"Human beings are very similar on a whole in every place," I told her, "while still being very different from each other. It's part of what makes them interesting."

"Have you seen—what is it called, where there is sand without end?"

"The desert?" I supplied. "You can see that right here if you just go farther south. The temperature shifts take some getting used to, but there's no shortage of sunlight, that's for sure."

"Well, I haven't traveled much beyond the enclave. Yet." She glanced down at her hands, which she'd twined in front of her. "Do you really find that—"

"Sunki." The coppery-haired fae returned in a flash of light. His voice was mildly chiding. "Our guest must come speak to Chimalis now."

The young woman shrank back so swiftly that I said, in as warm a voice as I could manage, "It was nice talking with you," if only just to annoy the other guy.

I followed the coppery-haired fae deeper into the forest, past tree trunks that glimmered with the outlines of doors. The homes they opened into, built and hidden by sorcery, would be far larger than the trees appeared capable of containing. The magic I'd bent my mind to studying and needed tools to fully use came to the fae as easily as breathing. Which made it even more irritating that they never used it for anything other than their very narrow priorities.

This forest was thriving, so what did it matter to them if another was being chopped down to make room for a subdivision, or if pollution was saturating the air everywhere else? What did it matter to them if this human king or that human president did well or poorly by his people?

My father had been different. He'd thought beyond his enclave. But even he hadn't been prepared for the commitments I'd been willing to make outside his kind. He'd wanted a child with human blood to ground it against the characteristic light fae flightiness and distraction, but he hadn't considered that his fae influence and teachings might not be enough to always sway that blood to his way of seeing things.

My guide stopped in a small clearing where sunlight pooled from a gap in the canopy. A table had been conjured there, set with sparkling cups of juice and cut fruits. They still offered me the basics of hospitality, at least. I sat on the oak stool.

The moment my rear touched the wood, another fae emerged from the forest. Like all her kind, she was lithe and elegant. But the fae did age. All the light fae looked a little faded around the edges to me, but as an elder, Chimalis was becoming nearly translucent, right to the core. As she passed into the pool of light, I could make out the darker shadows of the forest behind her through her glowing form.

She rested her tan hands, the slender fingers grown inhumanly long, on the table, a subtle reminder to respect her age and the status that came with it.

I bowed much as the young fae man had to me. I might have insulted her, or else those undoubtedly watching this meeting, by not prostrating myself lower— but then, if they were going to see me as a being unworthy of their full respect, why should they expect me to perfectly follow their customs?

"Daughter of Eóghan, what name do you carry now?" The elder fae's voice had the same translucent quality as her body, as if it came from much farther away than the other side of the table. Her misty blue eyes darted over me, never quite settling on one spot.

I wasn't sure if the question was politeness or a sign they didn't recognize me as who I'd once been enough to call me by the name my father had given me, but I'd rather they used my current human name anyway. "Emma."

"I'm told you come to us on this day with worries."

I nodded. "I've seen evidence of dark fae powers in the area. I believe a mercenary has set his sights on my… charge. He's attempted to do us harm. And on top of that, I ran into a gloom yesterday that was unusually strong."

"The darkness does shift," Chimalis murmured.

Right. I plowed onward. "My own ability to investigate is limited. I was hoping someone here might have sensed or heard more about what's going on. Why the mercenary is here. What his goals are." Beyond destroying my king, presumably.

The elder shivered on her stool. Her eyes went even more distant. "There are strange stirrings. A winter chill well before the winter."

A typical light fae answer. I bit back my impatience. "Do you think the Darkest One could be exerting some influence after all this time?" Dread gnawed at my gut at the thought.

Chimalis tipped her head to one side. "I have no sense of it. She is imprisoned far. Her sprouting is young. No point is fixed."

Was *that* answer supposed to be helpful? Swine crud, the New World fae were even loopier than the ones back in Britain. This was why I hadn't come out here earlier. But desperate times called for desperate measures.

"Can you tell me anything about the strange stirrings or the chill?" I said. "Or how to push them back, suppress them?"

"We can only know the shadows are longer than they once were, and the air grown colder," Chimalis said. "We keep to the enclave. The dark fae keep clear of us."

I frowned. "For now. If one is gathering power, making moves against *me*, he might decide to do more damage beyond that. He's obviously an enemy of the light."

"If he comes to us, he will find it impossible to do harm," the elder said placidly. "That is *why* we remain here. Tell me, daughter of Eóghan, why do you not give up your quest and stay here with the people of your soul?"

My spine stiffened. "I can't."

"Nothing prevents you. This wrenching from one life to the next so often, it's unnatural. It must cause you much pain. I can see it has." Her eyes sharpened, fixing for a moment on my face. "You know the darkness does not come for you. The other, he was a pillar once, but now he is nothing. Let them have him. Let your wandering end."

"My father believed it was important that we thwart their plans," I said. "That it was about more than just one human life. Why would the dark fae want him so badly if he doesn't matter more than that?"

Chimalis bowed her head. Her fine, shimmering hair slid over her narrow shoulders. "Eóghan had many wise ideas, but many odd ones as well. He did not always see as he should. Sometimes destruction must sweep through to bring new life from the ashes."

"Well, I'm not willing to risk who knows what kind of 'destruction' with fae philosophy as my only guarantee it'll end well." My voice shook. I shut my mouth and inhaled, collecting myself. "*I* was one of my father's odd ideas. The only reason I exist is so he could send me to unravel the darkness gathering around Arthur. I have no intention of giving that purpose up."

"You have so much loyalty to one long passed?" Chimalis asked with what sounded like honest curiosity. "You would continue to act as his tool?"

I bristled, gritting my teeth. She had never met my father and was in no position to judge him. He'd had uses for me, yes, and he hadn't always agreed with my decisions when they veered contrary to his intent, but he'd loved me. I knew that.

Anyway, it wasn't *him* I was staying loyal to. It was the soul still living inside that rather difficult man back on campus. My hand fell to my pocket, feeling the pouch of salt there. I was probably too far away from my magical alarm system for it to work. The risk hadn't been worth it. The light fae had nothing useful to tell me. I was on my own, as always.

I stood up. Now that I'd confirmed as much, I'd

better get home.

"If any of you *do* see signs of dark fae stepping beyond their usual practices, I'd appreciate a head's-up. I'm sure you could figure out where to find me."

Chimalis nodded, but I didn't really believe she or the others would seek me out. They kept to their enclave, as she'd already said.

How can they just sit by? I'd ranted to my father more than once, after it had become clear the Darkest One herself had some stake in my king. *They're lucky the dark fae have never yet taken a mind to slaughter* them, *or there'd be none of you left.*

You don't understand, he'd said in that slow, knowing voice of his. *That carelessness is our strength. The dark powers only understand order and certainty. They can't cope with the unexpected. And we always have chaos on our side.*

I'd never felt especially comforted by that response. The light fae's chaos simply meant they never pulled their heads out of their asses long enough to notice there might be problems worth applying it to.

"May your path be ever lit," Chimalis said. It was the light fae's standard farewell.

I gave her another truncated bow. "And yours in turn."

Arms tight at my sides, I marched back through the forest the way I'd come. I didn't need a guide to show me to the road. Then it'd be another mile or two before I made it to anywhere I could expect a cab to pick me up.

I'd nearly crossed the enclave when a slim figure flitted out of the trees toward me. The ebony-skinned fae who'd peppered me with questions earlier—Sunki. She bowed to me, more deeply than the others had.

"Might I speak?"

Not more questions. "Please make it quick," I said, suppressing a groan.

She took my instruction to heart. Her words tumbled from her tongue. "I listen to the animals. They have felt the darkness rising. Tendrils of it, sweeping like water grass in a stream, without aim."

"Searching," I said. She dipped her head. So the mercenary didn't know exactly where Darton was yet. That would explain why he hadn't traveled closer.

"And it feeds the glooms and the other lesser creatures of darkness," she said. "They grow fatter, and they follow the threads."

Creatures, plural. My gut twisted. The gloom I'd seen wasn't just a fluke. The dark rabble was absorbing the mercenary's power—and he was *sending* them searching for us? Lovely. But at least knowing that gave me a better chance of getting in his way.

"Thanks," I said, meaning it.

Sunki bowed again and tucked her hand behind her back. "It was such an honor to speak with you at all. If I could offer a gift that might make some small difference…"

She reached out to me, her fingers clasped around the hilt of a dagger. The power sealed inside it quivered through me. I caught my breath.

The blade, thick and lightly curved, was nothing more special than tarnished silver. But the holly-wood handle, polished smooth and carved with spiraling vines along the hilt, radiated life energy into my palm when I took it. Enchanted—live wood, like my wands—but from the feel, it had been made to hold the entire essence of the tree it had been cut from. It would have taken me months of concentrated effort to create a weapon like this.

"Thank you," I said again. A flash of a smile crossed Sunki's face. She gave me one last bow and slipped away.

I turned the dagger in my hand as I walked on. The shiver of its energy stayed with me, but as the awe of seeing it wore off, the knot in my gut remained.

It was a true gift, sure. A powerful weapon against the dark. I could slice through a gloom or any other piece of the dark rabble without drawing on any magic of my own. But only one at a time. And only those lesser beings. One half-fae wizard and one enchanted dagger were far from enough to take on the army of dark fae creatures this mercenary was empowering.

8

I'd gotten in the habit of arriving at fencing practice early so I could be suited up before Darton came around. I wasn't prepared to see him standing in the hall outside the gym door when I came around the corner. A little jolt ran through me, excitement and anxiety intertwined.

He'd been leaning against the wall with an open book in his hand. At the sound of my footsteps, he looked up, lowered the book, and pushed himself fully upright.

The way the lines of his body moved inside his fitted clothes set off a warmth inside me I had no control over. It really wasn't fair. My hand tightened around the strap of my backpack, but I kept walking steadily over.

"Emma," Darton said with a tip of his head.

"Darton." I stopped, longing to continue into the change room, knowing we were going to have this conversation sooner or later. I might as well get it over with.

"You really could have told me." His voice was light, but his indigo-blue eyes held mine intently.

"Told you what?" I said. "'By the way, I'm talented at both losing my grip on my saber *and* falling off tall

71

objects'? It didn't seem like vital information."

He looked as if he were biting back a grimace. "I wouldn't criticize the way you handle a sword *now*."

I shook my head. "It's not that big a deal. And if *you're* going to get better with those 'swords,' you might want to get ready for practice."

He paused, his gaze still fixed on me. If he didn't stop paying me so much attention, I was going to be flushed on the outside too, where he could see it. I turned toward the change room.

"Partner with me for the two-person drills?" Darton asked.

A persnickety part of me wanted to say no, just to irritate him. The weakest part wanted to ask why he'd made the request, with a little-too-much hopeful anticipation at the thought of his answer. I tensed against that hope, but I didn't say no either.

He was reaching out to me of his own accord. I could protect him far better from the threats I hadn't anticipated if he liked me. If he trusted me. Taking the stealthy route was impossible now anyway.

I'd just have to keep a tight rein on my impulses. I knew better than to entirely trust myself.

"Sure," I said, short and simple, and pushed past the door.

My heart had started thumping, but it slowed again when I slid on my mask. My little shield to ensure he didn't notice an accidental stare or an expression I'd rather stayed hidden.

And I needed it, because after our conversation in the hall, my awareness of his presence had only heightened. I felt each of his movements during the warm-up like an echo of my own, even though he was at the other end of the line.

"All right, folks—partner up," Coach said. Darton made a beeline for me as if he'd been just as aware of my position in the group as I'd been of his. I clamped down on my pleased shiver at the thought, lifted my mask to acknowledge him, and immediately tugged it back down.

Coach called out the first drill, and Darton stepped into the correct stance without hesitation. Even if he didn't see fencing as a serious sport, he'd obviously been paying attention. We shuffled back and forth in a rehearsed rhythm. Jab, parry, jab, parry. He drew in a breath, and just from the shape of it, I could tell he was smiling behind the black mesh.

"So you're a football fan?"

"What?" I said.

Darton chuckled. "You were watching the team practice that morning before you took your fall."

Oh. Of course. I'd steered clear of the stands ever since I'd had to introduce myself to him there. I shrugged around the motion of my saber. "Not really. Priya's the one more into it." From what she'd said, that had been true. Last year, at least.

"Priya?"

"My friend who was there with me." I peered at him through my mask. He'd remembered me but not her, even though she'd pushed the introductions? Well, I was the one who'd made the more dramatic *entrance*. There was no need to read more into it than that.

But if he wanted to talk through the drills, I had my own subjects to bring up. "How has your side been? It looked like you'd injured it the other day."

Darton's arm dipped, just slightly, but enough for me to know he was remembering that pain. The ghost of a deeper pain he couldn't have remembered yet.

"It's not bad," he said, which told me it wasn't *gone* yet. "I don't think there's any real damage."

How the heck could I ask about the discomfort in more detail—whether it was continuous or periodic; if the latter, what pattern there was to when it showed up—without sounding obsessively concerned? Before I'd figured that out, Coach ordered us to switch drills. Darton and I repositioned ourselves a little farther apart, our arms extended.

I tapped my blade against Darton's, and he began retreating from my mock charge. "Watch your footwork," I said automatically, like I would have any other beginner I was paired with. "Your front foot should be landing on the heel."

"Are you sure you're the best person to be advising on proper footwork?"

His tone was teasing but cocky enough to raise my hackles. I might like him better than I had on our first meeting, but he still had some jackass in there.

"I guess you'll find out if you ignore me and end up on your arse," I retorted.

We reached the wall and headed back in the other direction, me retreating now.

"So you just up and left Yale?" Darton said between slightly ragged breaths. "I bet your parents raised hell over that."

"Not really. They trust me to know what's best for myself." My gaze lifted to his face. For the first time, I found myself regretting the masks. "Are you only here because of *your* family?"

"Well, no."

We paused at the opposite wall. As if having sensed my wish, Darton shoved up his mask and swiped his sleeve across his face. Uncertainty had softened the usual cockiness in his expression. Something about this topic got to him.

Before I could scrutinize him further, he pulled the mask back down. "I know they wouldn't have been *happy* if I'd gone somewhere else. And my parents are covering most of the tuition—I'm not sure they would have anywhere else."

"There are these things called scholarships, you know." I motioned him backward to continue the drill. "Did you grow up near here?" *Do you have family around who you might go visiting sooner than I've planned for?* I wasn't sure exactly what I'd do if he ventured closer to the mercenary's territory, but it'd be nice to have a little warning.

"Upstate," he said. "Not close enough that I can drop in to do laundry like Keevan does. Where are you from, anyway?"

Not close enough he was likely to head home at random. One small concern I could cross off the growing list. "Here and there," I said. "We moved around a lot."

The truth was my parents had lived in the same house on the outskirts of Boston since before I was born. But I'd lived so many lives all over this continent and others, and accumulated so much random knowledge during them, that it was easier to pretend I was worldly in a more mundane way.

"You're a bit of a vagabond," Darton said in the same cocky-teasing tone as before. He almost sounded like he was… flirting with me. My pulse skipped, and an answer more honest than I would have preferred slipped out.

"Not by choice."

At least a little of my weariness must have slipped out too, because Darton fell silent. His advance when we switched directions didn't feel quite as aggressive as the last.

"It's pretty brave, changing your plans like that," he said after a moment. "I mean, a lot of people would think you're crazy to leave after getting into a place like Yale."

"I gathered that from your reaction when I mentioned it," I said dryly.

"I'm trying to give you a compliment."

"Well, maybe you need to try harder." Bugger it, *I* was flirting now. A smile had crept across my face, not that he could see it. I dropped the banter. "It's not that difficult to make a decision like that when you know for sure what you need to be doing with your life."

"Okay, drill time is over," Coach said from across the room.

Darton stopped, his saber drifting to his side. "And what is that?" he asked. "Biology and chemistry… Something to do with medicine?"

"You could say that." I was focused on saving lives, in a very specific sort of way. The question about what he wanted to be doing leapt to my tongue, but I caught it. My throat tightened. Hearing him talk about dreams I'd know he almost certainly wouldn't get to reach would only be painful.

Darton glanced across the gym. Coach had started instructing a small group of the beginner students. The senior fencers were pairing up to spar or working through some additional solo exercises on their own. Darton should have gone over to join the beginner group, but he turned back to me instead.

"Would you do me the honor of sparring with me? I'd appreciate the benefit of your expertise, and I'll do my best not to make a fool of myself in the process."

The teasing note hadn't entirely disappeared, but his voice was mostly serious. It held an echo of our first practice together, when I'd chided him for taking that swipe at me. An unspoken apology for that misstep.

Longing swelled in my chest—to accept that apology and his request. I swallowed hard.

I wanted it too much. I wanted to keep talking with him, not just to earn his trust and find openings to protect him, but just for the sake of knowing him better, being near him, feeling he'd chosen my company. But I couldn't forget what a mess I could make if the bare hand at my side brushed his even for an instant. Accidental contact during the controlled drills was easy to avoid. While free sparring with a novice? It was a much bigger risk.

"Maybe another time," I said before I stepped away. But I couldn't pretend I didn't see the way his shoulders stiffened, just a little, as if I'd slapped him.

9

I'd been a dedicated enough trainee for the last month and a half that Coach didn't blink when I stepped out of practice ten minutes early. I walked into the women's change room like I normally would have, headed straight out the door into the hallway, and ducked into the men's side.

The room smelled like floor polish and boy sweat. Wrinkling my nose, I scanned the benches. The clothes Darton had been wearing when he'd confronted me sat in a pile on one beside the wall. I pulled out the baggy of supplies I'd brought. Casting actual magic on anything of his was a bad idea—our dark fae mercenary might sense the resonance that would result. But plenty of things had their own power without my adding any oomph to it.

I grabbed his shoes. Brown suede sneakers—I could approve the style and the convenient texture of the material. Hopefully these were the ones he mainly wore. I could trust the average guy not to have a wide variety of shoes. I rubbed the sides and soles with the mixture of powdered salt and herbs I'd blended this morning. It wouldn't be enough to repel a really determined gloom, but it'd discourage most of them from getting too close.

When I blew at the sneakers, the visible powder drifted away. The suede showed only a faint scuffing, not so much I thought Darton would notice. I set the sneakers down and hightailed it out of there before the rest of the fencing club retired from the gym.

Between that and the large ring of enchanted salt I'd spent all yesterday laying down through town, I could rest a little easier even when Darton ventured a little off campus. But only a little. It wasn't enough. The mercenary's magic was reaching him somehow, if only with that vague pain. I wanted to cut it off completely.

I stewed over the problem as I changed. A salve, maybe. I could tell Darton it was for sore muscles—a special formula I'd brought a few containers of from back home. He might have warmed up to me enough to take it already. I could cook up something that really would soothe aches and pains while also providing a barrier against magical interference.

Perfect. Now I was imagining him rubbing his hands over his naked limbs. I yanked my head out of that daydream and hurried for the door.

"Emmaline!" a cheerful voice greeted me the second I stepped out. Priya was waiting in the hall. I'd been so busy worrying about Darton that I'd forgotten she often stopped by after practice on Mondays to walk home with me. She had an elective in the same building those afternoons.

For the first few seconds, her grin lifted my spirits. Then her smile turned sly. She hooked her arm around mine and tugged me down the hall, leaning in conspiratorially.

"You didn't tell me he joined fencing club. Sneaky girl. Please tell me you've made a move on him by now."

My face heated. And this was exactly *why* I hadn't told Priya about how often I was now seeing Darton.

"I haven't, and I'm not planning on it," I said. "I don't want to."

"Don't lie to me. I saw how you looked at him when he heroically came to your rescue."

"I don't want to make a move on him," I repeated firmly. I wasn't even lying… if we were only counting the decisions I made in my head and not the rest of my body's desires.

Priya sighed. "Fine. But we *are* going to sit down and have a talk about the problems with being all work and no play someday soon. Speaking of hangouts, what do you want to cook tomorrow?"

We usually handled our meals separately, but as we'd moved from roommates to tentative friends, we'd reserved Tuesday nights for what Priya called "girl time." We made dinner together, picked a movie to watch or one of her video games to play, and just relaxed. Deciding what to cook was a key component of the fun. Priya always wanted to experiment with new flavor combinations, and I liked to take on recipes that challenged my chemistry skills.

"There was that soufflé recipe we decided to hold off on last time," I said. "The one with the yam. Or if you're up for something spicy, I stumbled on a lamb curry with cream recipe that sounded good. Unless you had something else in mind?"

"Maybe, but I'm not sure it's up to your standards of difficulty." Priya gave me a teasing nudge. "Show me the curry one. I could go for lamb. It's my turn to do the grocery shopping, right?"

"Yep." Thankfully, because my other cooking project was going to take up most of my non-school time in the next twenty-four hours.

I found the bookmark on my phone and handed it to Priya as we walked. Newly fallen leaves scattered the sidewalks, dappling the pavement yellow and red. The crisp sunlight beaming down from the cloudless sky lit them up. The breeze that licked over my hair was tart but not outright cold.

This was my favorite part of fall—the colorful, refreshingly cool beginning. I wasn't all that fond of the end, when the trees had turned into skeletons and the leaves to rotting mush.

Would I get to see that end before my own came again? My chest clenched at the thought of starting over, waiting through all those childhood years, playing the game of being a regular human being, until I crossed paths with my king once more.

It used to be easier. We used to be reborn within a mile of each other. I'd find him sooner—but then he'd start to wake sooner, the darkness would descend on him sooner, and we'd both die sooner. So, okay, that hadn't been an ideal scenario either. But the time it took before the magic drew us back together stretched longer each time. I didn't like to think of what that might mean. What if someday I stopped finding him altogether?

Nope. Not following those depressing thoughts today. Maybe the mercenary would give up once I had my new protections in place and bugger off. Maybe the gods would reach down from the sky and tell me what the hell I'd been thinking when I'd cast this spell in the first place.

Hey, a wizard could dream.

At the apartment, I hustled into my bedroom to pop open the bin of supplies I'd hauled back from my storage locker. Priya had said she was going out to meet with a study partner after she ate, and then I'd have the kitchen to myself.

I retrieved and sorted the ingredients I'd need, pummeled the ones that needed grinding into submission, and carried everything out into the main room after I heard the front door click shut behind Priya. Making a salve that was effective for its declared purpose and my own secret ones was going to take several steps, but at least the work kept my hands and my mind busy. Less room to fret about what I'd do if this plan didn't work after all.

I was stirring the second pot, the steam dampening my bangs so they stuck to my forehead, when my phone rang where I'd left it on the counter. My parents' home number came up on the screen. I hesitated, but they were due for a call. I was going to need to talk to them soon if I didn't want *them* fretting. My stomach sank as I hit the accept button.

"Hey," I said in a false-chipper voice.

"Hi, honey," my mom said. "Is this a good time for us to chat?"

There probably wasn't going to be a truly good time again in this lifetime. I exhaled. "Yeah. This is perfect."

I wanted to talk to her—I really did. But there was so much I *couldn't* talk to her about now. This part of the cycle, the part where everything in my current life started falling apart, wasn't easy even in the crummy family situations I'd been born into sometimes in the past. And my parents in this life weren't crummy at all. What I'd said to Darton was true. Through my childhood oddities and the decisions I couldn't explain, they'd always accepted and supported me. Just hearing Mom's gentle voice sent a stab of homesickness through me.

I might never see them again. I'd known that when I'd said my good-byes in August, but now, after everything that had happened in the last two weeks, that possibility felt far too likely.

"Is everything still going well at the new school?" Mom said. "I guess you must be into midterms now."

The potion in the pot was thickening. I stirred harder. "Yep. Everything's going great. I aced my first two."

"Well, congratulations. You know we're so happy that the move has worked out for you, even if we don't get to see you as often."

"Five more weeks to go until Thanksgiving." I managed to keep my voice breezy, but I had to change the subject. "Did you get that problem with your art supplier worked out?" Mom ran an interior decorating business.

"Oh, I had to cut those ties, but I found a new company that seems more together." I could almost hear the shake of her head. "I've got to look out for my own customers, you know?"

"Of course."

I kept the conversation focused on what she and Dad were up to as I took the pot off the element to cool and mixed in a few additional ingredients. Finally, Mom said, "I know you're working hard to start off on the right foot there, but don't forget to take some time for yourself now and then, all right?"

The comment echoed Priya's about all work and no

play. I bit my lip, wondering what she'd think if she'd known I'd already skipped four classes in the last week while trying to stay on top of my other, more pressing responsibility. The one she'd never know about.

"Of course, Mom." I swallowed hard. If the situation escalated quickly, I might not even get another chance to *talk* to her or Dad. "I love you."

"Love you too, hon," Mom said, and then the salt in my pocket jittered against my thigh. I froze.

"I, um, actually have to get going," I said quickly.

"Is something wrong?"

Yes. So bloody much. "Nope, just got another call I was expecting coming in. A boy." She'd like that.

"Oh, well, don't let me keep you then." She chuckled, and then she was gone from the line.

I dropped my spoon and rested my hand over the fabric. The salt trembled against my fingers. I closed my eyes, absorbing the sense of it. The gloom had crossed the barrier I'd laid in the southwest end of town, heading east. Not too close to campus. Maybe it would do me a solid and head back in the opposite direction?

I'd barely had time to hope when a vision socked me between the eyes. An image flashed into my mind: Darton leaning against a bar stool with a beer glass in one hand, the reddish glow of the pub lighting tinted his sun-streaked hair and tanned skin. The grin on his face was probably melting the knees of every female person, and possibly some male, in a twenty-foot radius.

The vision faded as quickly as it had hit me, and I grasped the edge of the counter. My heart was racing and my stomach churning with the certainty that the spot I'd just seen was exactly where the gloom was headed.

10

The salt in my pocket jumped the second I stepped out of the cab into the ruddy lights of the pub. The gloom was close, but I'd gotten here fast enough to cut it off. Thank the light I'd caught the name of the place on Darton's coaster.

No one I recognized was standing near the front window, but I pulled my jacket's hood farther over my head anyway. Following the jittering in my pocket, I ducked down the alley toward the back of the building.

I emerged into a small, little-used courtyard. The aged wooden bench behind the pub was missing its middle backboard, and a tang of rotting garbage seeped into the cool evening air from the dumpster on the other side. Thin streaks of light from the streetlamps trickled into the space from the adjoining alleys.

But nowhere near enough light to deter a gloom. The one I'd come for was just slinking along the wall of the restaurant opposite the pub. My hand clenched around the twig I'd been carrying since I left the apartment.

I couldn't get down to serious business yet, not with Darton so close, but I should have at least a few minutes to myself back here in the dark. I'd trap the gloom, conceal myself, and wait until after closing when I could count on working uninterrupted. If the dark fae mercenary had lent this bit of vermin his magic, I might learn something about him from it.

"*Still you'll stay*," I murmured. The twig went brittle against my fingers. The gloom jerked to a stop where it had been wavering across the cracked pavement toward the pub. That minor enchantment would hold it in place while I completed the full binding spell.

I drew a vial of ambergris oil from my bag and sprinkled it on the ground in a circle around the scrap of living shadow, speaking the incantation under my breath as I went. Then I pulled out a wand. "*Through flesh, not bone,*" I said as I pressed the oak tip to my left palm. My skin split with a stinging pain. Blood welled up along the thin line I'd drawn. I squeezed my hand into a fist, winced, and let drop after drop fall along the ring I'd marked with the oil.

With the circle complete, I clapped both my hands together three times. I bowed my head, ready to call out the final threads of magic from the wand.

"Hey!"

The voice rang out through the darkness from just a few feet behind me. I fumbled with the wand and jerked it behind my arm. When I turned, a far-too-familiar figure was emerging from the shadows of the alley. My pulse lurched. I stepped between him and the circle I'd drawn—between Darton and the gloom that had come looking for him.

The guy I'd seen in my mind's eye less than half an hour ago peered at me and then beyond. My shoulders stiffened. Swine crud and cattle sod. Of all the people who might have wandered back at here at this exact moment, why had it needed to be *him*?

Darton squinted at me in the dim light. "Emma?"

He must not have recognized me until just now. He must've heard my clapping hands and come over to see who was back here. Down the alley, the pub's side door was slightly ajar, spilling an amber glow into the space.

"Darton." I kept my voice as even as I could. If he'd waited just a couple more minutes to come out for a smoke or whatever his original purpose had been, I'd have completed the spell. I could have made my excuses and left. Yet again, he'd caught me in the middle of business I couldn't leave unfinished.

"What are you doing?" he said.

A fair question to ask someone lurking in an abandoned courtyard, but that didn't mean I had to like answering it. I managed to maneuver the wand into my bag while gesturing with my other hand to distract him.

"A friend of mine's cat got out of her house a few days ago. I was walking by and thought I saw it run back here. I guess it took off faster than I could catch up."

A lost-pet scenario tended to provoke sympathy rather than suspicion—and it wasn't unbelievable. I really had chased after a runaway puppy of my cousin's down an alley back home when I was fifteen.

What I'd forgotten to consider was the state of my hand.

"Are you *bleeding*?" Darton took another step toward me. I dropped my palm to my side before he could try to examine it—to *touch* it—and groped for an excuse.

"I tripped, running after the cat. It's nothing. Just a scratch." I pulled my gloves on, hiding the wound.

Darton still looked skeptical. That was no good. I needed him to leave.

"What are *you* doing back here?" I asked pointedly.

He motioned vaguely toward the pub. "I just needed to duck out for a second. It gets... stuffy in there after a while." He paused. From his stance and the way he drew in his breath, I gathered he wasn't outright drunk but definitely a bit buzzed. "Funny, it seems like everywhere I go these days, there you are."

I crossed my arms. "I don't know. From my perspective, it's the other way around."

"Touché." He gave me a slanted smile. "I guess I invaded your fencing club first."

He didn't back off on his present invasion, though. He ambled over to the bench and sat down. Then he gave me an uncertain glance.

He didn't know how I felt about him, obviously. He wasn't sure whether our banter had been friendly, tolerant, or maybe even only irritated on my side. To be fair, it had kind of been all three.

He ducked his head, running a hand through his hair. There was something so lost in his expression, just for a second, that my heart squeezed. But I might still have resisted if his arm hadn't lowered a moment later so that his elbow could press against his side. That fatal spot. The mercenary was still getting to him.

I had no salve to give him yet. The best I could offer was my company, which for whatever reason, he seemed to want. And I did feel awkward standing there. So I meandered over to the bench and perched at the opposite end, leaving a space between us.

Darton rested his arm on the top of the bench as he

turned toward me. "You seem like a person who knows her own mind," he said. A little of his usual cockiness had come back into his tone.

"I don't know if I'd say that. There's far too much of it to keep track of."

His brow knit, and then he laughed. "And you're truly weird, you know that?"

I scuffed my shoe against the gritty concrete. "I've been told once or twice."

"I just meant—like you talked about changing colleges. You know what you want to do, and how to do it, and you don't let other people's opinions get in the way."

"Hmm," I said. "I've just learned that if there's something you want, other people's opinions *shouldn't* matter. Unless they know something you don't."

He nodded. "See, you say that, and it totally makes sense. But I've never heard anyone put it that way before. I can honestly say I've never met anyone quite like you."

I couldn't hold back my guffaw at that. I tried to cover the sound with a cough, but Darton caught my amusement anyway.

"You don't believe me?"

"No, it's not that. It's… never mind." I shook my head. No, he'd never met anyone like me, except all the dozens of times he'd met *me* before. But, gods willing, it'd be a long time before he could get that joke.

If we were going to chat, I'd rather we keep off the topic of me. "Is that a problem you run into a lot?" I added. "People's opinions getting in the way of what you want to do? Your friends don't seem all that judge-y, at least from the little I've talked to them." Keevan and Izzy had been friendlier to me than Darton had.

"Well, no, not my close ones… but I don't think even they would necessarily understand everything." Darton paused. That distant look came over his face again as he gazed across the courtyard. "Was that part of transferring schools hard for you?" he asked abruptly. "Leaving your friends behind?"

I shrugged. "There were people I enjoyed hanging out with now and then, but honestly, I'm kind of a loner."

A smile tugged at his lips. "You do give off that vibe. But you were with that friend of yours the other day. You came with her to watch a football practice even though you're not really into the game."

Why were we talking about me again? "Priya came with the apartment," I said, but even as the words came out, I didn't like how flippant they sounded. Pri deserved more than a careless dismissal. "And we get along well. I like her. But I don't need some huge social circle. Friend quota filled."

"No room for more then?" Darton teased before I could turn the conversation back to him.

A not entirely unpleasant prickle ran down my back. He was flirting again. I eyed him. "I decide that on a case-by-case basis."

"Sure. There are lots of ways you could vet potential candidates. Test their science knowledge. Check out their fencing skills…"

"I don't know. That could be a good idea." I'd meant to bounce his joke back at him, but my mind spun off in another direction. *Wouldn't* it be nice if I could set up a series of trials and have people clamoring to prove themselves? Not for me, but for him. My king had once had people competing to stand by his side and protect him back in our first lives. It'd certainly been convenient, even if they hadn't succeeded in the end.

It wasn't as if the job I'd done of protecting him had worked out all that well either.

Darton pointed a finger at me. "You're plotting something. I can tell."

"Nothing to do with you," I said airily to cover the bald lie.

He laughed. "I don't know if that should make me less worried or more." His gaze sharpened again. Those dark blue eyes caught and held mine. "Do you really not have anyone in your life who's important enough to miss?"

I pulled my gaze away. My throat had tightened. "My parents, I guess. But, you know, they're my parents."

And him. Always him. The person he was meant to be—the person he'd become, over and over. The person I still had to save—properly, this time.

Not that I could say anything like that to him in his present state.

"Emma," Darton said. Emotion colored his voice, raw and open, and I couldn't bear to find out how he was looking at me or to respond to whatever weakness he thought he'd discovered in me. So I let myself be a coward, keeping my eyes trained on the shadowy ground.

I didn't see him reaching out.

His fingertips grazed my cheek as if to brush my hair back from my face. I flinched away—too late. The spark of the contact, bare skin to bare skin, was already flaring into my brain. Memory flooded my head, almost as vivid as a vision.

The king's son, now king, settled his crown on his head. He

91

never looked totally comfortable wearing it in those moments when it was just the two of us before he stepped from his private chambers to greet whichever people had assembled to await his presence. Before them, as if by magic, the gold circlet would become as much a part of him as the dimple in his cheek when he shot a smile my way.

Today, that smile was slightly grim. "Have you seen any definite sign of a problem?"

I shifted on the padded chair. Bird chatter and joyful voices carried from outside. They didn't penetrate my uneasiness.

"No. But I know something is coming. I can feel it, Arthur. The fae all but confirmed it."

He nodded, the sunlight from the arched window catching on his bright hair. "I'll keep my eyes open, but I need to do this. The people need it, after all the fighting... Whatever happens, we'll face it, as we always do."

Did he fully believe that? I knew I didn't. But my king didn't have my instincts, hadn't seen my visions. And there amid the whitewashed walls and opulent fabrics of his chambers, it might have been hard to imagine anything could go wrong. Not here, not now.

But it would. It would.

The king stepped away from the mirror toward the door, and before I quite knew I was going to move, I'd grabbed his hand. He stopped and looked back at me. The shadow of our earlier argument crossed his face. I braced myself.

"Your Highness," I said, and then, because that sounded far too formal for what I meant to say, "Arthur. I just... I want you to know how much it's meant to me, to be able to serve you as long as I have. After everything we have faced, and no matter what happens next, there's nowhere I'd rather be."

His jaw twitched. The fear he'd been suppressing flickered in his eyes and melted away. He squeezed my fingers, and my pulse skipped. "Thank you," he said. And—

Darton scrambled off the bench. The sudden motion jerked me back to the present. He backed away, his eyes wide and his face pale. His hands shook as he tucked them under his folded arms.

"I've got to—" he said, catching himself on the verge of a stammer. I pushed to my feet, my stomach knotting. That touch would have sent a bolt of memory through him too, but one even stronger than the one that had hit me, because it was the first he'd ever had in this life. Because he couldn't have been remotely prepared.

It would have felt intensely real and yet absolutely alien. I didn't know *what* he'd seen, which part of that first life had hijacked his mind, but hijacking was the only word for it. He couldn't know I'd had anything to do with that strange sensation, but that didn't mean he'd want to be experiencing a mental breakdown in front of a relative stranger.

"It's getting late," he finally said without meeting my eyes. Then he swiveled on his heel and hurried down the alley toward the street.

My body ached to run after him, but I held myself back. One sliver of contact had only just cracked him open. If I didn't touch him again, he'd wake up by increments. Slowly.

Normally, I could have counted on having at least a week or two before his aura seeped through enough to draw the glooms directly to him... but the ones the mercenary had lent power to had been drawn to him already. I was going to have to stick extra close to him from here on—without him thinking I'd turned into a full-out stalker.

I pressed my hand to my forehead and dragged in a

rough breath. All wasn't lost. I still had ways I could at least try to protect him. I'd known this moment would eventually come.

I just hadn't expected it *tonight*.

There was no time now for extended experiments. I scowled at the gloom I'd trapped and fished out my wand. "*Darkness begone*," I snapped. The creature dissipated with a faint popping sound. I spun and jogged to the street, hailing a cab on my phone as I went.

II

Darton set off toward the football field in the hazy dawn light. He looked paler than usual but otherwise no worse for wear. A damp breeze tickled across my neck where I was watching him from under the awning of a campus cafe. I tugged my jacket tighter around me.

No more glooms had shown up overnight, but I wasn't counting on that luck holding. Now that my king's spirit had started waking up, there was no point in aiming for subtlety. I'd chucked the salve in the garbage last night. I had a spell that had served me well in the past, one that would create a sort of bubble around Darton that should at least slow the super-powered glooms down. Give me a chance to dispatch them before they got close enough to taste him.

If they got that first taste, the situation would be cocked up even without a fae mercenary breathing down our necks.

Unfortunately, the spell came with two problems. The first being that I needed part of Darton's physical essence to work the casting. And that wasn't the sort of thing I could just go up to a person and ask them for.

The second problem was I had to cast the spell right on him, in his presence, over the course of several minutes. The previous times I'd used it, it had been after Arthur's soul was awake enough to know who both he and I were. I hadn't figured out yet how I was going to pull it off without Darton deciding I was insane.

One challenge at a time.

I'd just drained the last of my bitter coffee, grimacing but grateful for the caffeine kick, when Keevan emerged from the residence building. My magical digging into school records had told me he and Darton were roomies—and that he had class at eight on Tuesday mornings.

As soon as his lanky frame had disappeared, I got up and headed for the residence building's entrance. The heavy stealth enchantment I'd cast over myself itched like a thick wool sweater, only one that covered me from head to toe. I hurried up to the third floor, around the corner and halfway down the hall, to Darton and Keevan's room. The students I passed brushed right by me as if I wasn't there.

By the time I reached the door, my skin was outright burning. Maintaining full invisibility was a pain in the ass. "*Open,*" I whispered to the lock, and then darted into the room.

I kicked the door shut behind me and shook off the stealth enchantment with a sigh of relief. I'd rather cast it again when I had to leave than conduct my search with it gnawing at me. Both guys should be occupied elsewhere for at least another couple hours.

The room was laid out in typical dorm fashion: a bed, a desk, and a shelving unit on either side. A glance at the shelves told me Darton's side was the left, where football strategy manuals squeezed up against politics, sociology, and law texts, and a bunch of novels that looked like legal thrillers. The lack of trophies and other badges of honor surprised me. He kept his things pretty spartan.

I pulled back the covers on his bed, but it appeared he was a bit of a neat freak in general. Not a single stray hair remained on his pillow or beneath his sheet. I frowned and smoothed the navy duvet back into place. The guy had to at least have a brush somewhere.

A caddy with shower supplies sat at the back of his desk, but it didn't supply me with a hair either. I shifted through the books stacked next to his computer. My hand paused over what looked like a sketchbook.

Darton *drew*? That didn't fit my impressions of the guy. I eased the sketchbook out of the stack and flipped it open.

The first several pages revealed nothing remarkable. He had some skill, but most of the pencil drawings looked unfinished, abandoned before he'd given them a real effort. Most of them were figures: a professor at the front of a lecture hall, a guy I thought was Keevan making a wild gesture, Izzy sitting at a table with the end of her pen pressed to her lips.

That last image gave my gut a little twist before I turned the page. Then my breath stopped completely.

He'd drawn *me*. From memory, obviously, and not an exact likeness by any means, but there I was in my fencing uniform, sabre in hand and mask in the other, my dark hair pulled back in my habitual ponytail. He'd barely marked my mouth, as if he hadn't been sure what expression to give me, but my eyes were carefully drawn. They peered from the page as if in thoughtful contemplation.

There were a couple more after. Lighter, hastier sketches: me standing by a tree, my arms crossed and hair lightly windblown—a memory from when Izzy had been doing her survey?—and a close-up of my face, the paper worn where he'd drawn and erased and drawn again, unsatisfied with the sharp line of my cheek, the slant of my jaw.

A shiver tickled through me. I shut the sketchbook and tucked it into place on the desk. My chest had gone tight.

He'd noticed me. He was intrigued. I could have guessed as much from our conversation last night.

There was always a connection between us. How could there not be, after the history we'd shared? It was never enough, though. I couldn't let myself dwell on it, let myself hope it meant more than it did. I wasn't going to be that selfish or that careless again.

A narrow basket wedged between the desk and the bookshelf caught my eye. Laundry hamper—jackpot!

I pawed through the small heap of clothes and found a polo shirt with a few gold-blond hairs clinging to it. I plucked them off and dropped them into a cloth bag. Then I dropped the shirt, turning to go.

The door swung open.

I froze. Keevan froze too, staring at me from the doorway. "*Don't see me, never did,*" I spat out over the thudding of my heart.

The air contracted around me, and a splintering pain jabbed through my nerves. All the twigs I'd hidden in various pockets crumbled to dust.

Keevan blinked. His forehead furrowed. "Art?" he

said. He stepped inside tentatively, his gaze searching the room. He probably still had the sense that something was wrong, even if he couldn't remember what he'd seen to make him think so.

I dodged him—he'd still feel me if I touched him—and sidled to the door, managing to dart out just before he pushed it closed. It thudded nearly as loud as my still-racing pulse. I stopped in the hallway, recovering my composure.

That had been much closer than I liked. I'd lost at least a week of life casting that spell so suddenly, unprepared.

And now I was out of magical materials. I hurried down the hall. I'd have to find a suitable tree on campus and relieve it of several twigs before I could even think about casting Darton's protection.

* * *

The clinking of test tubes and rasping of pens over paper settled my mind. I bent over my own notebook, studying the final results in the chemistry apparatus I'd set up for the day's lab. The acid gave off a pungent, soapy smell. As I wrote out my observations, a plan finally started to form in the back of my mind.

I needed to be within ten feet of Darton for the protection spell to work, but a physical barrier wouldn't affect my ability to cast. It was the middle of the afternoon now—hardly anyone was in the dorms. When he finished the second of his back-to-back lectures, I could conjure a little sleepiness in him, nudge him into taking a quick nap, and sneak into the room next to his to cast the spell through the wall.

It'd take a lot of energy, but he'd never have to know

I was even nearby. I could pull that off.

"Emma," Professor Kapoor called as I was passed his desk on my way out. I stopped. Uh oh. Had I forgotten an assignment amid the last two weeks' distractions?

He lowered his voice. "You missed our last class," he said. "And you looked somewhat… out of sorts when you came in today. If you don't want to talk, I'm not going to press, but I wanted to at least ask if everything is all right."

My face heated. I hadn't realized my angst had been that blatant. But I was touched by his concern, even if it meant I was going to have to lie to yet one more person in this life.

"Everything is fine." I forced a smile. I might not make it to even one more of these labs after today. "But thank you for asking."

"Okay," Professor Kapoor said. "You obviously have a lot of talent for this work. I try to support that when I see it in a student. If you ever do need extra time because of outside circumstances, please come talk to me."

A lump rose in my throat. By the light, how I wished I could get that kind of offer in the area I really did need extra time. "I will."

At least I had a plan now. I could make this work. My confidence crept back as I meandered over to Darton's lecture hall. His class wasn't over for another half hour, so I just staked out a secluded spot down the hall from the room and breathed slow and even to steady my nerves.

The minutes ticked by, but the door didn't open. Neither Darton nor his classmates emerged. Odd. When the next class of the afternoon started arriving and heading inside, I peeled myself off the wall and strolled over.

The seats in the hall were empty except for the few

scattered students who'd shown up for the next one. My stomach dropped.

What the hell had happened? Had the professor let them out extra early—or taken them on some sort of field trip? Or maybe the class had been outright cancelled.

It didn't matter. The result was the same—I had no idea where Darton was now. And no way of knowing where he might be before he decided to head back to his room for the night.

The campus was big. I didn't have much hope of simply stumbling on him, even though I'd managed to when it *wasn't* convenient. I checked the library, the football field, and the sandwich place he and Keevan appeared to be addicted to. No luck.

I wandered until I reached the front gate. The shadows were lengthening as the afternoon stretched toward evening. Tension wound through my gut.

I knew the soul of my king nearly as well as I knew my own. Now that it had started to stir inside Darton, I could reach out to it through my magic and know exactly where he was. The trouble with that approach was that connecting with him would release a little of that energy into the air. Any gloom tasked with searching for him would latch onto it in an instant.

I wavered for a minute, but then the glooms made my decision for me. The salt pouch in my pocket quivered. A gloom had drifted over one of my boundary lines—north of here.

It wasn't on campus yet, but I couldn't even say for sure Darton was still here. I slipped a twig into my hand, closed my eyes, and exhaled the ancient words. "*Where are you, my liege?*"

The awareness of him hit me like an elbow to the ribs. About a mile away, on the exact opposite side of campus.

Way too close to the gloom I'd sensed.

A knife of panic cut through me. My legs were already striding forward when my eyes popped open. I pushed myself into a run.

As I crossed the first major courtyard, the salt pouch jittered again. Two glooms—no, three—no, *four*. The first had been coincidence, but these had been drawn by my call. Damn it. I ran faster, ignoring the odd looks the other students were turning my way.

I could have run faster if I'd brought my magic into play, but I wasn't sure I'd make it to Darton if I put on a public display that obvious.

My sneakers thudded over the pavement. I dashed down the paths between the buildings, across a field, and around the horticultural department's conservatory. The salt vibrated at a continuous if erratic rhythm. I didn't have the wherewithal to keep count or track where each impulse was coming from. My chest was aching by the time I stumbled to a halt at the end of the garden on the other side of the greenhouse.

Darton was there, all right. Keevan and one of his other friends too. Darton was pointing out something in a sheaf of papers to them as they ambled between the beds of half-wilted flowers. Izzy had wandered a little apart from the boys to eye the glossy apples in a hunched tree. Some other students were laughing as they kicked around a hacky sack to my left, but they weren't the company I was worried about.

No, what concerned me were the five glooms

crawling across the garden from various directions—converging on the spot where Darton now stood.

Before I could spring forward, before I could do *any*thing, three of them drifted right against his legs.

12

No! The protest echoed in my head, but I didn't let it escape my mouth.

I could still fix this. As long as none of the glooms drifted back to their master to report what they'd found, we were safe. Relatively speaking.

The glooms were too far away for the fae dagger I'd stuffed in my bag to be of any use. I palmed a handful of twigs and cast a quick distraction spell over me to divert casual attention. In the few seconds that took, the glooms that had touched Darton whirled around and rippled away across the garden, hugging the patches of shadow along the flowerbeds. The two latecomers twisted around his ankles and quivered giddily.

"*Darkness begone,*" I whispered and jabbed my hand toward the closest gloom. It wisped apart into the air. Another had just streaked past Izzy's apple tree. Her head jerked around as if she'd seen it from the corner of her eye. I pointed and spoke the dispelling words again.

One of the two latecomers tumbled across the wilted flowers toward me. I exterminated it with a mutter and a slice of my arm. Two left.

That pair had darted in the opposite direction, farther away from me. I skirted a rose bush, the lingering floral perfume cloying in my nose. The leading gloom whipped between the thumping feet of the hacky sack players, and I managed to throw my magic across the distance after it. The effort drained the life from all but the last of my twigs.

The last gloom had flitted out of view beyond the ring of students. I hurried after it, my heart pounding. There—it was making for the hedge at the far end of the garden. I grasped my final twig. My arm jerked up.

And a body rammed into my side.

I tripped, my feet tangling, and hit the ground. The hacky sack player who'd dashed backward into me stumbled and swayed around. He raised his hands, his face flushing red.

"Sorry! Crap. Are you okay?"

I didn't care about his apology or his question. I scrambled onto my feet and groped after the twig I'd dropped. Where was the gloom? I threw myself around his group, toward the hedge.

Nothing but bare, regular grass and leaves met my gaze. My heart plummeted.

It was gone.

It was gone, and it had touched Darton before it had fled. Tasted the soul inside him and the magic that bound it there. Escaped to carry the message to every creature of darkness that might be eager to share in that tasting. Which experience told me was an awful lot of them.

We might be dead before our mercenary even got here.

My throat had constricted. I fought to swallow. The guy who'd bumped into me had followed me.

"Hey," he said. "Is everything all right?"

Why the hell wouldn't people stop asking me that?

"Yes," I bit out. "Fine." Other than the part where everything was absolutely wretched. The sun was sinking behind the conservatory. When night fell, all the creatures of the dark rabble would be at their fullest power—and I'd be at my weakest.

And it was all my fault. Something in the spell I'd used to sustain our lives and bind the Darkest One away spoke to the lesser darkness. Maybe they sensed a thread of their highest master in it. Or that Arthur's spirit lived on in defiance of her. Whatever the case, they would try to do what she had failed to—wipe him from this world. They'd nearly succeeded more than a hundred times over.

I'd failed him again. We'd barely even come together in this life and I'd already failed him.

My fingers tightened around the remaining twig, not that I had much use for it now. I glanced over at Darton. He was still laughing away with Keevan and the other guy, his back to me now. The distraction spell had been enough to stop him from noticing me even in my collision with the hacky sack guy.

Izzy had come up beside him. Her hand rested on his arm with a familiarity that dragged the feelings I'd been suppressing—and *really* didn't have room for right now—into my chest. I gritted my teeth.

I wasn't going to give up yet. The protection spell I'd planned wouldn't repel the glooms now that they'd had a taste of the king's spirit, but I could shred any that came near him. Over and over, as long as it took, until I figured out a new plan.

Of course, that meant *I* had to be near him too.

Darton and his friends headed toward the edge of the garden. I shook off the distraction spell, pushed aside my doubts, and propelled myself forward. I'd made it halfway over before the sound of my feet must have caught Darton's attention. He was the first of them to look my way.

Our eyes met. In that first instant, I saw an echo of last night's bewilderment. My steps slowed. He blinked, and just like that, he looked more like the cocky, assured guy I'd met in the middle of fencing practice.

He said something to the others and headed my way while they continued across campus. Whatever he wanted to say to me, he apparently didn't want them hearing it. I stopped and let him come to me.

He halted a few feet away from me. "Emma."

"Darton."

"So we run into each other again," he said. "Are you looking for another lost cat?"

His tone was teasing, but his gaze stayed wary as he waited for my response. Was he suspicious of me or worried he'd offended me?

"No," I said, and found my mind was too scattered to produce a halfway decent excuse. "Just stretching my legs. Too much time sitting in class today."

He nodded and lowered his eyes. "Thank you. For sticking around with me while I was rambling last night. I must have had more to drink than I realized."

The tension in my body eased. He was only worried. Well, why would he assume some weird vision that had popped into his head had come *because* of me?

Even if I'd been fairly useless in the last ten minutes, I could at least do this one thing for him. "It was fine," I said, offering him a slight smile. "I think I kind of like little-bit-buzzed Darton."

He raised an eyebrow. "*Only* that Darton?"

"I'm withholding judgment on the sober one pending further information." I gathered my nerve. "Maybe— partly in the interests of collecting said information—the bunch of us could grab dinner? If you all don't have something else lined up." I motioned to his friends, who'd just reached the conservatory.

Darton hesitated, but before I could think my suggestion had come out badly, a grin sprang onto his face. "Sure. I don't think we'd nailed anything down for tonight. Let me see what everyone's up for."

I let out my breath as he loped away to check in with his friends. Suggesting a group hangout had felt like a safer bet than trying to convince him to spend the whole evening with me alone.

My phone buzzed. I pulled it out and winced.

At the grocery store, Priya had texted me. *Was it ground or whole coriander we needed?*

I'm so sorry, I typed back. *I'm going to have to bail on dinner.* My fingers hovered over the screen. This once, going with the truth was probably the excuse she'd take the easiest. *I'm going out with Darton and his friends.*

A string of winking and thumbs-up emojis blew up my phone. *Go you! It's about time. Hey, I'll clear out for the night. Don't want worries about thin walls giving you an excuse not to seal the deal.*

It's not a DATE, I replied. Gods, even over the phone, she'd managed to make me blush.

Sure, sure. It's all good. I've been meaning to drop in on my cousin anyway.

There was no point in arguing with her. I shoved my phone into my bag and turned toward Darton's group.

The moment I looked their way, Keevan and Izzy waved to me. They turned and walked away as Darton strode back over. A prickle ran down my back.

"It turns out they've got someplace else to be, so it's just the two of us, I guess." Darton cocked his head. "If you think I'll be good enough company on my own."

Sod it. It practically *was* a date. I willed my legs not to start backing away.

I could handle this. I could keep myself in check. I *had* to—for Darton and the king he didn't know he was.

"I guess we'll see," I said, reflecting his casual air back at him. "If you start boring me, we'll just have to get some drinks into you."

13

"And *then*," I said, sweeping my arm for dramatic effect, "after all that trouble, they come running across the parking lot to realize they've been chasing the wrong bus the whole time. It's a bunch of high schoolers partying after prom, not the band."

Darton tipped his head back as he laughed. "God, Emma, I wish my parents had stories half that entertaining.

I smiled, running my finger through the sheen of condensation on the outside of my beer mug and making a concentrated effort not to ogle the slope of his neck from his throat to the V-neck of his sweater. My goal for the evening had been to keep Darton entertained enough that he'd want to stick around. So far that was working out, although I'd had to dig into my admittedly large stash of hippie-dippy stories from my parents' pre-parental escapades.

The campus bistro we'd ended up in was warm and bright enough to be falsely comforting, with a jangle of country music carrying over the chatter around us. Darton had eaten his way through a burger and fries and was now on his third beer. As far as he knew, I was on my second. Actually, I'd surreptitiously enchanted them into colored water. I wasn't going to risk impairing my own judgment any more than sharing the warmth of his presence did on its own.

"What did they do when they figured out the mistake?" Darton asked.

I leaned back in my chair. "My mom always gets a little vague at that point. I kind of suspect they talked their way onto the bus and partied like teenagers until the chaperone noticed and tossed them off.

"My dad was the kind of college guy who'd have been watching the hippies having the time of their lives and silently plotting how he'd 'show' them once he was rich." Darton took a swig from his beer and set it down on the wooden table with a thump. "He managed the rich part. I don't know if any of the kids who had more fun than him ever cared."

"And here I figured he must have been captain of the football team," I said lightly. "So you're not following in his footsteps?"

"Well... Same school, same major, same projected career path. I'm not straying very far."

"It seems like a pretty sweet path." Earlier in the evening, Darton had mentioned he was pre-law. Apparently his dad was a big-time corporate lawyer. "Nothing wrong with that."

A shadow crossed Darton's face. "Is life supposed to be that easy?"

I hesitated. I hadn't anticipated the shift in his mood. "What do you mean?"

"Honestly?" He looked at his beer mug instead of

me. "I wish I could feel the way you do. Like I knew where I wanted to go with my life, to be sure I'm heading in the right direction and not just coasting along. This probably sounds like entitled whining, but no matter what I do... I always have this gnawing impression that it's not enough. Or not important enough."

A pang of sympathy filled my chest. That was the Arthur in him. The knowledge he was meant for greatness, as present as if it were written into his DNA.

He had been great. I just hadn't managed to preserve him in the time he was meant for.

"Why not do something that does feel important?" I said gently.

"I try." Darton laughed again, but this time without much humor. "But once I get going, nothing ever feels exactly right."

Because the sense of direction that's compelling you is fifteen hundred years out of date.

"You know the one thing I've done that feels like a real accomplishment?" he went on. "When I was nine, my little sister fell in the pool. No one else was around. I jumped in and got her out. Did CPR and managed to get her breathing again. She'd have drowned if I hadn't moved that fast, if I hadn't remembered all that first aid training I learned in Boy Scouts."

"Saving someone's life is *definitely* an accomplishment."

"Yeah." He rubbed the back of his neck. "But I don't know how I'm ever going to do anything better than that. So is that it? I was at my best at nine? Like I said, I know this sounds stupid. I'm not normally this woe-is-me. But I really do admire that about you. The certainty you have.

Maybe that's why I like talking to you—hoping some of it might rub off on me."

He gave me a smile that was a little more relaxed, but I could still see the longing in the depths of his eyes. My throat tightened.

A real friend would have been able to comfort him. Reached across the table and squeezed his hand. Told him he'd find his way. But even with my gloves on—"My hands get cold all the time," I'd told him when he'd teased—I didn't want to take the chance of even that small physical gesture going wrong. And I couldn't bear to lie to him that blatantly.

He wasn't going to find his way—not as Darton Rowe, not as his father's son.

I could say *something* true, at least.

"I think I've given you the wrong impression," I said. "I knew what I wanted to study in college. With most other things… I have no idea what direction to go in. I just keep trying and hoping I'll eventually stumble on the right thing."

Darton bobbed his head, but I suspected he thought I was humoring him more than empathizing. He beckoned our waitress as she slipped by. "Check?"

My heart lurched, my gaze jerking to the window. It was fully dark outside now. No more glooms had come hunting Darton yet, but they'd be on their way. How was I going to keep him safe for the rest of the night? I couldn't expect him to stay up into the wee hours just chatting with a girl he barely knew.

The waitress dropped the receipt on the table, and Darton pulled out his wallet. I grabbed mine before he could try to pay for both our meals.

"Where are you heading now?" I asked as we waited for our change. I could have tried staking out his dorm room within a concealment spell, but that wouldn't help if the glooms seeped through the outer wall or the window or—

"I've got practice tomorrow morning," Darton said. "I should probably call it a night. But I'm glad we did this, Emma."

"Me too." I could lose him tonight, just like that. It all came down to the next few minutes.

He stood up to shrug on his jacket. I scooted to the end of the bench and scrambled to my feet so hastily my heel snagged on the table leg. I wobbled, and Darton caught my arm. My gaze fixed on his bare hand against the fabric of my shirt, and inspiration hit.

He wanted to be a hero. Deep down, that was what he'd always wanted.

I waited until we'd stepped outside and he turned to me to say his good-byes. The chill of the night air twisted around me. I braced myself. My gloved hand closed around his.

"Don't go."

I relaxed the careful control I'd been keeping over my expression, my emotions, and without even trying, nervous tears sprang to my eyes. Darton took one look at me and frowned.

"What's wrong?"

"I..." I sucked in a breath. "My roommate is out of town. It'll just be me at home. I don't know if I'll be okay on my own. I'm sorry, I realize it'd be a huge hassle, and I wouldn't ask if I knew anyone else I could—"

"Hold on." Darton looked confused, but at the same

time, a heat had crept into his voice that did something funny to my stomach. "Are you asking me to come back to your place and spend the night?"

Darkness take me. That wasn't how I'd meant the request to sound. "No," I said quickly. I didn't have to fake my embarrassed stammering. "I mean—yes, I'm asking if you'd stay, but—on the couch, not, like, *sleeping together.*"

Darton eased his hand from mine to run it comfortingly up my arm. Sparks shot over my skin at the contact, even with the layers of my jacket and shirt in between. Oh, some part of me very much wished I had meant the proposition the way he'd first taken it.

"What's going on, Emma?" he said.

I made myself stare him right in the face and let the last memory of my last life swim up out of my consciousness. The broken and bruised body the dark rabble had left behind when they were done with him, because I hadn't been there like I should have been. A different man, but the same one.

"I don't think it's safe." My voice trembled of its own accord. "I'd just… I'll feel so much better if you're there with me. Just this once. Priya will be back tomorrow."

Darton's expression softened. "Okay. You've got nothing to worry about. I'll be there. It's not even that big a deal."

You don't have a clue. I smiled gratefully, blinking back the tears. Now how was I going to deal with the other half of the problem?

14

Darton snored. It wasn't a particularly obnoxious snore, at least—just a low rumble that rose and ebbed with his breaths. After several minutes, I started to find it somewhat comforting, mainly because it told me he *was* still breathing.

I'd managed to put off any questions Darton might have had after we'd gotten to the apartment by bustling around making up the couch and thanking him profusely every time he'd opened his mouth. Ducking into my bedroom with a minimum of socializing had fit my frightened act, thank the light.

Of course, my fright wasn't entirely an act. I sat on my bed as Darton washed up and hunkered down on the sofa, tracking his movements by sound. My hand rested on the salt pouch in my pocket.

Not even a gloom had trailed Darton here. So far. In some ways, that worried me more. I'd have expected one or two that had been in the area to have headed this way by now.

But these weren't glooms following their normal impulses. The mercenary wasn't just lending them power.

He was also controlling them. To what end?

When Darton had been snoring long enough that I felt sure he was staying asleep, I inched open my bedroom door. I couldn't see him from that angle, but the thin light from the streetlamps beyond the living room window outlined the back of the couch, the entertainment unit, the kitchen island, and the front door. Settling myself on the hard floor where I could keep watch, I opened my bag and pulled out the supplies I'd been hauling around.

Maybe the spell I'd planned wouldn't hold off any gloom eager for the king's essence, but it might still slow them down a little. And damn it, I needed to do *some*thing.

I measured out the herbs on a silver plate, laid a circle of twigs around them, drew the symbols, and added the stolen hairs. The words of the incantation whispered over my lips. I closed the door just for a minute to light a flame on the plate. Then I blew the acrid smoke toward the living room, willing it through the door, across the floor, and around Darton's sleeping form.

There. It might not buy me more than an extra minute or two, but even a second's grace could make the difference between life and death.

I studied the shifting shadows in the main room and contemplated my next steps. If none of the dark rabble had come for Darton by morning, I could probably allow him a little distance by daylight. My salt warning system was still in place. It was the nights when he needed protection the most.

I grabbed my laptop. With a little magical finesse, I made my way into the college residence records. Ah. There was one empty room in Darton's building, scheduled for repairs after its original occupants had bashed several holes into the walls. Lovely. But useful. I could camp out there until I came up with a better plan.

I redirected the repair order and cloaked the record of the room so it wouldn't show up if someone else searched. Amazing how anything and any place could nearly cease to exist if it wasn't visible on a computer screen. And people thought *magic* was creepy.

Dawn light started to creep through the windows. My salt pouch lay still. I bit my lip, rubbed my hand over my weary face, and allowed myself to crawl into bed to snatch a couple hours of much-needed rest.

Sleep sucked me down into a deep, black void. In the midst of it, a vision unfurled, too stark to be just a dream.

Two trees swam into view, their trunks leaning so one crossed in front of the other like an X. My heart was thumping hard, the taste of adrenaline filling my mouth. Grit dug into my palms. *Give them hell,* a gruff voice I couldn't place hollered. A flare of heat seared over me.

I woke up with a jolt, my pulse still thudding. My head felt as if it'd been stuffed full of wool. I turned my bleary eyes toward the clock and swallowed a groan.

No more sleep for me. Darton had practice in an hour.

I pulled on a clean shirt and jeans and pawed briefly at my hair before shoving it into its usual ponytail. I stepped into the main room already debating how to best wake Darton up. He struck me as the sleeping-in type.

It threw me for a second when I found the couch empty and a very-awake Darton standing in the kitchen, stirring something in a pot on the stove. His hair was sleep rumpled in a way that provoked a tug of fondness in my gut.

A sweet, bready smell crept into my nose. My mouth watered. But the scene was far too domestic. Too cozy. The tug inside me turned into a painful twist.

"What are you doing?" I blurted out before I could catch myself.

Darton turned and gave me a sheepish smile. "Good morning. I, ah, hope you don't mind—I poked around in the cupboards and saw the bag of oats in there. When I was a kid and home sick from school, my mom always made me oatmeal. It's kind of comforting. I figured maybe you could use something like that."

Right. Because of how I'd freaked out in front of him last night. I managed a smile. "Yeah. Thank you."

"You're right on time," he said, more confidently now. "I just added the sugar." He spooned the thick mixture into two bowls and shot me a glance as he checked a couple drawers before locating the cutlery. "Fifteen kinds of tea and only instant coffee is a travesty, just so you know."

"I don't even drink the coffee," I admitted. "That's Priya's. I prefer being eased into alertness rather than kicked in the head."

"Hmm. With that attitude, you must have drunk the wrong coffee." He arched an eyebrow teasingly as he carried the bowls over to the table. "I'll forgive you if you tell me the truth about whose book that is."

He nodded to the corner of the counter by the fridge… where one of my historical romance novels was sitting out. My cheeks warmed. I'd been reading it while making dinner a few days ago and totally forgotten it since. At least it was one with a subdued cover, no blatant man chest or cleavage on the verge of bursting out.

"That's mine," I said shortly. "I like them more for the historical parts than the romance."

A total lie—though I did *like* the historical context, as wrong as the authors often got the details.

Darton grinned. "Ah-ha! So you do have at least one vice."

The conversation ebbed when I joined him at the table. We ate in silence, Darton gulping the instant coffee he'd resorted to between bites. He'd done a decent job with the oatmeal, actually—a little on the sticky side, but cooked well and with a lot of sugar—but it sat heavy in my stomach.

I liked seeing him sitting at my table. Liked the little teasing comments. But I couldn't have this, not really.

I forced down everything in my bowl, grateful he'd only filled mine halfway. As I set down my spoon, Darton leaned his elbows onto the table and fixed me with that inescapable indigo-blue gaze.

"Emma," he said, quiet and serious. "Are you going to tell me what you were so scared of last night?"

Somehow, I'd let myself think I'd successfully evaded this conversation. Since I was done eating, at least I didn't choke.

"I don't really want to talk about it," I said.

His eyebrows rose. "You had me spend the night on your couch to protect you and you're not even going to tell me why?"

I had you spend the night on my couch so I could protect you. Obviously, I couldn't say that. Instead, I hedged. "It's personal. I really appreciate that you stayed. Thank you. Priya will be home soon, and everything will be okay."

I wished. But at least I'd circumvented the most

immediate potential disaster.

Darton shook his head. "No. I want to know what's going on. I think you owe me that much, Emma. I saw how worried you were. Do you think you're in danger? Has someone tried to hurt you?"

Going along with that story would have been the easiest route in the moment, but it would only lead to complications. He'd want to take the matter to campus security or even get the police involved. I'd have to pile on lie after lie when I had more important things to focus on.

"I just don't do well at night on my own," I said. "It's not about anything that's happening right now."

"Bullshit. Something was going on last night. It freaked you right out."

I shrugged. "Maybe it looked that way to you, but that's not true. I'm sorry I made a big hassle for you. You want vices—there's my big one. Okay?"

His jaw set. "No, it's not okay. And it's not about you making a hassle for me. Staying wasn't a big deal. It *is* a big deal if you're in trouble."

The look he was giving me, so full of concern, did a number on my heart. I fumbled to find a response, and he reached across the table toward me.

His bare hand reached toward mine.

I jerked my arm back with a lurch of my stomach. Oh, no. This was too close, too intense. I needed him out of here, now, before any hope I had of keeping him safe unraveled.

I pushed away from the table and picked up my bowl. "Don't you have practice to get to?" I asked as I walked it over to the sink.

"I can skip one to help a friend."

My throat tightened. The words I was about to say burned in it, but I didn't see any other way.

"Your *friend*? You barely know me, Darton."

"I know you well enough," he insisted, standing up.

I summoned the chilliest tone I had in me. "I don't think you do at all. My roommate took off unexpectedly. I was nervous about being on my own all night, so I glommed onto you. You were there. That's all there was to it. That doesn't mean I want to start exchanging friendship bracelets."

Darton stiffened. "Don't do this."

He was never going to want to talk to me again after this, at least not until he woke up enough to understand why I'd had to push him away. But it was probably safer for both of us if I stuck to lurking around the edges of his life until that time. I'd already gotten too tangled up in his for either of our good.

"Do what?" I said, throwing my hands in the air. "Tell you the truth? I thought that's what you were asking me for."

"Emma."

"Just *go*. You'll find lots more kittens up trees to make you feel like you're doing something important with your life. You don't need me."

I suppressed a wince as the words fell from my mouth. I'd cut a little deeper than I'd planned.

Darton's expression shuttered. He strode across the room, grabbed his jacket off the hook, and set his hand on the doorknob. But even then, he gave me one last look.

I stared back at him defiantly, my teeth clenched to keep my chin from trembling. He yanked open the door and stormed out.

15

The door banged shut. A sob broke from my throat. My fingers closed around the kitchen counter as if I needed it to hold me up.

It'd be all right. I'd had to do it. I'd had to hurt him so I'd have some chance of preventing a far worse outcome later.

I stood there until my shakiness subsided. Each breath drew in the sweet smell of the oatmeal he'd cooked for me. An ache lingered in my chest, but I had to ignore it.

I needed to give Darton a head start before I followed him onto campus. *He* couldn't know I was sneaking into his residence. I had to focus on that. Focus on the real danger here.

First, I tugged on my gloves. No matter how strange I looked, I was *not* going without them in Darton's presence again. Then I headed into my bedroom to grab my duffel bag.

In went a crapload of magical supplies to supplement the ones already packed in my knapsack, followed by the sleeping bag I'd thankfully brought from home. There probably wouldn't be much furniture in a vacant dorm room.

A change of clothes. Some snacks from the kitchen, in case I got hungry in the middle of my surveillance. No pizza deliveries possible.

I zipped the bag shut and leaned over it. My head was spinning. Two hours of vision-interrupted sleep was really not enough to put me at my best. But I'd just have to make do. Once I was set up in Darton's residence building, I could sneak in a nap.

I pushed myself upright—and a quiver ran through the pouch of salt at my hip. My hand dropped to it.

The quiver didn't stop. It heightened, jittering erratically, as if it were being jerked from rhythm to rhythm at a frantic pace.

My pulse stuttered. I threw myself to the window.

The day had turned overcast while Darton and I were eating breakfast. Only thin sunlight washed over the street outside. And amid the dull shadows of the buildings and cars, clots of darkness were streaming by. Dozens of glooms.

All of them heading toward campus.

There were too many of them, coming too quickly. How could they—

I knew before I'd even finished thinking the question. My dark fae enemy was behind this. The mercenary had held the dark rabble in check, and then sent them at us in a horde.

I scrambled for my backpack. A wand. The light fae dagger, which I shoved into my pocket where I could reach it easily. I tossed the pack over my shoulder and clenched the wand in my hands.

I couldn't outrun the glooms. I'd just have to hope no one was around at this early hour where I planned to descend. I knew exactly where Darton should be.

Closing my eyes, I pictured the building and the lawn. "*Like the wind, carry me*," I said, and snapped the living wood of the wand in half.

A whirlwind of energy whipped out from it into the core of my body. My ribs shuddered, and my lungs seared. Everything emptied from my head but blackness and a roar of sound. With a lurch, I found myself stumbling on the grass at the north end of the football field. The athletic building loomed in front of me.

I'd barely made it in time. Patches of shadow were swarming across the field toward me. I grabbed the dagger in one hand and another wand in the other.

"*Darkness begone!*" My voice rasped, my throat still sore from the teleportation spell, but a wave of light split through the glooms. It shredded them apart across the field.

The salt in my pouch hadn't stopped quaking for a second. There were more coming—so many more.

The wand had gone brittle in my hand. I tossed it away, and it disintegrated where it hit the grass. Pulling another from my bag, I ran for the athletic building doors. The dark rabble could be approaching from all sides. I had to get to Darton to protect him.

My sneakers squeaked on the waxed linoleum floor inside. Where were the locker rooms? My gaze flicked over the signs as I pounded down the hall. There—the women's… and the men's. I burst inside.

Male voices and laughter echoed between the lockers. The guys in the row closest to the door, each in differing stages of undress, stopped to gape at the girl who'd charged into their midst. I dashed down the aisle, ignoring the startled shouts that rang after me.

Darton mustn't have arrived much earlier than I had. He was standing beside an open locker three rows down, the sweater he'd worn to my apartment crumpled on the bench beside him, his shoes kicked off. His hands were just falling to the buckle of his jeans. I skidded to a halt at the sight of him—in all that muscular, bare-chested glory—and his head jerked up. His arms flinched to his sides.

"*Emma?*" he said, his expression incredulous. "What the—what the *hell* are you doing here?"

For a split second, I entertained the idea that we might make a stand right here in the locker room. But even with the bright florescent lights beaming overhead, shadows pooled beneath the benches and along the bases of the lockers. The dark rabble would find plenty of paths to travel along.

"We've got to go," I said. A shout and a yelp carried from another row. I spun around as a shape like a jaguar made from shadow sprang from the wall. It landed on the end of a bench, smashing the wood to splinters, and swiped a paw at a guy who'd been too shocked to fully dodge. He stumbled backward with a cry of pain.

Shit.

"*Darkness begone,*" I hollered at it, flinging the wand out to encompass any creatures already in the room. Then I lunged forward and grabbed Darton's wrist.

They were after him. If I got him away, they'd leave everyone else alone.

"Come *on*," I said. He stared blankly at me. His head

jerked around at the screech of claws cutting through metal. I hauled on his arm. "We have to go, *now!*"

I dragged him into the aisle just as another creature of darkness rounded the opposite end. Darton flinched at its lupine snarl and spun around. I didn't have to drag him quite so much to make it to the doorway.

"W-what is going *on?*" he sputtered. I tugged him down the hall the way I'd come. "Where are we going?"

A good question. My mind whirled and latched onto an answer. "The track." Open ground, too flat to hold sheltering shadows. The dark rabble might not be frenzied enough to cross that much ground yet.

A dark beast leapt at me from the doorway. I swiped at it with the fae dagger, and it winced backward, its form splintering into the air. Another swing of the blade scattered the glooms crowding around the entrance.

Darton's jaw was still slack, but I didn't have to pull him after me on the way outside. Apparently he'd seen enough to want to get away without further prodding.

We raced across the grass to the broad ruddy swath of the track. Darton crossed his arms over his bare chest with a shiver. The chill of the morning air bit into my own face. I glanced at the sky, and my heart sank.

The sun was merely a spot of light glowing through the clouds. It wasn't going to be enough.

I stopped halfway across the track. "This is crazy," Darton was saying. "Oh, God."

The dark rabble had followed us, as I'd expected. Glooms and larger creatures of darkness rippled out of the athletic building and across the campus grounds, surrounding us in a wave. My stomach lurched.

I'd never seen so many coming for my king all at

once. He'd died before under the weight of a tenth this many. But the mercenary had obviously inflamed their urge to destroy. And now they'd caught wind of their prey.

The first few creatures to reach the edge of the track hesitated. My fingers tightened around the hilt of the dagger. One by one, they crept forward into the dim sunlight.

I reached to my bag to grope for another of my wands. We needed a place that we could flood with full light from end to end. Where near here— Oh. Yes, that could work.

But as I dragged the wand out, my grip on the polished wood wavered. Darton was staring at the dark rabble approaching us, but when I paused, he looked over at me. His face was white, his eyes wide. And I was about to frighten him even more.

The cat was already out of the bag, wasn't it? If we survived, there'd be no coming back from this, no convincing Darton I was some ordinary student, regardless of what I did next. And if I didn't act now, our chances of survival were nil. I inhaled sharply.

"*Darkness begone,*" I shouted with every bit of desperation in me. The wand cracked apart between my fingers as light blazed through it. A rush of brilliance seared across the field. The glooms and their dark companions shuddered and vanished.

Darton swayed on his feet. "What the hell?" he managed to say. As if I had time to explain. I set my gloved hand on his back and shoved.

"This way," I said with a gasp for breath. "*Run.*"

16

Darton didn't need a second push. We tore around the athletic building. I pointed across the green toward the campus theater. "There. We have to make it there."

More glooms and other dark creatures were creeping around the edges of the buildings and stalking across the grass. A few of the students strolling to their early morning activities caught sight of them and bolted for the theoretical safety of the nearest doorway. Others froze like rabbits in a hawk's shadow.

"Get out of here!" I yelled at them as we raced by. That was enough to break most from their dazes. But they didn't all dodge fast enough. One of the creatures leapt between a couple and knocked them to the ground. An enormous snake-like beast slithered past a girl who'd tripped in her panic, snapping its tail against her legs. She cried out in pain. My gut twisted.

If we could get into the theater building and clear everyone else out, the dark rabble would congregate there. Away from the bystanders who never should have been drawn into this conflict.

A winged shadow dove at me from above. I slashed

upward with the fae dagger, but the creature's filmy talons raked across my forearm before the light energy sliced through it. A sharp burn radiated through skin and muscle. I hissed in a breath, yanking my arm to my belly. My sleeve gaped open, the flesh beneath where the creature had touched it turning dead and gray.

Darton glanced over and blanched even whiter. "Are you going to be all right?" he said, his voice ragged from the run.

"Let's hope so," I muttered.

We reached the theater doors just as the dark rabble surrounded us. I spun around with a swing of the dagger, scattering the closest forms, and Darton heaved open the doors. Inside, I dove for the fire alarm.

The pulsing blare echoed down the hall and rattled my ears, but it'd get anyone else in here to leave. Darton had halted behind me, waiting for my cue. I took off toward the main auditorium, and he followed at my heels.

"You have to tell me what's going on," he said. "What *are* those things? You knew they were coming. How did you... do whatever you did that killed them? *Where* did they come from? What do they want?"

"All you need to know right now is that if they catch us, they'll kill us." I yanked open the auditorium door. "If we survive the next hour, I'll explain the rest."

We sprinted up the aisle to the stage. I swung myself onto the wooden platform rather than bothering with the stairs. As Darton clambered after me, I dashed into the wings.

The light controls had to be around here somewhere. I ducked between the curtains, a dusty smell tickling my nose, and caught sight of a broad black panel covered with switches. Bingo! Thank the light this school wasn't artsy enough to have an ultra-complicated setup.

My hands whipped across the panel to snap all the switches on. The lights crackled overhead and flooded the stage with light from every possible angle. Darton swayed in the mist of it, blinking and probably momentarily blinded.

The breath rushed out of me. I'd done it. The entire stage was lit so thoroughly not a single shred of shadow darkened the floor.

I hurried across the polished wood to Darton's side. The fire alarm wailed on. I tuned the racket out as well as I could as I peered beyond the stage. A couple of the lights had been pointed toward the area at its foot, so I could make out the front row of seats, but beyond that, the rest of the auditorium blurred into a black mass.

A gloom rippled along the edge of the light as if testing how much its shadowy body could tolerate. It flinched away into the deeper darkness. More shapes shifted across the tops of the chairs and the fringes of the aisles, but nothing ventured out far enough to become fully visible.

My shoulders eased down, but the rest of my body stayed tense. My gambit was working—for now. More glooms and dark creatures would be converging on us with every minute we stood here. It wasn't as if we could live on this stage for the rest of our lives. I was going to have to come up with a more permanent solution. But at least I had space to think.

Darton had started to pace. His steps took him close to the edge of the stage, and he veered to the side abruptly. The muscles in his bare shoulders flexed. He only stilled when a creature with a knobby head sank its jaws into the cushion of one of the chairs and ripped out a chunk of fabric and stuffing.

"What. The. Hell. Are those things? What is going on? Why are we in here? Shouldn't we, I don't know, call the police or something?"

A laugh burst out of me. It sounded so hysterical I clamped my mouth shut. Breathe. In and out.

"The police don't have any clue how to deal with a situation like this," I said. "These are the things that go bump in the night, Darton. Creatures people have pretty much forgotten really exist thanks to our modern-day 'advances.' But they never really went away. They just got quieter. Until they see something they want."

"What are *we* going to do about it, then?"

I grimaced. "I'm *trying* to figure that out."

Darton fell into an uneasy silence. I scanned the auditorium again. One of the snake-like creatures slithered along the edge of the light in an undulating line. Another shadow beast pawed at the lit floor by the end of an aisle. The thing on the seatbacks was still wrenching shreds of stuffing out of the cushions.

A mass of glooms lurked behind the distinctive creatures. I couldn't tell how many had already gathered in the blackness, but their presence grated against the light fae essence woven into my soul. My fingernails dug into my palms.

The fire alarm trailed off, and the hum of the overhead lights filled my ears. I tipped my head back, eyeing them. A glimmer of an idea sparked in my mind. I'd used up most of my living wood, but electric energy was still energy. Running through those manmade machines and wires, it didn't hold the natural power to kill the dark rabble on its own, but I could channel it through *my* natural body with a little effort, convert it into conjured sunlight

"Stay there," I said to Darton before he could launch into more questions. I swapped the dagger for one of my few remaining wands and stalked closer to the front of the stage. Inhaling deeply, I raised one hand toward the lights. I pointed the other, holding the wand, at the darkness.

"*Stream fast, stream far, and burn*," I commanded, and jerked the wand.

A bolt of crackling brilliance shot from the stick's tip and blazed across the first several rows of seats. Every dark creature in its path dissolved. So did the wand. I flicked the crumbled wood from my hand and reached into my bag for another.

The flash of light had revealed the rest of the theater, all the way to the writhing mass of darkness that was blotting out the seats and the walls, as even more poured inside. In the few seconds it took to pull out my next wand, the dark rabble surged forward. It filled the space I'd just cleared as if I'd accomplished nothing at all. Behind me, Darton swore.

There had to be a limit to them. They couldn't keep coming forever in these numbers. But I didn't know how many the fae mercenary might have drawn from distant grounds to serve his purpose. We might have an entire continent's worth of dark rabble to deal with.

"*Burn*," I called out, propelling another sizzling wave over the creatures in the shadows. My hand shook as the electric energy flowed through me, but I managed to throw light nearly halfway up the auditorium this time.

The luminescence faded, and the rest of the monsters swarmed forward. Were they at least a little thinner where they squirmed by the base of the stage? I reached into my pack. Three more wands. A bunch of twigs. Was that going to be enough?

Two of the spotlights flickered. Not so much that the glow on the stage visibly dimmed, but the jitter caught my eye. I glanced up at them, and a few more quavered. My back stiffened.

I'd only turned them on, what, ten minutes ago? Fifteen? No way should the bulbs be burning out just like that. I'd drawn my power from the wires, not the bulbs themselves, and I could still feel the electricity streaming through the cables. Something else was going on.

I stepped closer to Darton.

"What?" he said.

"The lights." Another flickered, and then another. A ripple of darkness crossed them in a shuddering chain, just as my sense of the electricity hiccupped. My mouth went dry. "They're eating through the electric supply."

"*What?*" Darton repeated. He raised his hands as if he thought he could fight off our attackers with his fists.

If I could find them... If I could pinpoint the spot where they were working at it...

I extended my awareness into the space around us, beyond the walls and below the stage floor. The thrum of electricity buzzed against my nerves. Where was it stuttering?

I followed the hitch in the energy down into the ground and out... to where a pack of the dark creatures had burrowed down into the lawn beside the theater. I winced at the feel of their shadowy teeth and claws scraping at the cable and the wires within.

Sparks danced behind my eyes. The stage lights wavered and dimmed. *No!*

I groped for a wand and opened my mouth, the words to blast light across that distance and shred those creatures into nothingness already rising in my throat—

Every bulb above us snapped off.

In that first instant, in the sudden black, my mind blanked with shock and horror. The emptiness of the dead lines laced through the building, the fixtures overhead dulled of light, echoed through me. With a rising hiss, the wave of monsters barreled toward us.

The sound of our impending doom sent my mind spinning into action. Darton grabbed my arm, his tight grip both protective and seeking protection.

I could still touch the sputtering flow of electricity in the far end of the cable the creatures had split. I could reach it, pull it, if I extended myself far enough, and bridge the gap they'd cut.

My fingers closed around my last three remaining wands. No time to second-guess—no room for moderation. I knew, even as I swung my arm, that either I took every creature in and around this building down in this fell swoop—or we were dead, because I wasn't going to be conscious to try again.

"*Come to me and burn,*" I hollered, heaving at every particle of electricity in the line with all the life inside my body.

The energy walloped me across the back of my head and ripped through my chest, tearing the breath from my lungs. A brilliant sear exploded around me, as if the sun itself had fallen through the theater's roof.

My vision filled with the yellow-white glare. Inside my head, everything went dark. My knees gave, and then I knew nothing at all.

17

A shadowed figure stood by the decrepit carcass of a cabin in the woods. Tall and lanky with black hair and pale skin—but it was a paleness that seemed to swallow the light that touched it, leaving a haze of darkness in its wake.

Just as the light fae exuded a natural glow, the dark fae dampened any radiance in the air. They deepened shadows and drained the vibrancy from everything around them.

The figure turned, revealing a masculine face, a profile of harsh angles. His lips curled with a smirk.

"I feel you spying on me, would-be protector. But you are not here. Your magic is not here. What will you do to me, hmm?"

His low, ringing voice washed over me. I couldn't move. Couldn't answer. My limbs, my tongue, were someplace else.

Somewhere I was needed. I had to get back.

"Nothing, yes," the dark fae mercenary—who else could it be?—remarked. "Poor thing. You'll just have to watch as my shadows claim my prize and carry him back to me. I can't believe it took me so long to stumble on the two of you. The one you're guarding is a great one. I can feel that there's nothing the darkness I honor would appreciate more than the chance to devour every hint of his soul. And I *will* deliver him to her."

No. I had no throat to force the word from.

"It's just a matter of time. I'm sure we'll see each other soon—for as brief a moment as you manage to survive the meeting."

The dark fae laughed, a hollow sound, and the vision fell away. I spun into a thicker blackness, the chill of his words wrapped around me. *Devour every hint of his soul.*

If the mercenary captured Darton—if he wrenched my king's soul from that body in whatever ritual sacrifice he had planned—he might destroy not just Darton's life but whatever was left of Arthur's.

My thoughts whirled and blurred. Then my eyes blinked open to a panicked face lit by an eerie glow.

"Emma!" Darton's grip on my shoulders tightened. I was lying flat on the floor. No, not the floor—the polished wood of the stage where we'd made our stand. My back hurt, probably because I'd fallen on it when the effort of that last casting had knocked me out.

I'd given up at least a year of this mortal life with that one blast. Maybe two. Not that it mattered if we didn't live through the next few hours.

I pushed myself into a sitting position. "I'm not sure—" Darton started to protest, but I ignored him. An ache ran down my spine and up the back of my head. I forced myself to think past it.

"Are they gone? The glooms and the—the creatures that were trying to attack us. They're all gone?"

Darton nodded. The light shifted over the planes of

his face. It was streaming from a cell phone screen—he'd turned his on and set it on the stage beside us. Otherwise, the auditorium was dark, but also still. If any of the dark rabble *had* remained, we wouldn't be having this conversation.

"Are you all right?" Darton said. "You've been passed out for a couple minutes. We should get you to the health center—"

"No!" I shoved myself onto my feet, swayed, and managed to steady myself as Darton grabbed my elbow.

The dark fae mercenary wasn't planning to give up. He'd be sending even more of his minions after us. And if they caught Darton…

"We can't stay here. More of those things are coming."

Where could we go? Anywhere in the city, we'd be putting even more innocents in the line of fire. I needed more supplies. Damn it, I needed time to prepare.

The light fae enclave. They would take us in if I forced the issue—if I pressed hard enough on the allegiance they owed to my father. I didn't know if they'd actively *help* us, but at least if the mercenary and his creatures found us there, the fae would be able to defend themselves.

"We have to go." I motioned for Darton to pick up his phone. "We can stop at your dorm room and my apartment to grab essentials, and then—" I wasn't sure about the bus schedule. Where was the closest car rental place? I'd burned away all the dark rabble within a large distance, but there was no telling how much time we had before the next wave hit us.

"Emma, stop." Darton's hand clenched around my

elbow. "I'm not going *anywhere* until you explain what's going on. I don't understand any of this. What those things were. What you did to get rid of them. Why they came after you in the first place. Who you even *are*."

I looked at him in the thin light. The fear he was trying to cover leaked into the twitch of his eyes, the sharp slant of his mouth. He wanted to be strong, because that was what he did, what he'd always done. But he couldn't take on this problem, not really, not when he didn't even have a clue what we were up against.

I couldn't keep lying to him. We weren't getting anywhere if he didn't believe enough to fight for his life alongside me instead of fighting *with* me.

"They aren't coming after me," I said. "They're coming after you."

Darton's forehead furrowed. "What? I've never seen anything like those... bogeymen before in my life."

"Not in this life," I said as evenly as I could manage. "This isn't your first one. Do you remember the other night outside the pub? An image rushed into your head—a scene that would have felt unfamiliar but also... as vivid as if it belonged to your past. That was a memory, Darton. A memory from the first life you lived, more than a thousand years ago."

His expression had frozen in place. He shook his head. "That's crazy."

"It sounds crazy when I have to lay it on you all at once, but that doesn't mean it's not true. It's the whole reason I'm *here*. You made a dangerous enemy in that past life. An enemy who's still making trouble for you, one way or another, even now. I've been trying to keep you safe."

"We'd never even met before *I* decided to join your

fencing club," Darton said.

I laughed weakly. "Darton, I told you I left Yale to come here because I knew I had something else I needed to do with my life. That was finding you. Believe me, I'd have gotten here earlier if I'd known where to go before then."

The skepticism in his face hadn't softened. If anything, he looked more incredulous. "*You're* crazy."

Bloody hell. We didn't have time for a debate. The passing seconds gnawed at me.

But all the same, my body balked. I knew what I had to do. But the more he woke up, the more easily the mercenary would be able to track him.

I dragged in a breath and yanked off my right glove.

"I can show you. When that memory hit you the other night, it was because you touched me, skin to skin. We're connected, and the contact triggered that connection. We can make it happen again. It's easy."

I held out my bare hand. Darton stared at it. For a second, I thought he was going to turn and stalk off, that I'd have to force the waking on him.

His jaw flexed. He slid his hand down from my elbow to fold his fingers around mine.

A little jolt raced up my arm, even though I'd been fully prepared for his touch this time. My own memories trickled up, much more gently than the ones that would be racing into Darton's mind. His eyes glazed over as I watched. He was hardly even here.

The impressions of a time long past washed over me, and I let them come. The image swelling inside my mind was totally out of tune with our current situation—bright and happy. By the light, how I wished our lives had stayed that simple.

The prince and I lounged at the edge of his estate's orchard—a moment of rest after a long, hard ride. There was something wonderful about feeling, if only briefly, that we were two ordinary young men simply sharing a summer's day. My muscles were aching, true, but the brilliant warmth of the noon sun made up for that. It beamed down on us from above and radiated from within the golden stalks of the scratchy bale of hay we were leaning against. The rich, dry smell filled my nose.

"So what can you do with this magic of yours?" Arthur said casually.

"Whatever you like," I said, flushing with eagerness for his approval. "Are you hungry?"

I gestured to the nearest tree and murmured. A large, ripe apple snapped off its stem and sailed through the air to hand in the hand Arthur extended. He tossed it up, caught it, and chuckled. Then he bit in, as if it were a fruit gathered by completely normal means. A knot in my gut I hadn't noticed loosened.

That memory blurred into another.

My prince dragged me into the castle's stables. Our feet clattered over the straw-strewn floor. Swine crud, *I thought as I hurried to keep pace.* Not another ride.

We came to a stop in front of one of the stalls. A bay mare with wide, dark eyes peered out.

"There," Arthur said, as if I were supposed to know what was going on.

"What?" I said.

"She's yours." He reached to rub her nose. The mare whickered with a contented hum. "The seller trained her specifically as a child's horse—all patience, no skittishness. Since you ride about as well as a small child, I figured you'd suit each other."

His tone was teasing but his gaze intent as he stepped back. I eased forward, braced for the mare's reaction. Every animal sensed my fae heritage, and every domesticated horse I'd encountered so far had objected to it with rolling eyes and stomped hooves.

But this one didn't shy away from my reaching fingers. I held my breath as I scratched her chin. She emitted the same pleased sound she had for the prince. He looked exceedingly pleased with himself, but I didn't mind. My own face had split with a smile I couldn't contain.

He'd gone out of his way to find a horse I wouldn't dread handling, even though his family already owned dozens. He'd arranged this gift just for me. For me and all that damned time we spent riding together.

I opened my mouth to ask the mare's name…

The memory shifted again.

I was lying on my back on a camping roll, cool air on my face and lumpy ground beneath me, gazing at the night sky. A campfire crackled beyond my feet. Beside me, the man who was now my king waved his hand toward the stars.

"What do you think they are, really? All those lights we only see when the sun is away."

I tilted my head, considering. "Maybe they're suns too, just farther away."

"That must be awfully far. Do you suppose people will ever travel all that way? Perhaps by using magic like yours?"

I snorted. "I don't know, but I'm sure that's nothing we'll ever see. It's looking to be a long day tomorrow. Go to sleep, my liege."

Arthur harrumphed, but he rolled onto his side, his back to me. I studied that back in the dim light of the fire. Exhaustion hazed my thoughts. As if of its own accord, my fingers crept across the short distance between us and rested on the fabric of my king's blanket.

The warmth of his body beneath bled through the wool at the faint pressure. My heart thudded. Arthur didn't stir. He probably hadn't noticed. I wasn't sure whether I wanted him to or not.

No, I did. I wanted him to—

I jerked my consciousness out of that memory into the present to find my pulse thumping here too. Okay, that one had delved a little deeper than I'd have preferred.

Darton's grasp on my hand had faltered. With relief, I decided he must have seen enough. I tugged my arm away, breaking the contact.

Darton shuddered, blinked, and the glaze faded from his eyes. They fixed on my face as intently as if he were looking straight through my skin and skull to the mind that had lived alongside his so many times before. His lips parted.

"Merlin?"

18

Hearing Darton say my name—my first name, my true name—sent a rush of warmth through me that I should have been prepared for, but wasn't. I bowed my head, my throat suddenly tight. "Your Highness."

"*Merlin.*"

He grasped my shoulder and pulled me to him, clapping one arm around my back. My breath hitched at the feel of that bare, sculpted chest against my body, but I hugged him back, clenching my hands so my fingers didn't brush his skin again. A tremble ran through him as he held on to me. What memory had he seen?

Enough to convince him, at least.

It felt good, being that close to him. Breathing in the citrusy fabric softener smell that was only Darton's and the earthy, masculine musk that had belonged just as much to Arthur.

It felt good because this embrace meant more to me than it ever would to him. My heart squeezed.

"Darton," I said.

He stepped back, his expression abashed. "Sorry. I just… I still don't understand, not really, even though I

145

know… What is going on?"

I drew myself up straighter. "Look, I know it's a lot—it *is*—and that's exactly why I can't get into every detail right now. The most important thing you need to understand is that there are dark powers that want very much to kill you, and they know you're here now, so we have to leave. The faster we get moving, the harder it'll be for them to track you. Once we're on our way, there'll be more time to talk."

"Okay," Darton said. "But I expect you to explain *every*thing."

I nodded. "I promise. Now let's hurry."

* * *

I gave Darton five minutes to pull on a new shirt—as much as I enjoyed the eye candy, I'd rather he didn't get hypothermia—and to stuff a few essentials into a bag in his dorm room.

"How long will we be gone for?" he asked as we ducked out of the residence building and started to jog across the courtyard. "*Where* are we going?"

"To the first question, I'm not exactly sure." We were going to be lucky to survive more than a couple days with the dark rabble this close on our heels, but I wasn't going to tell Darton that, not this early in his waking. "But if you need more basics, I've got money. We just need to stop by my apartment so I can grab some supplies, and then there's a place I think we might be safe, south of here. I need to check the bus schedules. Maybe we'll have to rent a car."

"If we have to go somewhere farther than we can walk, Keevan would help. He's got his own car."

"No," I said firmly. "It's safest if we're alone. I don't

want to bring him into this mess."

"Bring me into what mess?" said a voice behind us.

I swung around, my pulse skipping. Keevan and Izzy, her arms crossed tightly over her chest, stopped a few feet away from us. They'd obviously just caught up.

"What are you doing here?" I blurted out.

"What are *you* two doing?" Keevan demanded. "We heard…" He paused, looking almost embarrassed now. "Well, we heard that there were some sort of *monsters* chasing Darton—that he ran off—so we came looking to make sure he was okay and to figure out what the hell everyone is *on*."

His gaze dropped to my arm. To the slashes in my jacket and the slivers of dead gray skin that showed through it. The shadow creature's wound didn't hurt anymore, because there were no nerves left in the spots where its claws had raked to feel anything. I tugged my sleeve to cover them, and his gaze flicked up to meet mine.

"There *was* something after you." Shock had colored his tone. He hadn't believed it when he'd said it before. "And—now you're talking about taking off somewhere?"

"It's hard to explain," Darton said, which was easy for him to say when even he didn't really understand.

"You can't get involved," I put in. "There are monsters, yeah, if you want to call them that, and they're dangerous. But once we're out of here, they shouldn't hassle anyone on campus. So you're better off here."

Keevan frowned. "This is totally wacko, but Darton's my best friend. If something dangerous is going down that could hurt him, I'm not hanging back to protect myself. You need help, I'm there, Art. You gotta drive somewhere? Name the place."

Izzy nodded, looking scared but determined. "Everything he said. I saw the way the lawn looked behind the athletic building... I don't want whatever did that getting to Darton. I'll do whatever I can."

I suppressed a groan. We didn't have time for an extended argument. And having the use of a car would make the next few hours so much easier.

Keevan could drop us off by the enclave, and then I'd send him right back here.

"All right," I said to Keevan. "We *could* use your help. Thank you." I glanced at Izzy. "But that's just for the car. You've got to stay here."

"No way." Her hands dropped to her sides, balling into fists. "There'll be something I can do."

"Izzy," Darton began. She shook her head, her chin set.

I sighed. "Fine, fine. The whole gang can come. Why not? Keevan, you and Izzy go get your car and meet us at my apartment."

As soon as I'd given them the address, they hustled off. Darton loped along beside me the rest of the way across campus. I could tell from the way his jaw worked that he was simmering with questions, but the dark rabble's attack must have shocked him enough that he was wary of distracting me.

Inside the apartment, I strode straight to my room. Darton leaned against one of my bedposts as I stuffed a few final items into the duffel bag I'd already mostly packed. Then I organized the equipment I was keeping on me. Fae dagger in my pocket, the hilt jutting out for easy access. A wand tucked into my belt loop. That was as good as it was going to get.

I turned toward the doorway. At the exact same moment, Priya stepped into it.

I froze. I hadn't even heard her approaching.

Her gaze darted through the room, taking in the bulging bag I'd just slung over my shoulder, the bewildered guy beside me, and the tension that must have blared from my own expression. "What's going on?"

"Nothing important," I said. Guilt gnawed at my stomach at the lie, but it was for her own protection. "We were just leaving."

I moved toward the main room, but she blocked the doorway. "For how long? You look like you've packed half the bedroom."

My hand tightened around the bag's strap. "I'm not sure. But we really do have to get going."

Priya finally stepped to the side, but she grabbed my arm when I tried to pass her. "Emmaline. What happened? You're acting so weird. Don't say it's nothing. It's obviously not."

The sense of time slipping away from us loosened my tongue. "I can't get into the details, but something bad is going down, and Darton and I need to get out of here for… a while. You don't need to worry. I know what I'm doing. I'll make sure my half of the rent gets paid."

"I'm not worried about the *rent*." Priya stomped her foot. "Geez, Emmaline. Where are you going? How are you getting there?"

"One of my friends is picking us up in his car." Darton's voice sounded creaky after his long silence. I appreciated him speaking up for us, but not the way Priya's eyes narrowed at that statement.

"Oh, so *his* friends are allowed to know what's going

on?"

"It's not like that. Pri…"

Priya tugged me a little to the side. Her voice dropped. "I'm not blowing smoke up your skirt. If something's gone wrong, I might be able to lend a hand."

She raised the sleeve of her sweater, calmly and deliberately, just high enough for me to see the leather band wrapped around the brown skin of her forearm right below the elbow. A leather band that was etched with lines so familiar my heart stopped. I stared at them and then at her as she shook her sleeve back down. Priya gazed back at me steadily, her mouth pressed flat.

She was wearing a fae armlet, marked with fae runes. Where the hell had my sweet, bubbly roommate from the suburbs of Seattle gotten *that*?

And how had she known *I'd* know what it meant?

"I think we have a lot to talk about," I said. "But not right now." I sucked in a breath. Screw it. "Come on. Let's hope Keevan's car has room for five."

A grin stretched across Priya's face, so brilliant it was as if I'd invited her on a road trip to Palm Beach and not to flee some unspecified mortal danger. She clapped her hands, bounded into her bedroom, and emerged with a large satchel before I'd even walked the whole way to the front door.

"Do you really think it's a good idea for her to come too?" Darton murmured to me.

"No," I said. "I wanted it to be just you and me. But it looks like I'm not getting much choice in the matter."

A honk carried from the road below the living room window. Our ride was here. I just hoped it wasn't the last one we took together.

19

The backseat of Keevan's red Toyota wasn't the largest space I've ever been squeezed into. I'd taken the middle spot between Priya and Darton so I could see through the windshield while still having Darton within immediate reach, and while she was thin as a whip, I was so close to him that I felt every slight movement he made. The solid muscles in his arm pressed against mine. The thump of his pulse echoed through his body.

With my gloves on, I wasn't too worried about accidental skin contact. The problem was more how much I wanted that contact purposefully.

Inside the boy I was becoming fond of in his own right, my king was stirring. It had been far too long since I'd spoken to him outside a memory, since I'd been able to look into his eyes and know he knew exactly who he was looking back at.

My mind darted to the last memory I had of his weight over me, caressing hands, and tangled sheets, some two lives past. A flush I really did not need to be dealing with right now flooded my skin. I bit my lip and focused on the map I'd brought up on my phone.

Keevan filled the car with the buoyant melodies of a classic pop radio station for the first couple hours of the drive. As we neared the state line, the reception started to break into static. He switched it off. The quiet that followed felt ominous. Apparently not just to me, because after a minute, he cleared his throat.

"So. Emma. I'm hoping I speak for us all when I say I'd really like a little more explanation about shadowy monsters that can rip through locker room benches, and how we're going to make sure they don't rip through us."

My throat tightened. I'd known I was going to have to tell him and Izzy something. The truth—part of it, at least—was easiest. If they didn't believe me, that was their problem.

"There are fae living in the world," I said. "Some of them are a lot like us, like people, but most of them are more like animals, or even less conscious than that."

"Fae," Izzy repeated. "You mean *fairies?*"

"Not like something out of a Disney movie." I rubbed the streaks of deadened flesh on my left forearm. "They're just part of... another side of the world that people have mostly dismissed these days. Anyway, there are two kinds—light and dark. The light loves chaos and energy and the dark loves order and stillness, so they tend to be at odds. Although there are few enough left that they don't get in each other's way too often anymore."

"Order versus chaos," Keevan said. "It sounds like we should be on the dark's side."

I smiled thinly. "I wouldn't recommend that. Life is chaos, and nothing is quite as orderly as deathly oblivion. So you can guess which direction each side likes to push the rest of us toward."

A nervous giggle slipped from Izzy's mouth. "Okay, in that case, I'll vote for light."

Darton shifted, the brush of his knee sending a fresh tingle of warmth up my leg. "It's the dark ones that came after us, right?"

I nodded. "Came after *you*."

"Why would they want Darton?" Keevan said. "I mean, he's a great guy and all, no complaints here, but I didn't think he was such a big superstar that he'd have fairy things knocking down his door."

That was the part I didn't think it was wise to get into. There was no way they were going to wrap their heads around *that* truth, even if I'd wanted to get into it.

"You could say he's got a connection to someone who has caused a lot of trouble for the dark fae in the past," I said. "An ancestor, a *long* time in the past. They're very good at holding on to grudges. And now they've noticed he's around."

"And they want to… to kill him?" Izzy's voice dropped with the last two words.

"That's the general idea."

"What are you going to do about it?" Priya asked, the question simple and soft. She hadn't questioned my story at all. How much of what I'd said had she already known? I eyed her, my shoulders tensing. We *really* needed to have a talk—a private one.

"We're heading to a light fae enclave," I said. "It's about another hour from here, if the traffic doesn't interfere. I don't know how much they'll help us, but just being around them will make it harder for the dark rabble to find Darton again."

Izzy turned in her seat to peer at me. "And how do

you know about all this stuff? Are you one of—"

"No," I said quickly. Better to keep that part of my explanation simple too. In a literal sense, the life I'd been born into was completely human, spiritual heritage aside. "I've been friendly with the light fae for a while. It's a long story. They'll let us in. That's all that matters."

Darton's friends fell silent. I couldn't tell whether they were merely absorbing what I'd said or wondering what to do about the lunatic in the backseat.

At least I seemed to have stunned them out of asking anything else. What they thought about it didn't matter.

Darton's hand crept over his thigh to clasp my fingers. My heart squeezed as I returned the pressure. He was here with me. Confused and torn, no doubt, but here, and that was all I really needed.

The roads I directed Keevan down grew narrow and lonely. Finally, I had him pull the car off onto a large patch of grass facing a little wooden shack that served as a fruit and vegetable stand during the warmer months.

"This is as far as we can go by car," I said. "Darton and I will walk the rest of the way. I really appreciate the drive and the company—but the rest of you should head back now. I don't know for sure how long we'll be safe here, but the dark fae shouldn't hassle anyone else on campus now that we're gone."

"Nuh-uh," Keevan said firmly. "This may be the wackiest story I've ever heard, but that's more reason to stick with it to the end."

"But if Izzy—"

Izzy shook her head. "I can handle a walk in the woods. Let's go."

My gaze slid to Priya, whose slightly arched eyebrow

was all the answer I needed from her. Biting back a groan, I glanced at Darton. He spread his hands as if to say, *What can we do?*

Not much, apparently. I could have bound the bunch of them to the car, but I couldn't force them all the way home. If they were out here at all, they were safer with me.

I sighed and motioned for Darton to open the door.

The fae weren't likely to appear to me when I had human company, but my recent visit here had left me with a concrete sense of where the enclave began. We'd tramped maybe a mile and a half into the forest when a tingling passed over my skin. I stopped and scanned the trees before giving a short bow.

"As the daughter of Eóghan, I request sanctuary for myself and my friends from Chimalis of the light fae. We swear to do no harm. Our need is urgent."

Energy rippled around us. Izzy shivered, pulling her cardigan tighter around her. The young fae man who'd greeted me on my last arrival shimmered into sight beside one of the trees, and she gasped. Next to me, Darton's jaw dropped open. Keevan let out a low whistle.

Priya just stood there, cool and casual, as if this were old hat to her.

The filmy, gleaming figure stepped forward and bowed lower than I had. "Daughter of Eóghan, you are welcome here. Your guests must stay in this spot until you've discussed the matter with Chimalis, but they will come to no harm from us."

That was very different from promising to *protect* my friends. I hesitated, reluctant to leave Darton behind, but I'd known our abrupt arrival would require additional smoothing over. Bracing myself, I followed the sentry deeper into the enclave.

The young fae led me to the clearing where I'd met Chimalis before. The same table and chairs awaited, with cups of the cool, nectar-laced tea the light fae enjoyed.

This time, I didn't sit. I wasn't interested in having a relaxed chat.

A few torturous minutes ticked by before Chimalis glided out to meet me. Two other elders, not quite as old or translucent as she was, flanked her. I went through the motions of a formal greeting, but impatience gripped my chest.

"The trouble I came to speak to you about before— it's gotten worse," I said. "The dark fae pursuing us sent an onslaught of dark creatures after us, and he lent them enough power that they made the charge in clouded daylight. He spoke to me in a vision. I believe he's attempting to please the Darkest One. Her influence is seeping from her prison somehow."

"We heard word of a shadow passing," Chimalis acknowledged—whatever the hell *that* was supposed to mean. "But it has not extended far. An ocean is safety enough."

My hands clenched. Didn't they care what dark fae did in their own lands? Didn't they care what *might* happen if the Darkest One shook off her bindings even slightly?

Of course, Chimalis and her brethren here might never have faced the Darkest One when she moved freely. Most of them wouldn't have even been born before I'd sealed her away all those centuries ago. But now the mercenary was right on their doorstep.

"It isn't safe enough for Arthur and me," I said. "The dark rabble nearly killed him. Their master means to try again."

"Then that which was to pass will find itself completed."

"He wasn't *supposed* to die," I snapped. "I made a mistake. If I'd cast properly... but that's beside the point. The dark rabble is tracking him now. We couldn't stay where we were living. Will you allow us to put ourselves under your protection?"

The three elders drew back to murmur to each other. I shifted from foot to foot as I waited.

Chimalis turned to me. "The boundaries of our home may obscure the trail. We offer you lodging and sustenance here in respect to your father. But I will not ask my own people to put themselves at risk if the danger comes upon you here."

I inclined my head. I hadn't really hoped for a more generous offer, as much as I'd have welcomed it.

"With luck, it won't come to that." But I knew just how much luck we'd need to keep the dark mercenary away. It wasn't as if Darton could live his life out in the forest anyway. If we were going to have any hope of surviving longer than the next few days, extreme measures were required.

"I need something else," I said. "Is there anyone here who could advise me on how to kill a dark fae?"

The glow that imbued Chimalis flickered, as if the idea of death offended her very essence. Well, it probably did. She pursed her lips. The man at her right stepped back, his mouth curling with disgust. The other woman crossed her arms over her chest.

"The path of life flows onward with our blessing."

I grimaced. "I know, I know. But *this* life wants to cut

short a whole lot of other lives. Doesn't that make any difference to you?"

"It isn't done," the man said. By which he'd meant, they hadn't done it. I gritted my teeth.

"If your journey takes you away from the light, it is not in light you will find the answers," Chimalis said in her not-at-all-helpful way. "Now, to accommodate your—"

A crystal-clear voice pealed from amid the trees. "Wait!" A young fae stepped out—the tall, ebony-skinned woman who'd given me the dagger now stuffed in my pocket. Sunki. She must have heard about my arrival and come to watch the meeting.

She bowed low to the elders, quivering. Interrupting them had been a major breech of decorum. "May I speak? I have information that may be of use to our guests."

Chimalis's stance had gone rigid. "Sunki, you forget your roots. This is a discussion for those long grown."

The young fae shrank back, spun, and darted away into the trees. Sod it. Just with that one sentence, she'd given me more reason to hope than anything these "wise" old husks had offered.

Well, they'd already given their word that we could stay, and they hadn't been likely to offer more. I gave the elders a swift bow. "Thank you for your kindness." Then I hurried after Sunki, not caring if I'd offended them.

Her form had already started to haze away into the streaks of sunlight. "Sunki!" I called, and she stopped. Her pale eyes fixed on me and widened. She dipped down.

"Daughter of Eóghan."

"Emma will do," I said. "I want to hear this useful information of yours."

A smile crossed her face. "I can't answer the question

you asked, but I listen to the tales that pass this way. I've heard there's a human who hunts the dark fae. Near the great gouge in the earth, it's said he lives."

The great gouge… "The Grand Canyon?"

She shrugged. How would she know? She'd never left this forest.

"All I know is what I just told you," she said, "and that he lives where two trees cross. I'm not sure how old the stories are, or whether he's even still living, but perhaps he would know what you need."

Where two trees cross. My mind leapt back to that vision in my brief sleep this morning—to a dark crossing of trunks flashing before my eyes. My pulse skipped.

"Thank you," I said, meaning it so much more than I had when I'd said the same words to the elders. The vision had been showing me the way, and Sunki had offered the vital clue to piece it together. There *had* to be someone there who could help me defeat the mercenary.

Now I just had to find out if any other fae had heard more of this story, because I didn't like our chances of trying to track down a single house around the entire Grand Canyon.

20

Keevan tipped his head to study the cup of nectar tea one of the light fae had offered him. The waning afternoon light filtered through the trees around the clearing we'd settled in and glinted off the pale liquid. Its steam carried a tangy sweetness.

"Do the 'standard' rules apply around here?" Keevan asked in his usual joking tone. "Isn't there some trick about how you're not supposed to eat fairy food or you'll be stuck in their world forever?"

"The fae do have that power," I said, "but it's not automatic. And I'm sure this bunch has no interest in kidnapping us."

They'd prefer we left as soon as possible was more like it. But the information I'd been able to scare up so far was slight. Sunki had brought me around to speak with the fae who were willing to entertain my questions, but while a few others did remember hearing about this human who hunted dark fae, only one had recalled anything more than she had.

"I crossed paths with an elder on a scouting venture south of here a few years ago," that young man had told me. "She spoke of the hunter in passing—said there was talk he lived near a town of petals, by the east end of the gouge."

Not the most helpful tip. A town of petals? Presumably that was human information filtered through at least three layers of a telephone game slanted by the light fae tendency toward metaphor and vagueness. I might be able to work with it, but I needed a map, and my cell phone didn't get any service out here.

When I'd made it back to the clearing, the shadows had been growing long. If we tried to make it to the car, the sun might set before we got there. My fatigue was already wearing on me, and I'd rather spend the night here than on the road with who-knew-what lurking in the shadows. The fae would just have to put up with us until morning.

Sunki had promised to inquire farther afield. Maybe she'd bring me something more concrete. For a fae, she wasn't bad.

Keevan took a sip of his tea and grimaced. "Well, that is... interesting." He leaned against the broad oak he was standing by. Near his feet, Izzy took a bite of the baked roll she'd been brought. Their gazes roved through the clearing, watching the shimmering forms of the fae ambling around.

"How long will we wait here?" Izzy said. "Is there a point when we can assume this dark fae thing has decided to leave Darton alone?" Her eyes had gotten even wider since we'd entered the enclave, but she was sitting with a calm I couldn't help admiring. Was that what had attracted Darton to her—the quiet composure behind her flower-child looks?

She wouldn't keep that composure long if I answered her honestly. The mercenary had no intention of leaving Arthur's soul alone now that he'd gotten my king in his sights.

"I have to find a way to stop the dark fae so he can't keep after Darton," I said. "And I'm working on a strategy for that."

On the other side of the clearing, Priya had fallen into conversation with a couple of our hosts. The glow they exuded glinted off her dark hair, flickering as they laughed in twinkling tones at something she'd said. Priya grinned back at them.

She looked completely at home, as at ease as she did in our apartment. My stomach twisted.

Keevan waved his half-empty cup toward me. "So who exactly was this ancestor of Darton's who got him in all this trouble? That's got to be quite the story."

Yes, and not one I had any interest in sharing. "I'll leave it up to him whether he wants to tell you about it," I said, which seemed a fair answer. My attention was still fixed on Priya. There was no point in putting *that* conversation off any longer. "Are the two of you all right for now?"

Izzy nodded, and Keevan gave me a pensive look but a thumbs-up as well. I stalked across the clearing with a small weight lifted from my chest. I hadn't wanted Darton's friends along—it was their own fault if they were uncomfortable—but I felt a little protective all the same. This place wasn't my home any more than it was theirs, but at least I understood it.

Priya's shoulders tensed before I'd made it halfway to her. She made some comment to her fae companions, and they brushed hands with her before they slipped away. The knot in my stomach tightened. That was an awfully familiar gesture for a fae to offer any human.

I came to a halt in front of her. "What's going on, Priya?"

She looked at me for just a second before lowering her eyes. "I thought, while we're here, I might as well make friends."

"You know what I mean. You know *how* to make friends with them. You've got that—" I motioned to her arm. "That band with the runes. You're not going to convince me this is your first experience with the fae. I'd be surprised if it's only your *tenth*."

"Emmaline." She sighed and rubbed her mouth. Then she raised her head. "Don't be angry. It was better that I didn't tell you before. You wouldn't have understood."

"Understood what exactly?"

"I grew up with the fae," she said. "An enclave not that far from Seattle—that part wasn't a total lie. I never could get them to tell me how I'd ended up there as a baby, whether my parents had left me or they'd abducted me or what." She laughed haltingly. "Sometimes I got the impression they didn't totally remember. But they kept me until I was eight, and I kept visiting after they managed to bring me back into the human world."

I stared at her. "You're a changeling. Not in the usual direction, but…"

She shrugged. "'Foster child' is more how I'd describe it."

"That doesn't explain why you ended up rooming with me. Why you didn't tell me. By the light, Pri, you must have known I was working magic. You had to have sensed something was up with me before today."

Her gaze darted away from me again. She sucked in her lower lip. Then she said, quiet and careful, "I knew everything."

I'd tried to anticipate what she might say, but that statement stopped me in my tracks. All I managed to spit out was, "*What?*"

A glitter of fae wildness sparked in her eyes, so distinctive it was a wonder I'd never made the connection before. Eight years raised by them—that would leave a mark. But how could I have guessed?

"They knew about you," she said. "My enclave—well, *all* the light fae know about you. The daughter of Eóghan who lives over and over, tied to the long-dead-but-never-dying king. They knew the dark creatures come where you appear. It worried them. When you transferred, they asked me to, well, to keep an eye on you. To watch what was happening."

It took me a second to recover my tongue. When I did, it felt laced with ice. "You were spying on me."

Priya winced. "It wasn't like *that*. They only wanted me to be able to let them know if there was danger coming that they should prepare for. Obviously concern about outside affairs isn't common across all enclaves." She shot a critical glance at the clearing at large.

Oh, no. She wasn't changing the subject just like that. "That still sounds like spying to me. Especially when you didn't tell me. When you pretended you didn't have a clue what I was worried about. You did know, didn't you? Why I was so distracted?"

"I guessed." Her eyes fixed on mine again. "I didn't

know how to tell you, Emmaline. But I always thought maybe I could help you, even if that part didn't seem to matter much to the fae. I still think I can help. Why do you think I came with you?"

I shook my head. "I don't know. Apparently I don't know much of anything."

"We've really been friends," Priya insisted. "I didn't *pretend* to enjoy hanging out with you. I didn't pretend to care that something was going wrong."

"It doesn't matter." Sure, she hadn't pretended—but she'd cared because she'd wanted to know what to tell her fae family. All that time she'd chummed up to me, tried to draw me out, without ever sharing the most vital piece of information about herself, or that she already knew so much about me—

I backed up a step.

"Emmaline," Priya started.

"No," I said. "Not right now. Maybe not ever. You don't get to hide something that big from me and then act like nothing's changed two seconds later. People don't work like that."

A lump had risen in my throat. I whirled and strode away before she could protest further.

I should have known better. I shouldn't have cared as much as I had. Trying to make friends had never worked out well for me—why should that change now?

21

My feet carried me straight to the only person I'd ever been able to count on in any of my lives. Darton had wandered apart from the others earlier for some space to think, but I'd been aware of his presence the entire time, laced through the whispers of fae magic that twined in the air.

He was sprawled on the coarse grass in a smaller glade, gazing at the clouds streaking across the sky. A few of the light fae hovered amid the trees around him. Arthur's host was as much a curiosity as I was—*long-dead-but-never-dying*, as Priya had put it—and they weren't at all afraid of *him*.

I frowned at them and made a jerking motion with my hand. A shudder of irritation ran through their glow of life, but they retreated, leaving us to the bird song and the cool tickle of the late afternoon breeze.

"May I join you?" I said.

"Sure," Darton said, sounding a little dazed. "Why not?"

Offering him as much distance as I could in the small space afforded between the trees, I sat down on the grass a couple feet from him and leaned back on my elbows. A disconcerting sense of déjà vu stole over me. So many days and nights my king and I had stolen a moment to recline and contemplate the sky that stretched above us.

I pointed to a particularly puffy bit of cloud. "What do you think—a rabbit or a mitten?"

Darton gave a choked laugh. "Just like old times," he said, and I knew a sliver of one of the memories he'd glimpsed.

"It's a lot to take in," I said. "I'm sorry I had to lay it on you all at once. Usually the revelation is a little more... gradual."

"But you've known all along."

I nodded. "I need to, if I'm going to look out for you. And you *don't* need to, not right away. As soon as that part of you starts waking up, the dark rabble can sense it."

Darton frowned. "Why do I even still matter to them? I mean, whatever I might have done... before, that was centuries ago, wasn't it?"

"I don't know," I admitted. "I don't even know why you were so important to them in the first place." I didn't know why my father had wanted me to seek out the prince and future king all that time ago. But something had tied the Darkest One to Arthur's future.

"So we've lived and died, lived and died, over and over again? Do you always manage to find me?"

"The spell I cast—you were dying, and I was trying to stop that from happening—ties our souls to this world and to each other. The bond has frayed a little. I used to be able to count on finding you while we were still children. But it always brings me to you before too long."

"Before I start remembering on my own."

My throat tightened. In all but the unluckiest circumstances. "Usually. Yes."

He rubbed his forehead. "This seems so insane. If I hadn't seen—felt—whatever those memories were… I can hardly believe it anyway."

"As long as you believe you need to stay far away from the dark rabble and not get killed, that's all that really matters."

"Well, that's inspiring."

"Hey," I said. "I'm here to be your wizard and your defender, not your life coach."

A laugh sputtered out of him, one that sounded more authentic than his last effort. "Am I going to remember any of the lives other than my first one?"

"I don't think so." Maybe if I kept him alive long enough, just this once, we'd find out. "You never have before. So just assume they were all full of me being brilliant and saving your arse repeatedly."

"Do *you* remember them?"

"The earlier ones have faded. With the more recent ones, I've retained a few fragments." A pale body set upon by shadows. Any humor I'd summoned fled me. "And I keep written records, as well as I can."

Darton set his hands behind his head to cushion it. "Were you watching me from the beginning—after you transferred? I don't remember seeing you until a few weeks ago."

"I hadn't 'found' you until you walked into fencing practice," I said. "Our paths hadn't crossed. But I knew you when I saw you."

His smile turned teasing. "So that's why you were so 'friendly.'"

"I was making the best I could from the situation handed to us," I retorted. "It's hard, you know. I don't *want* to wake up that part of you and bring the dark forces down on us. But I've got to stick close enough to you to be ready when you start to wake up of your own accord. Sometimes I don't get the balance quite right."

Darton was silent for a moment. Then he said, abruptly, "Isn't it lonely?"

I looked at him, but he was still staring at the sky. "What?"

"For you," he said. "Living over and over again, knowing who you are, not being able to tell anyone. Not even me, when you first meet me. That's an incredibly big secret to have to shoulder."

"Technically, you keep secrets and shoulder burdens," I informed him.

He shifted over on the grass so he was close enough to elbow me. "Have you always been annoyingly pedantic?"

"Yes," I said, deadpan. "You love it. You just haven't remembered that yet."

He shook his head, but I could tell he was fighting a chuckle. "Well, whatever the correct terminology, I stand by the observation. And I'm sorry if I made things harder for you."

His sympathy tugged at a soft spot inside me. I scooted a little forward so I could lie all the way back on the grass, imitating his pose with my arms bent behind my head. "I appreciate that," I said. "If it makes you feel any better, as far as I recall, you haven't made it particularly harder than usual this time around."

"It does, actually." He exhaled. "So what was I really

like back then? Are all the legends true? Was I as great as they say?"

He was trying to keep his tone jaunty, but a note of yearning rang through it, so heavy with need I hesitated before choosing my words.

"The legends are almost entirely fiction," I said. "No Lancelot, no questing after holy grails, your table was not round. Those are literary inventions built up around the small scraps of the real history that survived the ages. But the one thing the tales do get right is that you were a damned good king. And I think I was in a position to judge that accurately."

He made a noncommittal sound. "What is that judgment based on?"

What was it not? A rush of past moments poured through my mind.

"You were compassionate," I said. "Always looking out for your people. But smart about it. You knew how to weigh the good of the many over that of the few, when it came down to that. The country was at war when you were crowned, our neighbors vying for territory and the local lords beginning to squabble in the wake of it, and you managed to unite them against the common enemy. That was always your commitment—to establish peace and maintain it. To let people live without fear that their fields would be razed or their homes ransacked. I'm not going to lie and say everyone was happy, but a lot more were happy after you than had been before."

"That does sound pretty great," Darton murmured.

"It was an honor to stand beside you." I looked at him again. His face was less than a foot away now. My heartbeat kicked up in tempo with a yearning of my own, one I couldn't entirely suppress. "Then and since and now, still. Always."

This time, he turned to gaze back at me. I couldn't read the emotion in his eyes, but I recognized it. I'd seen a glimpse of it that night behind the pub. The night he'd touched my cheek and started waking.

Before that memory could act as a warning, Darton moved. He rolled onto me, bracing his weight on his forearms. In an instant, his body covered mine from the chest down—not crushingly, but firmly enough that I lost my breath all the same. I stared up at him, at that face that was becoming familiar in its own right. In that moment, it held an expression I'd known for fifteen hundred years, set with passionate determination.

His fingers stroked over my hair with a gentleness that felt contradictory. I still couldn't breathe, not with the feel of him against me as I'd tried not to remember it just a few hours ago, different and yet the same. Not with his eyes searching mine so intently.

"Tell me to stop." His voice came out low and almost harsh as he tried to tame the tremor in it. "Tell me you don't want this too."

My lips parted—he'd given me the words I needed to say—but the lie was too big to work quickly from my throat. At my silence, Darton bent down and caught my mouth with his.

His kiss was everything I always wanted, hot and fierce, as if he were trying to fit ten kisses into this one. A shudder of longing—for more, for anything he would give me—ran through my body. My hand swept into his hair of its own accord and pulled him even closer. His lips coaxed mine apart to deepen the kiss. The taste of the nectar tea he'd drank earlier slipped from his mouth into mine, and a memory swam into my head.

"She's just... she's lovely." The prince paced his chamber, his shoes rasping against the stone floor and muting when they hit the rug. *"That hair of hers, like a dark waterfall, and those eyes, so fathomless... I can hardly think of what to say when I'm with her."*

"I think you should scratch 'poet' off your list of possible careers, Your Highness," I remarked with a touch of rancor I hadn't intended.

"Yes, yes," Arthur said. The wave of his wave dismissed my joke without so much as a smile. *"I thought, maybe, there was some way you could help. With your particular skills and so on."*

A chill passed through me that was deeper than the cool autumn air. *"Are you asking me for a* love *potion, Arthur? You can forget about that. Do you have any idea how unconscionable—"*

"No!" The prince's eyes widened with horror. *"Oh, gods, no. I would never— Do you really think that of me?"*

I didn't. But then... *"I've never seen you moon over a lady like this before,"* I pointed out. *"How am I to know how that might have addled your mind?"*

He snorted, some of his usual humor returning. *"I* admire *her. I'm hardly addled. I simply thought you might be able to offer something to bolster my confidence. So I can remember how to find my tongue when I have a chance to talk to her."*

The rancor inside me clenched at my chest. *Why did I feel so uneasy over such a simple request? I shook the discomfort off.* *"All right. That much I can do. First, we must—"*

Darton's lips brushed over mine again, and I yanked myself out of the memory and away from his kiss in the same motion.

"We can't do this," I said tightly, tipping my head to the side. "Please get off me."

Darton blinked at me, his eyes hazy. Still immersed in whatever recollection this physical contact had stirred up in his head.

Then his gaze cleared. He shoved himself off me and scrambled upright. An ache ran down my body at the loss, but that was exactly why I'd had to stop this interlude. That and—

"You feel it." Darton wavered on his feet. "You kissed me back."

Oh, my king. I felt whatever you did and so much more. I pushed off the ground, shaking away bits of stray grass that clung to my clothes.

"Every time we touch directly, the contact wakes up more memories in you," I said. "And the more that part of you wakes up, the louder it calls to the creatures tracking you. Do you really *want* them finding you?"

"I thought we were safe here."

"Not completely. Not forever. I'm not taking that risk."

Darton's jaw clenched. "What if *I* want to take it? Every time... There's so much I'm missing that I don't know, that I don't understand. Maybe it's worth the risk to fill in those blanks."

"Everything you could remember, I already know," I said. "Nothing could be worth it."

"But what if *I* want to understand—"

A shout echoed through the forest. I tensed, and Darton's mouth snapped shut. A shriek split the air, so panicked it turned my blood cold. I leapt up.

"The dark rabble is here," I said. "They've already found us."

22

"What?" Darton said, but the paling of his face told me he knew exactly what I was talking about. I hurried to the edge of the glade. More shouts rang out, mingled with a startled hiss, a cry, and the rustling of fae legs flitting through the underbrush.

I couldn't see any sign of the attack. The dusk was deepening with a chill in the breeze that stung my skin. Glints of light darted between the trees in the distance.

Darton came up beside me, and I held out my gloved hand to keep him a little behind. My heart thumped.

The dark fae had found us here so quickly. The enclave had barely provided any shelter at all—or the mercenary had so much power he could track even the slightest hint of Arthur's essence, even when obscured by other energies. I bit my lip.

My first and only real concern was keeping the man beside me safe. We'd managed to fend the dark rabble off so far. They were *not* taking him here.

"I need my bag," I said. I'd dropped it in the clearing where I'd left our other companions, not expecting to have any immediate use for it. I caught Darton's hand with my left and brandished the fae dagger with my right. "Come on."

"I thought we were protected here," Darton said as we hurried through the thicker forest. "Isn't that why we came? Can't these other... fae do anything?"

"I'm sure they're trying. I didn't expect this, but things are a little different this time around." I tugged him faster. "It's not just the shadow creatures after you. There's a full dark fae directing them. That hasn't happened before, at least not recently enough that I have a record of it. Obviously I underestimated the danger."

Darton's jaw tensed. "And those things out there— they still want to kill me."

No. They wanted to carry him back to the dark fae mercenary so he could perform whatever ritual would dedicate Arthur's soul to the Darkest One. But I was not letting that happen, so knowing that wouldn't do Darton any good.

"Yes," I said instead. And then, because I was, "I'm sorry."

Darton's eyes flicked to me, startled. "No. Em, don't even think you have anything to apologize for. It's because of you I'm alive right now at all."

More of the light fae streaked by us as we plunged into the clearing. Their forms were little more than wavering sunbeams amid the dusk. They streamed this way and that, some toward the hollers still carrying from the edge of the enclave and some fleeing away. Others whirled around us as if they couldn't decide which tack to take.

"What's happening?" I called out to them. "How many creatures are out there? Can you hold them off?"

None of them slowed long enough to answer me.

"Darton!" Izzy leapt to our side and grasped Darton's arm. Her cool had vanished, not that I could blame her for that. She trembled as she clung to him. Keevan bounded over, slapping his hands together as if eager for a fight, but fear shone in the whites of his eyes.

"What the hell is going on?" he said. "I'm guessing it's not good."

Priya came up behind me. "The enclave is being attacked by glooms and shadow beasts. Part of the pack that came after you on campus, I'd guess."

Izzy outright shuddered. "What do we *do*?"

I'd already crouched down by my duffel bag. I snatched out a few wands, shoved the extras into my back pocket, and retrieved a bag of crushed salt to supplement their power. I didn't have enough hands to hold all of that and the dagger too, but salt didn't require a skilled touch. I held it out to the others.

"The dark creatures don't like salt. It won't keep them off us completely, but you can make them back off for a moment if they get right in your face. And then I'll take care of the rest."

Keevan reached for the bag, but Darton got there first. He tore the corner open. I straightened up and swung the duffel over my shoulder.

"Are we going to *have* to go face to face with these things?" Izzy's voice quavered. "I thought—"

Chimalis materialized in the middle of the clearing. She glided over to us, the filmy edges of her body rippling. Her expression was profoundly sad but unshakably firm. I knew what she was going to say before she opened her mouth.

"The creatures of the dark have sought you out here," she said. "We are doing what we can to slow their progress, but we are not prepared for combat of this magnitude. You must go, and then they will leave us too."

And I was sure this burned through any favors I could ever have expected to beg from them, in this life or the next several, assuming I got that far. Oh well. At this point I'd be happy just to be around that long in the first place.

I glanced at Darton, as if to reassure myself he hadn't vanished in the second my attention had been elsewhere. "We have to get to the car."

Chimalis nodded. "We will attempt to clear a path to the humans' road. But you must move quickly. It is a long way and holding against the dark tires us."

"Okay." I sucked in a breath. "Let's move. Fast. Everyone, follow me."

"May your paths be ever lit," Chimalis murmured. She was already drifting away. The farewell had never sounded more ridiculous than now as we hurried off into the dark ahead.

"This way." Sunki appeared ahead of me and beckoned. "I'll help as much as I can."

We sped up to a lope, crossing the uneven ground between the trees as quickly as we could without risking a fall. Our feet thudded over the packed earth. More and more light fae blinked in and out of sight amid the trunks on either side of us. The dark rabble must have been too deep in the shadows for me to make them out.

Good. Let them stay there.

I'd barely had time to think that when a light fae man toppled onto the ground ahead of us. Izzy shrieked. Glooms twisted around his limbs and neck. A pained grunt escaped him.

Priya dashed forward. I twitched my wand without

177

pausing to think. "*Darkness begone.*"

The patches of shadow clutching at the fae man blinked away into the air. He heaved himself upright with a rasp before throwing himself into the forest again. I swallowed thickly.

Whatever Chimalis had said, some of her kind were fighting hard. Fighting for us. Even though this was our war, not theirs, and we'd brought it to their doorstep.

We hustled on. Other glooms started to trickle through the lines of fae defense. I jerked my wand and sliced out with my dagger, destroying them one by one. The tingle of energy running through the wand's wood began to fade, but it wasn't gone yet.

A shadow creature shaped like a giant hawk swooped down at Darton out of nowhere. "Art!" I shouted automatically. His head jerked up. Izzy staggered backward, and Keevan swore.

Before I'd even spat out my casting, Darton tossed a handful of salt into the air. The creature recoiled. My spell hit it, and it burst apart into the air.

My wand crumbled in my hand. Keevan stared at my now-empty fingers. "Is that a bad sign?"

"There's a reason I brought backups. Keep moving!" I pulled another wand from my pocket. My pulse raced in time with our feet. I caught Sunki's eye. "Is it just the lower creatures?" I said. "Has anyone seen an actual dark fae?"

She shook her head. "He comes like a shadow, here and yet not."

More fae vagueness, but I thought I knew what she meant. Our pursuer had imbued these creatures with his power, but he had stayed distant. A bit of a lazy one, apparently. But then, given the army he was commanding, I supposed he could reasonably afford to take it easy.

"Can't you cast the same spell you did in the theater?" Darton said. He panted as he ran. "Blast them all away as far as we need to go?"

A hoarse laugh slipped out of me. "If I have to, I will. But I prefer not to go around knocking years off my life left and right." And if I threw out that much energy and failed, then I wouldn't be conscious to protect Darton or the other three tagging along.

"You mean—" Keevan started.

At the same moment, another creature, this one in a wolf's form, knocked over one of our fae defenders and sprang through the trees at Darton.

I dropped my wand to clutch his arm and yank him backward as I leapt in front of him. My hand whipped out with the fae dagger. Its blade sliced through the creature's neck. The shadow wolf crumpled, spilling darkness across the brush.

The trees ahead were thinning. Hope thrummed through me alongside my heartbeat. "Have your key ready," I said to Keevan as I hauled Darton faster. My hand slipped from his arm. He groped after mine, and his fingers closed around my wrist where my sleeve had ridden up during the fighting. Skin to bare skin.

A spark shot through my nerves. Sod it. Getting him out of here mattered more than keeping his soul in its slumber. I let him hold on as we rushed forward.

Darton stumbled, but he stayed on his feet, his grip tightening. Priya dashed around to his other side. She looked ready to grasp his other arm if she needed to.

Impressions of past times welled up in my mind, but

the blare of adrenaline kept me moving, focused on the present. The memory played out in the back of my head, echoing the panic of our mad flight.

My king was standing in the western field, his head bent close to a man I didn't recognize. He was tall and long-faced with tan skin and slate-gray hair, his shoulders slightly hunched. The man motioned with his arm, and my hand tensed against the edge of the castle window where I'd stopped to glance outside.

The shadows on the ground near him had twisted, as if drawn to his movement.

I scrambled over the windowsill and jumped. The air rushed past me. Some witness below gasped as I plummeted, but I'd already muttered the words to cushion my fall. My plunge slowed, and I hit the ground with only a light jarring of my knees. And then I was running.

"So you can see," the dark fae man was saying, "it is merely a matter of—"

"Your Highness," I blurted out, stumbling to a halt beside them. I hesitated to be as familiar as to grab my king's arm in front of a stranger, but there were other ways of getting his immediate attention. I threw myself prostrate at his feet, which was the last thing I'd ever have done in any normal circumstances.

As Arthur well knew. He crouched in an instant. "Whatever is the matter, Merlin?"

"You must come," I said, my head still low. The ground smelled of rich earth and summer grass, but a trickle of the fae's deathly chill seeped into my nose. "Back to the castle. Now."

The urgency in my voice must have convinced him. I scrambled upright as he tossed out a brief apology to his companion, and then he was hurrying with me to the gate I'd leapt over in my charge from the window.

"Tell me what's the matter."

"Not here." Not in the yard beyond the gate, not in the castle hall, not until I'd slammed the door to his chambers shut behind us.

I spun around to face my king. "That man you were talking to was not a man. If you see him or anyone like him again, you must stay away. Don't talk to them. Don't even look *at them."*

Arthur frowned. "He hardly seemed a threat, especially on that scale."

"He wouldn't. He wouldn't want you to see it. They're a part of my old world, not yours. You have to trust me, Arthur. There's nothing so dangerous on all the Earth as a dark fae who wants something."

A heap of glooms spilled out into our path, and my mind jerked fully out of its reverie. Sunki cried out a few words, but only a few of the creatures quivered apart. Damn, the light fae around here really didn't go in for much combat training, did they? I guessed they rarely saw the need for it.

The faint smell of asphalt reached my fae-touched senses. We were almost to the road, to the car. I took in the sprawl of glooms rippling along the path toward us, Keevan and Izzy drawing up short, the stretch of woodland between us and our goal. My stomach balled. I had one wand left in reach, no time to dig in the bag for more. Between that and my own power, could I manage this much while staying conscious?

I didn't have much choice but to find out.

I tugged my arm from Darton's to snatch up that last wand and thrust it forward. *"Burn and banish,"* I shouted with a heave of power.

A blaze of light washed from my body and the wand. It careened across the brush and seared through the mass of glooms and whatever else lurked amid the trees. My legs wavered. It was *my* elbow Priya had to catch. But she did.

"Are you okay?" she asked.

"Yes." I jerked my arm back, my head spinning. "I just bought us about a hundred yards' grace. Let's not waste it talking."

We took off at a sprint. Izzy let out a choked sound of relief at the sight of the car. Keevan hit the unlock button, and we dove in different doors, me pushing Darton ahead of me.

Sunki pressed her ebony hand to the window, and I nodded my thanks as I barked out the order.

"Drive!"

23

"So…" Keevan said after the car had been roaring down the lonely highway for several minutes. "Should I assume those shadows with minds of their own can't outrun a car?"

"They can't if you're driving this fast," I said. "So, you know, definitely keep that up."

"Aye, aye, Captain." His joviality sounded so forced I didn't think any of us believed it. "And where exactly are we driving *to* now?"

I shifted, squeezed between Darton and Priya on the backseat's worn faux leather again. "I'm trying to figure that out. For now, keep heading south."

I skimmed my fingers over my phone's screen. Where was the east end of the Grand Canyon? Gods, that had *better* be what the fae had meant by the "great gouge."

Eastern Arizona. *Here we go*. I zoomed in on the map.

Priya leaned over, her narrow shoulder bumping mine. "What are you looking for? Maybe I can help."

My back tensed. "That's all right," I said, sharper than I'd intended. But then, I wasn't even totally sure what she was still doing here. Making sure she saw this entire disaster through so she could make a full report?

Darton sank down in his seat, gazing blankly at the one in front of him in silence. He rubbed his jaw. "I saw something."

"What?" My attention was still focused on the map. Petals... Petals... I hoped that word hadn't been too literal. Arizona might be dry, but I was sure there were still plenty of gardens around.

"In my... um... when I grabbed your arm," Darton said hesitantly, as if even he weren't all that sure about what he was trying to say. "You said there was nothing from before that you didn't know about, but I don't think you knew about this."

"Anything I wasn't present for, you'd have told me about. At least if it were important."

"Because I was so hopeless without you?" A little drollness had come back into his voice. I guessed he wasn't totally shell-shocked.

"*True friends don't keep secrets*," I said. "Your words." Ones I hadn't lived up to quite as fully as my king would have liked, but I'd been as open with him as I could without threatening the greater priority of his safety.

My finger stilled over the screen. Just beyond the eastern tip of the canyon was a little dot of a town named Peddleton. *A town of petals.* That was exactly how the fae would have bastardized a name like that in the telling from one to another.

"Okay," I said. "There's a man who lives in Arizona, probably near a placed called Peddleton, who knows how to take on the dark fae better than I do." *I hope.* Light willing, he'd at least be *alive* and not long dead from a story decades old. "We're going to pay him a visit and see what he has to say. We should be able to stay on this highway for a while yet."

Keevan gave a jerky nod. Beside him, Izzy sat with her shoulders stiff against the seatback. A grayish bruise I hadn't noticed before marked the back of her hand, which was clenched against her leg.

One of the glooms had brushed against her hard enough to do damage.

Darton prodded me with his elbow. "Apparently at times I was more of a 'do as I say, not as I do' type, because whatever I was doing in the place I saw, the one thing I remembered for sure was that I was worried you'd find out I'd come there. So I doubt I was in a hurry to tell you about it."

My head snapped around. He'd never mentioned a memory in which he was hiding things from me in any of his past lives... at least not the ones I could remember or the moments from those previous I'd been able to note down before the end. Granted, he didn't often have the chance to recover more than a fraction of that first life before the shadows took him, and me with him.

"Where *were* you?" I asked.

"I don't know." Darton frowned. "It was a long, narrow room with lots of shelves covered in bottles, all different colors. It smelled like dust and... kind of like my mom's herbal tea. My mom now, I mean. I haven't—" He cut himself off, his gaze darting to his friends at the front of the car as if he'd only just remembered them. "You know what I mean."

And you barely knew your mother then. The queen had passed when Arthur was two. But his description recalled a place I could identify. Ffion's workshop—the alchemist.

"What were you doing there?"

185

"I didn't remember that much," Darton said. "It was just a glimpse and a feeling… But it felt important. I was hoping whatever I was going to accomplish there would fix something. For you, I think."

I'd been the one who stepped in to fix the problems my king couldn't solve, not the other way around. I hadn't *had* any problems except the ones that continually arrived at his door.

Unless… unless he'd known. Might he have thought an alchemist could cure me of *that* sentimentality? My throat tightened.

Arthur had never mentioned a visit to Ffion's workshop to me—I was sure of that much.

Darton ducked his head. "Anyway, I thought we could… try again? And maybe I'll see more, get a better idea of what I was up to."

"You can't control what will surface," I said. "Not with any accuracy. You can try to focus on the other memory, and maybe that'll tug one up that's related, but especially this early, when there's so much still buried—"

"What the *hell* are you two going on about?" Keevan broke in. "All this stuff about memories buried and surfacing—and you're talking as if you've known each other for ages. What am I missing here?"

Priya glanced at me, but she kept her mouth shut. I groped for an answer. The thought of getting into the past lives of legendary kings made my chest clench up. How well was *that* likely to go over, even given recent events?

But I already had a thread I could use in the vague explanation I'd offered him and Izzy earlier.

"I told you that Darton is connected to a past ancestor that the dark fae clashed with. Some of that man's memories have passed along to him. And I have a comparable situation through an ancestor of mine, who helped back then, which is why I'm here to help now. Sometimes it can feel as if the things that happened back then really did happen to us."

"Uh-huh." I couldn't tell if Keevan bought my half-lie or if he simply didn't have the bandwidth to push harder. "So you're having old-timey memories, Art? That sounds pretty psychedelic."

"It definitely feels weird." Darton let out a stilted laugh. He was going to need more practice with the lying thing. He adjusted his weight next to me, bringing me back into all-too-clear awareness of his closeness. The citrusy smell from his shirt tickled my nose. I swallowed the flicker of desire down—and he rested his hand on my leg just above my knee, palm up. His voice lowered as he bent his head beside mine.

"I think we should try. Right now, we need all the information we can get, don't we?"

It was hard to believe I was making the clearest decision ever with his breath heating the side of my face— the lips that had been pressed against mine less than an hour ago nearly brushing my ear—but I gave it a champion's effort. The thought that my king might have been keeping secrets gnawed at me. Just a brief touch, just hands, wouldn't stir the soul inside Darton that much.

And it wasn't as if the mercenary and his dark army weren't tracking us quite closely already. I wasn't sure we *could* make the situation much worse.

"Just for a minute, then."

I pulled off my glove and laid my hand over his. His fingers twined with mine, his skin dry and warm. A fluttering energy ran up my arm and shivered around my heart.

Sights and sounds of past times rose in the back of my mind, but I kept my awareness firmly focused on my current body. On the feel of Darton's hand and the pressure of the seat belt across my chest, the headlights streaking across the darkening road ahead of us, Keevan's staccato breaths, the rustle as Izzy swiveled to peer at us, her mouth flattening before she turned to face the road again. I wanted to stay here, in the moment, so I could detach myself before this experiment carried on too long.

Darton's fingers gripped mine. His head bobbed with the motion of the car. The new memories springing up in his head would become less intense each time, but he'd only experienced a few so far. He'd still barely be aware of anything around him in the thick of one. It'd take several more of these moments before I could hope he'd be able to talk to me during one.

One minute slipped by and then another, and Darton stayed lost in his recollection. His lips twitched. His eyes opened, and I drew my hand back. The deep blue of his irises glinted when he looked at me.

"That really was a waste of a good boot," he said, incredulous and amused.

A laugh burst out of me. I clapped my hand over my mouth to try to contain it. Yes, that had been… quite an adventure. Darton grinned, clearly pleased with himself for provoking that reaction in me.

"So not a very helpful memory then," I said when I'd recovered my self-control.

"I tried, but…" He spread his hands apologetically.

Keevan drummed his fingers against the steering

wheel. "Okay. Look. Darton, I'm in this for however long you need me, but I just can't—it doesn't make sense. I don't know."

Darton's face fell. "Keevan, man, I—I don't know either. What do you want me to say?"

"Is there anything you *can* say that'll let me wrap my head around this craziness?"

Silence filled the car. Keevan grimaced. "Yeah. That's what I thought."

"Does it have to make sense?" Priya said softly. "Can't you just believe there are some things in the world that don't, not in the way you're used to?"

"I don't know." Keevan's voice sounded broken. "Beasties made from shadows and magical ancestor connections and… I don't know."

My jaw set. This was why I'd wanted to go it alone. Priya, at least, had some clue what she was getting into. Darton's friends couldn't have imagined this by half. And the fact was that this race across the country might very well be a suicide run. They hadn't agreed to witness that.

I had to protect Darton. I didn't have the capacity to take responsibility for anyone else.

"You can drop us off at the next town," I said. "We'll figure something out. We can rent a car, grab a train or a bus, whatever's there. It's okay. You've already done a heck of a lot."

Izzy jerked around so abruptly I had to suppress a flinch. She stared at me. "We should leave Darton with *you*? It doesn't matter what your ancestors or whoever did. You don't know him, not really. And he doesn't know you. It's—it's your fault he's mixed up in all this stuff, isn't it? Maybe we should drop *you* off."

I could only stare at her. Her normally gentle features had gone rigid with resolve. Darton's eyes widened.

"Isabel..."

"Don't 'Isabel' me," Izzy snapped. "You're in danger, and it started when she came along—and the farther she makes us go, the worse it gets."

My hands balled at my sides. "I'm trying to get him *away* from the danger. Could *you* have blasted away the things that came after him on campus? Or ripped up the glooms back there in the forest?" How the hell did she think they'd have made it out of there without me?

Her gaze turned dagger sharp. "Would they have *been* there if you hadn't? If we hadn't followed you out here into the middle of nowhere?"

"Darton is the one they're following."

"We only know that because you've said it," Keevan put in. "Izzy is right."

Did they even have eyes? Light above, I should never have agreed to let them come.

"I trust Emmaline," Priya said. "I've known her longer than any of you. I know she's telling the truth."

Keevan guffawed roughly. "We don't know *you* at all."

"*Stop it.*"

Darton's voice cut through the car, ragged but unyielding. Everyone else shut up.

"You know me," he said. "You came all this way because you were worried about me. I can't tell you how much I appreciate that, from both of you. A lot of what's going on seems crazy to me too. But Emma is on our side. On *my* side. Even if you don't trust her yet, trust me enough to know what I'm talking about. I wouldn't say that if I wasn't sure."

He squeezed my knee, and it was hard to say whether it was that contact or the passionate defense he'd just given me that sent more heat through my body.

Izzy sucked in her lower lip. Keevan rubbed his hand over his forehead.

"We're going to need to sleep at some point," Izzy said finally. "It's getting late. We can at least do that, can't we? We'll all be thinking clearer after we've had some rest."

"Anywhere we stop, we give the dark rabble a chance to catch up," I said.

"If we don't stop for that, we'll end up stopping because we've crashed into something, and we'll really be stuck then. I know there's no way I'm getting any sleep in the car. After everything today…" She shoved her hands through the auburn waves of her hair. "It's going to be hard enough in a bed."

I couldn't say I didn't sympathize. My awareness of the dark army closing in behind us jittered through my nerves even when I wasn't directly thinking about it. And Keevan looked worn out already. But…

Darton's thumb ran up and down the side of my leg. "Can't you set down some sort of magical protection?"

"Not exactly." Nothing even a mere gloom couldn't leap right over in their current super-powered state.

But I could cast down another line of salt, a supernatural trip wire that would give us warning when the dark rabble was close. I stared down at the phone map, the lines of the roads blurring and re-sharpening before our eyes. At our current pace, we'd reach Peddleton in the wee hours of the morning, when we couldn't exactly drop in on strangers to make inquiries anyway.

I let out my breath. "All right. But it's not *that* late. I'd like as much of a head start as we can get. We should be well into Utah by midnight. I'll switch off with you at the wheel before then if you need it, Keevan. At midnight, we'll look for a place to stop off for the rest of the night."

My gut had twisted as I made the concession, but Keevan's shoulders sank down and some of the tension left Izzy's face. Apparently I wasn't getting rid of them. I hoped I could keep working around them.

24

"Why here?" Keevan asked, frowning at the sprawl of low fields on the other side of the windshield. The highway light on the post where we'd stopped lit the grass with an eerie yellow glow.

I held up my phone. "The motel is another ten miles down the road. If I lay down a line here, we'll have plenty of warning—and time to get going—if the dark rabble catches up with us before morning."

Keevan's frown didn't budge, but he didn't say anything else, just swiped his hand past his drooping eyelids. He'd insisted on staying at the wheel, but now, at just past midnight, he looked too exhausted to argue about anything. Izzy nodded where she was curled up in the passenger seat.

Darton pushed open his door, the hinges squeaking. "I'm coming with you."

That suited me fine. The car wouldn't be much protection if the glooms were closer behind us than I'd have guessed.

"Grab the salt," I said with a nod. Then, to the others, "This shouldn't take too long. Try to relax for a bit."

Keevan slumped in his seat.

"Are you sure I can't—" Priya started, her expression beseeching, and I cut my gaze toward her.

"Do you know how to work magic? Because if you do, you should have been using it when we were running out of the enclave."

Her mouth twisted. "No. Well, I'll shout if anything bad starts going down here."

It wouldn't. If the dark rabble came, they'd come to Darton and me. They didn't give a sow's arse about the three people we were leaving behind in the car.

Our elongated shadows wavered in the lamplight as we tramped over the ditch and into the thicker darkness across the field. I peered to the north. Had I seen an unnatural movement, or had that just been a trick of my own weary eyes? The night stayed still and blank, but my pulse kept skittering. The mercenary had already surprised me more than once. We'd cut it far too close too many times.

Darton seemed more interested in the sky, where a dappling of stars peeked between the streaks of cloud. I made for a skeletal electrical tower that stood about a quarter mile from the highway, and he kept pace. After a minute, he glanced over at me.

"Did you and Priya have an argument I missed?"

"Yes," I said. "But I'd rather not talk about it."

"Fair enough." He shifted the bag of salt in his hands. The fine grains hissed against each other. The wind licked over us, chilly and laced with the scents of dry earth and dying grass. It reminded me of the chill the mercenary carried around him even in my visions.

"Have you had any more of that pain?" I asked. "In your side, where it was bothering you before?"

Darton tipped his head as he considered. "Not today. Not that I can remember. I guess I should be glad it's not acting up even more with all the dashing around we've been doing."

I was glad for that, but I didn't think it was a coincidence. The dark fae must have been using the moment of Arthur's near death to seek out his essence. He might not have known the significance, only felt some impression from the Darkest One that had guided him. But he didn't need to search for Darton like that anymore. His creatures had all the scent they required.

For a moment, we walked in silence, but then Darton cleared his throat. "When you were using your... abilities, getting us out of the forest, you said something odd. Is it true that doing magic takes away from your life? The more you do, the sooner you'll die?"

"Yep." I didn't have to force the breeziness of my answer. After shaking hands with my physical mortality a hundred times, it was hard to get emotional about it. "It hasn't really mattered. It's not as if I'm ever around anywhere near long enough to die of old age."

Darton's stride faltered with a sudden hitch. He caught himself.

"What happens to me if something happens to you?"

"Oh, you don't have to worry about that. I go when you do, not the other way around."

He stopped dead then, and I could have smacked myself. Between my fatigue and the stress of the last few days, I hadn't watched my words. Mortality might be a well-worn concept to *me*, but Darton had never thought about death with that much familiarity.

His face looked gray in the wan glow that barely reached us this far from the road. His gaze didn't waver from mine. "So how long do we normally make it?"

"Keep walking," I said. "We don't want to waste time." When he didn't move, I grabbed his forearm and tugged. He came along, his posture tense.

I dragged in a breath. How to put this without provoking a total existential panic? "I told you before it's taken longer each time for you to wake up on your own. The dark rabble never comes after you before you know who you are. So when you became aware at a younger age, we had fewer years to live. At the beginning, we wouldn't have been more than kids. More recently… From what I can remember and what I've recorded, in the last century or so, the oldest birthday I've made it to is twenty-two."

"Twenty-two," Darton repeated in a hollow voice. I felt him doing the calculations. Our birthdays would be within a day or two of each other. A year and a half—that was how far off twenty-two was. As if we had much chance of making it even that far with the mercenary breathing down our necks. A shiver ran down my back, as if that breath had touched me right now. I walked faster.

We reached the foot of the electrical tower. Darton passed over the salt when I reached for it, but he stood rigidly. His jaw worked.

"I always try to extend that time," I said. "I try everything I can. You have no idea how many—" My voice caught. I swallowed. "But there's only one of me, and who knows how many thousands of glooms and the rest."

"Yeah."

I didn't know what else to say, and there wasn't really time for delays. I drew out the spare wand I'd brought with me—gods, how was I already running low on those?—and pointed it at the bag of salt. During the drive, I'd mixed in the necessary herbs. I murmured the incantation to command the salt to react to any shadow creature's crossing.

Darton stirred out of his daze as I headed toward the car, sprinkling the salt along the ground.

"What am I usually doing while you're working your magic and so on?"

I shrugged. "Not a whole lot. Offering emotional support? Our enemies are my kind, not yours. It was my spell that got us stuck in this cycle. I'm the one who has to untangle it."

"So I was a great king, but I'm utterly useless now."

"You're not *useless*," I said. "I'd imagine you could do plenty more important things if you had the chance to. We just—we all have separate roles. The magical arena is my domain."

His voice dropped. "I feel useless. You've been the one doing all the work here, Emma. I'm barely managing not to get in your way."

The pain in that admission squeezed my heart. My mind darted back to our conversation in the restaurant yesterday evening. The lack of direction he'd talked about, that *need* to know he was contributing something important to the world.

How much harder must that desperation be hitting him now, watching me battle forces he could barely understand, telling him it was all for his sake? No wonder he was groping after a fragment of memory, a slight chance he might offer *some*thing I couldn't.

"I doubt it'll make you feel any better," I said, "but I will point out that if I hadn't cocked up the spell in the first place, we wouldn't have to be fending off the entire dark rabble instead of focusing on the sorts of things you *will* be great at again. At least useless is better than active ruination."

"Don't say that," Darton said with more force than I expected. With a tone that sounded almost like my king's. "You've done so much—back then and now, while I— God. Last night. Even then, I thought you wanted me there to make *you* feel better, but it was for me, wasn't it? You were scared for *me*." He paused. "Did you sleep at all?"

With his eyes intent on me, I found I couldn't lie. "A couple hours. After the sun came up. The dark rabble can't move as quickly in daylight."

"*Two* hours!" he burst out. "You've been going all day on two hours of sleep? How are you not falling over?"

"Practice." I dug out another handful of salt. "And staying alive is an excellent motivator. I probably will fall over when we get to that motel." His question stirred up other memories from this morning, though. "I'm sorry about afterward, just so you know. I was only being mean because I needed you to leave so I could get the rest of my plans in order. That was before I knew that whole army was coming for you right then."

"That's the last thing you need to apologize for. God." Darton shook his head. "So we really are running for our lives."

A laugh sputtered out of me. "Have you only just figured that out?"

"I don't know. None of this has seemed completely real, to be honest. It's still sinking in." He raked his fingers through his hair. "What do you figure our chances of making it past twenty-two are this time around?"

My throat closed. Darton gave a hoarse chuckle. "That bad, then. Okay."

"Honestly," I said. "I didn't think we were going to make it out of the theater, so I'll be grateful for every hour farther we're still living."

25

I only gave myself a minute in the motel room shower, even though I'd left the new pouch of salt on the counter where I expected to hear it rattling if it stirred. But between that short interlude and a quick change of clothes, I walked out into the main room feeling infinitely less manky than when I'd walked in.

Darton was sitting on the second bed, flipping through channels on the tiny flat-screen TV. He switched it off when I emerged and turned to face me. The eye contact alone was enough to send a little tingle over my skin. Sharing a room with him felt dangerous in a totally separate way, but if the dark rabble arrived, I couldn't risk having even one wall between us.

"I tried to call my parents," he said. "Only got voice mail."

"Well, it is pretty late." Almost one in the morning now. But I could understand him hoping for one last conversation before his probable death. A lump rose in my throat. "If you want to shower, you should do it now. We don't know how quickly we might have to leave."

He got up and crossed the room. I stepped to the

side to clear his way, but instead of heading to the bathroom, he stopped in front of me. His gaze locked with mine.

"I've been thinking."

"Always a hazardous activity," I joked, partly because the husky note in his voice had amplified the earlier tingling.

He took a step closer—close enough that if he'd stretched out his arm, he could have touched me. My pulse thumped.

"Darton—"

"I've been thinking," he interrupted, "that I need to dig up more of that one memory and find out what I knew that you didn't. And I've also been thinking that the deepest I've gotten into my memories wasn't when we were just holding hands. It was when we were kissing."

My skin flushed from head to toe. "What's your point?" I asked as innocently as I could manage.

He moved forward, and I backed up—right into the wall. He set his hand a few inches from my head, leaning on that arm. He bent toward me, and if I'd thought his voice was husky before, now it was low enough to melt me.

"You have fifteen hundred years of accumulated wizardly wisdom, Em. I think you know what my point is."

Of course I did. And it was just like him to find a way of presenting this proposition as if it were an act of heroism.

If he'd had any clue how much every particle in me was screaming for me to touch him, trail my hands up his chest, pull his mouth that last short distance down to mine—but I'd been down that road before. It never led anywhere good for either of us.

My body stiffened. Darton hesitated. He straightened up enough to give me room to breathe. His eyes searched mine.

"You said before that we shouldn't because it'll make me more of a beacon to the dark creatures. But those things are obviously following me wherever I go anyway. The more I remember, the more I'll be able to pitch in. So is there something else stopping you? If you really don't— if it's *me*—I wouldn't force the issue."

"No," I broke in. "I know you wouldn't. It's not that. I just—" *I know how much it hurts to act out a love beyond any you'll ever return.* As if I could say that to him. "All those hundreds of years of keeping my distance so I didn't wake you up early—it's a hard habit to break."

He cocked his head. "Has it normally taken a lot of effort to keep your distance from something like this?" He made a vague gesture between himself and me. "Do we often…"

Memories flitted through my head—other sets of hands, other eyes, other mouths, traveling over other bodies I'd inhabited. "Sometimes," I hedged. *Almost always if I let it happen*, would have been the truth. We were inevitably pulled toward each other. But how easily *he* gave in to that desire depended somewhat on what sort of body *I* was in. "There's a connection between us, magic and history."

And I'm never sure how much you come to me merely because of that rather than any real wanting.

Darton's gaze dropped. I felt the imminent question and braced myself.

"Is it strange," he said, "being a woman, now, when, before… At least if I'm remembering correctly…"

"You are," I said, "and no. The specific bits that come with any physical body, male or female, never mattered all that much to me even before this swapping started. I'm Merlin. That's all I need to know. Wherever my soul ends up, I'll still *be* Merlin, so I'm not much fussed as long as I'm human. A lemur or a warthog or something I'd take some issue with."

He paused. "Do *I* go back and forth too?"

I had to laugh at his uncertain expression, feeling a little relief. I'd take uncertainty over disgust or abhorrence any day. "Not much. Apparently yours is a man's soul through and through. It's only been a few times, I guess when circumstances threw fate for a bit of a loop… You do make an interesting woman on those rare occasions, as I recall."

"Hmm." He looked down at himself, at the shape of the space between our bodies. I held my breath as I waited to see where this line of thinking would take him. Whether he would be the one to stiffen now and draw back from me.

Instead, he said, "This isn't just about who we were before, though. This is about Darton and Emma too."

I guessed that was how he needed to frame what he was feeling to get around the memories in which he wouldn't have thought of me that way even for a moment. But I couldn't help asking, like prodding a canker sore, "Are you sure?"

"Well, maybe I can't be sure how mystical connections or whatever might be affecting me." His voice dropped again. "All I know is that there's been *something* there from the beginning. From before I even saw your face behind that fencing mask. A spark. A partly antagonistic one at the start, maybe…"

He smiled, and darkness take me, he did have a smile worth every wonder known to humankind.

"You are so… enigmatic. In an intoxicating way."

"Those are some nice SAT words there," I said.

Darton shook his head, still smiling. "You know what? I think I like you even more, somehow, when you're putting me in my place. I like that you do it. I like *you*. I *want* you. So what if I don't know exactly why? Does anyone with anyone? Does it *matter*?"

As I gazed at him with the raw honesty in his words washing over me, it didn't. Not in that moment, at least. Because he was right—the dark rabble was hot on our trail no matter what we did. Because that memory he was chasing really might be useful to us. Because his remarks from an hour ago were still ringing through my head—*I'm utterly useless now*—and I wanted him to be able take them back almost as much as he did.

We'd already come this far. Giving in always felt almost as good as it hurt.

My answer came out in a whisper. "No. I want you too."

A gleam lit in those indigo-blue eyes. Darton leaned in. The tip of his nose brushed mine. He traced his free hand down my side, and my pulse pounded even harder.

"You want this?"

"Yes," I murmured, lost in his gaze.

His palm settled on my waist. He tugged my hips forward to meet his. "And this?"

"Yes."

His head dipped. His breath teased over my lips. "And—"

Good gods, enough of this torture. I clutched the back of his neck and pulled him to me.

Our mouths collided in a crash of heat and tongues. I couldn't kiss him hard enough, deeply enough, to feel satisfied. My hand slid to cup his cheek, to trace down his neck and over those football-player muscles I hadn't gotten to properly explore when they'd been on view before. An urgent, needy sound worked itself from Darton's throat. He pressed me against the wall, kissing me back just as fervently.

But then the forcefulness of his lips eased. He kept kissing me, so gently the tenderness of it made my heart ache, but I knew his mind had come unmoored. I stayed there with him, trading breath for soft breath, waiting for him to come back.

His mouth drifted away from mine to tease along my jaw. He grazed it over the crook of my neck. Then he paused with a shaky inhale.

"You really were terribly, terribly bad with horses, weren't you?"

A giggle jolted out of me. "Despite your best efforts."

He nuzzled my hair, nipped my earlobe, and blazed a scorching path to my lips. We'd only kissed once more before I felt him fade a second time.

I let my mouth linger against his for a moment, and then I just held him. He hugged me back as if I were his anchor amid the rush of ancient history. His thumb stroked up and down my spine. I buried my head in his shoulder, soaking in the mingled scents of citrus and earth in the warmth of his body.

He was far away right now, but that distance meant my king was returning to me, bit by bit.

His embrace relaxed, and he bowed his head next to mine. "The whole flashback thing does make hooking up a little tricky, doesn't it?"

I snorted. "It's early days. You'll get better at staying present."

"With practice?" he suggested hopefully.

As tempting as that idea was, I knew it was time to stop. Under the giddy thump of my pulse, the ache in my chest was growing. And there were logistics to consider too.

I swatted his arm. "I think we've had enough of that tonight. I would actually like to add to that two-hour store of sleep I've been running on."

"Well, I can't argue with that." He smiled against my cheek. "I got back to it. To the memory, in the alchemist's shop. I remembered enough this time to know that's where I was."

I pulled back to watch his expression. "And?" Whatever he'd recalled couldn't have changed his opinion of me if he was still making hook-up jokes, but I'd tensed all the same.

Darton's gaze drifted away as he slipped back into the memory. He frowned. "He was showing me pieces of… glass? I think. Round ones, laid out on the workbench."

That image tugged at my mind with a vague sense of familiarity. *Had* he mentioned this moment to me in another life and I'd simply not had the chance to record it?

"What were they for?" I asked.

"I'm not sure. I'm going to have to try to bring up more next time. I had the impression, the bit I fell into, that he and I had already discussed whatever my purpose was. But I know I was excited about what he'd told me. I was going to make something easier for you, something you'd been worried about." His brow furrowed. "There was a man I'd talked to who'd frightened you. The alchemist was saying that he'd never seen 'one,' that he could only rely on 'fairy stories.'"

My skin turned cold. "Not a man. A dark fae. You never told me you went to Ffion to ask about them."

Was that why this memory had surfaced for him now—because of the mercenary's magic that had already touched him?

"I think I wanted to handle the situation by myself," Darton said. "Make less work for you. Or something like that. I just wish I remembered how the hell a bunch of glass shards was supposed to accomplish that. You don't have any idea?"

I shook my head. What were the chances a human alchemist who'd never even seen a dark fae had held some secret knowledge that would defeat them? It was grasping at straws.

"We'll try again if we can't find out anything from this hunter the light fae talked about," I said, more for Darton's benefit than because I had any real hope we'd find our answers there.

26

The pouch of salt in my pocket shuddered. I jerked awake.

A thin gray light seeped through the gap between the curtains beyond the red glow of the clock. It was six fifteen. We'd made it to morning, if not with a whole lot of sleep to show for it. I blinked blearily, and the salt jittered again. My body jolted into full awareness.

I shoved off the comforter and leapt out of the bed. "Darton, we've got to go. Now."

A defiant muttering filtered through the pillow his face was buried in. He pushed upright with a groan. He'd taken off his sweater to sleep, and his undershirt showed off his muscular arms and chest to full effect.

I yanked my gaze away. This was not an appropriate time to be getting distracted.

"The sooner we leave, the better," I told him. "Get dressed."

I ran to the bathroom to relieve myself and splash cool water on my face. When I returned, somewhat revived, Darton was standing outside the bathroom door, his sweater and shoes on. His face looked sleep worn, but his eyes were alert.

Alert and somber. His voice came out with a rasp. "I was dreaming. I don't remember it all but— I don't know whether they *were* just dreams or real."

I paused. "What did you dream?"

His head bowed. I was about to order him to hurry up or leave it for later when he brought his hand to his abdomen. To the spot on his gut where he'd felt that pain before. My pulse hiccupped.

"The woman," he said. "The dark fae? Who killed me. She stabbed me here?"

I swallowed thickly. "Yes. But she didn't *kill* you. You're not dead. You've lived more lives than she ever will. I stopped her."

For the time being, at least.

"Right," Darton said, but the shadow in his expression lingered. I wanted to say something more comforting, but comfort wasn't my specialty even at the best of times. And right now, we had barely any time at all. I gripped his arm with what I hoped was a reassuring pressure.

"Do your business, fast. I'll get the others. If you've got more questions, we'll get to them once we're on the road."

The benefit of holing up in a random motel in between nowhere and nothing was we'd been able to get rooms right next to each other. I rapped on the door of the one the other three had shared. On the other side, someone—it sounded like Priya—cursed, and someone else—Izzy, no doubt—gave a resigned-sounding yawn. It was Izzy who opened the door a few seconds later, tugging on her cardigan.

"Already?" She ran her hand through her pale auburn

waves to untangle them.

I nodded. "It's not bright enough yet to slow the dark things down much. If we're lucky, we've got fifteen minutes before the first ones turn up—but we might not be lucky."

She darted off to grab her things. Keevan slunk past the door without glancing my way. Darton strode over, his cowlicks ineffectively tamed with water.

When Izzy and Priya emerged onto the concrete walk, Keevan was nowhere to be seen. "He went into the bathroom a few minutes ago," Izzy said with a frown.

Darton stepped inside and knocked on the bathroom door. "Come on, Keev! Let's get a move on."

He didn't answer. My chest clenched. What if he was having second thoughts? Or third or fourth thoughts, really. He'd acted pretty fed up with me and my stories last night.

Izzy bit her lip. Darton banged on the door again, loud enough that Priya winced—and finally Keevan jerked it open.

He stood there on the threshold of the room, looking blankly at Darton. The blood vessels stood out in his eyes, and his dark skin had a grayish cast. He listed to the side.

Izzy's eyes widened. "Are you okay?"

"I'm fucking tired," Keevan grumbled. "It took me forever to get to sleep. If I even did. Feels like I was staring at the ceiling and then you were knocking on the door."

I felt bad for him, but sympathy wasn't going to keep Darton alive. "We're going. Are you coming?"

His gaze focused on me. "Yeah," he said roughly. "Of course. Yeah."

"You're not in any condition to drive," Darton said.

Priya raised her hand. "I'm feeling pretty good. I can take over for the morning." She looked at me. "It's not too much farther, right?"

My instinctive reaction to her offer was skepticism, but we'd already wasted too much time. I stuffed the twigs in my pocket and hefted my duffel. "Fine. Keevan, try to sleep some more in the car."

Priya's driving did reflect her personality, but not as worryingly as I'd feared. She worked the gas and took her turns with a brisk, carefree air that suggested nothing could possibly go wrong—and the car went along with it. As we pulled onto the highway, I thought I made out a flickering darkness in the distance behind us. I pulled a few twigs from my duffel bag, but after a minute or two, we'd left even that hint of pursuit behind. For now.

The sun rose higher, burning off the darker, longer shadows the dark rabble preferred to travel along. I eyed the sky through the windshield. Hardly a cloud touched the blue. We should pull away from them quickly. At least while we could drive fast.

We reached Peddleton midmorning and cruised down the main street, which was a blink-and-miss-it type of deal. The vegetation was sparse too. "We're looking for two large trees leaning together to make an X," I said as we looped back around town. I hadn't seen anything like that. We trundled around the outskirts and ventured out along the back roads without any luck.

"Any idea where to from here?" Priya asked.

"No," I admitted. My stomach knotted. The sun would have slowed down the dark rabble, but with the mercenary's lent power, they'd still be on our trail. With each circle of the countryside we made, they were drawing closer.

A lark swooped past the windshield. Izzy squeaked in surprise, and I went still. There was a more efficient way I could search. But I'd be leaving myself totally helpless in the car.

My body balked. Priya veered down yet another side street. A stand of poplars fluttered leaves in the breeze. Still nothing. Keevan sighed, and my fingers tightened around the twigs I was still holding.

It was better to leave myself to the mercy of Darton's friends than to the dark rabble, wasn't it?

I reached over the seatback to fumble with my duffel. My groping hand found the incense I'd stuffed in one of the smaller pockets.

"I'm going to do some magic," I said to the car at large. "I need to find the place we're looking for. I won't be able to talk to you while I'm doing it. Just keep driving around. Hopefully it won't take very long." I handed the stick of incense to Darton. "Hold this?"

He took it. I lit the end with my lighter and lay the twigs across my lap and around me. It wasn't as formal a circle as I preferred, but it'd do for a quick flight.

I sank back against the seat and closed my eyes. The herbal smoke of the incense filled my nose. I breathed it in and murmured the sight-riding incantation under my breath.

My mind lifted from my body, through the roof of the car, and up toward the sky. A robin was just darting past. I leapt into its head.

The world with its sprawl of interlocking roads and stubby buildings stretched beneath me. I urged the bird higher, turning to scan the ground below. The wind buffeted the robin's wings and pushed it even higher, and its gaze caught on a wave of motion far to the north.

The shadows were shifting. Even from that distance, the bird's eyes picked up the shiver in the dark spaces amid the scrub and farmland. Its muscles tensed at the sight.

Oh yes, the dark rabble was coming for us.

I nudged the bird around to swoop in a broad circle well beyond the edge of town. Where were those damned trees? The robin's gaze flitted over fences and billboards and—

There. I tugged it to the left, and the crisscrossing trunks of two old elms came more sharply into view. My thoughts twitched with excitement, but I held myself within the bird and took in the entire landscape. A tingling in the back of my mind told me where the car that held my body was. If we turned here, and then there… Yes. That would take us to those trees and the squat gray building set down the dirt drive behind it.

I released the robin and plummeted. My spirit fell back into my body with a lurch, and my eyes popped open.

The stick of incense Darton was holding had burned an inch down. He was staring at me, his expression tensed. At my other side, Izzy let out a sharp breath. Keevan had turned in the front seat, his face looking even grayer than before. When I met his gaze, his eyes jerked away.

"That," he said in a creaky voice, "was really creepy."

"What *happened* to you?" Izzy said. "You went so still… Priya honked the horn at a dog, but you didn't move even then. It was like you were just gone."

Because I was *gone.* But given how shaken up everyone looked, I didn't think confirming that would help matters.

"I was vision-riding," I said. "It's no big deal. And I know where we need to go now. Priya, take the next left. Then a right three roads down."

Darton let me pluck the incense from his fingers. I snuffed it out against the canvas of my duffel and tucked the rest away. No point in wasting it.

I'd settled into my seat when Priya made the second turn. A giggle slipped from her lips.

"Well, what do you know?"

Just ahead of us, the two elms leaned past each other against the hazy blue of the sky. Keevan let out a sputtered chuckle. Priya eased on the gas.

The building that stood a quarter mile down the potholed driveway looked more like a large garage than anything I'd have called a house. The ground between the trees and its walls and all around it was barren, just dry dirt and a few patchy shrubs.

Priya drove up the driveway and stopped the car in front of the building. The engine's growl was still fading when a door in the side swung open.

A tall man with a mane of white hair and a hawkish nose stepped out. He raised the shotgun he was carrying, but not quite high enough to aim it at us. Just to show he could if he decided to.

I motioned for Darton to get out so I could. He emerged holding his hands up in submission. I rolled my eyes at him and scrambled out onto the dusty earth.

"What are you doing here?" the man demanded in a gravelly baritone. He took a step forward, out of the building's shade. The sunlight caught on a spider web of scars etched across his cheeks and chin, nearly as pale as his hair. "I don't have any business with strangers."

I eased in front of Darton. "I'd appreciate it if you made an exception. I've been told the man who lives here knows how to kill dark fae."

Beside me, Priya opened the driver's door and slipped out. She peered at the man with a curious tilt of her head. Keevan and Izzy didn't stir, but I couldn't blame them.

The man's jaw clenched. He squinted at the bunch of us, his narrow gaze lingering on me and then Priya. Did the traces of our fae association cling to us in some way his eyes could perceive?

He shifted the gun in his hands. For a second, I expected him to point it at us after all, but he lowered the muzzle toward the ground.

"Back the car up to the trees, and then come in. This sounds like an inside conversation."

27

"So you *do* know how to kill these things?" Keevan jumped in. His shoulders had straightened and the color had come back into his face as he'd gulped down the cereal our host—who went by Jagger—had offered us. I'd only just finished my truncated story of why and how we'd ended up at the building behind the crossed trees.

Jagger rubbed his chapped lips where he was standing by the fridge. The rest of us were sitting around a polished oak table in a kitchen that was a lot neater than I'd expected given the grungy exterior. One wall was concrete, but the other three looked like regular plasterboard, painted pale yellow, and the bowls felt like real china. No windows in the place, but light streamed down on us from panels that covered the entire ceiling, bathing us in a steady, thorough glow. It banished all but the most tenacious shadows.

Seeing that had set me a little more at ease, but the glimpse I'd gotten of the dark rabble rippling toward us from upstate lingered in the back of my mind. The milk residue in my mouth turned sour. I shifted on the hard wooden chair, waiting for the fae hunter's answer.

"It depends on what things you mean," Jagger said.

"The first thing you've got to know is I've never actually killed a *fae*. Not the human-looking kind. The amount of power those sort have…" He shook his head with a rough chuckle.

My heart sank. Fingers tensed around my spoon, I gathered myself to probe further, but Keevan beat me to it again.

"Would it be a wild guess to say it looks like one of them tried to kill you?" He offered a goofy grin.

Jagger's hand twitched toward the interlacing scars on his cheek. I cleared my throat sharply.

"Forget that. What we really need to know is what you can tell us about hunting any of the dark creatures and about fending off the fae at the very least."

"That I can do," Jagger said. "The lesser dark creatures—the things you're calling glooms and the ones like animals—that's what I hunt. Those I've killed."

Izzy lifted her head. "Those are the things that have been after Darton so far. If we just knew how to get those to stop—"

By the light, could they not leave the conversation to the people who knew what the hell they were talking about?

"It's a dark fae that's urging the rabble after Darton," I interrupted. "The mercenary is lending them power— they wouldn't be half as much a threat without him behind them. We'll need to deal with him. But the strategies may be similar." I studied Jagger's spare, wiry frame. "Do you have magic?"

Few full humans did, but he might not be full human any more than I was.

Jagger gave me a crooked grin. "Nah. I leave sorcery

out of it. The drill is simple. Natural light destroys the dark. On open terrain, a flamethrower with a proper flint will do the trick. You've just got to amp it hot enough."

Our mercenary, like most fae-kind, had seemed rather attached to his woodland habitat. "And when you don't want to burn down an entire national park?"

"Now that used to be a complicated matter of lures and traps. But some ten years ago, new findings started coming down the pipe."

"Down the pipe?" Priya repeated with an arch of her eyebrows.

"There are a few of us hunters scattered around," Jagger said. "We check in and exchange strategies over the internet."

"Wait," Darton said, sounding more bemused than he had any right to be when I was trying to figure out how to keep him *alive*. He poked my arm. "You could have just Googled the answers and saved us the road trip?"

"Of course not." I'd searched the internet in this life, even though the new tech felt more byzantine than the language I spoke magic in. It never hurt to dig around a little in case some human development revealed new secrets. I hadn't found any chatter about fae that remotely aligned with my reality.

Jagger leaned back against the wall. "We keep our communications private. The better not to have any thrill-seekers interfering. In any case, one of us discovered another way to make use of the sun. Solar energy can be captured in cells and passed on to a focused light source. The process only gets more efficient every year. I've got several guns soaking up the rays on the roof right now."

"Sun guns!" Keevan said. "So if we get ourselves a

bunch of those—"

I cut him what I hoped was a silencing glance. We didn't have time for joking around.

"Do those really work?" I asked. "Even with the battery as a stepping stone?" My focus might have been on the biological and chemical sciences, but I knew enough about physics to understand the basics of solar power. Electrical light on its own could repel glooms and their kin, but it didn't outright harm them. I'd only managed to use the electricity in the theater by transforming it through the magic in my living body.

Jagger nodded. "The effectiveness fades the longer you keep the energy trapped in the cell. It's best for daylight hunting in dark areas, or evenings. But we've found ways to amplify the effect using crystals inside the chamber to keep the light bouncing around until we're ready to fire. That extends the usefulness somewhat.

"And the solar panels are helpful in other ways." He motioned to the ceiling lights. "But even if you caught a full dark fae amid daylight, and you'd just charged my best gun a moment ago, I don't think you'd do more than annoy it."

"That's a start," Keevan said, but my stomach had knotted.

I didn't need a *start*. I needed an end.

Jagger pointed at me. "It's Emma, right? Come with me. I'll show you what I've got."

The others started to get up, but I waved them down. "Finish eating. Who knows when we're going to get another chance to. I'll handle the shop talk."

Jagger led me down a brightly lit hallway to a narrow flight of stairs that stopped at a short ladder and a hatch above. We climbed out onto his roof.

Other than the small concrete square where the hatch opened, the entire surface gleamed with glossy black panes baking in the sun. A rack of guns, mostly rifle-sized, stood at the edge of the bare spot. My gaze immediately leapt from them to the landscape around us, but the shadows of the telephone poles and the sparse vegetation on the other side of the road lay still. For now.

Jagger hefted the largest weapon—practically a bazooka. A narrow pane ran down the top of its length, presumably feeding sunlight into whatever battery he'd hooked it up with.

"It functions a lot like a regular gun," he said. "Not that you look as if you've played much with those either. You squeeze the trigger, and the seal on the end opens. The crystals at the back focus the light into a beam straight down the muzzle. Aim it well, with fresh light, and you can shear apart a gloom. Or wound one of the bigger creatures enough to get it in a better position for torching."

I took the gun from him. The metal shape felt awkward in my hands, so much heavier and bulkier than a wand.

"So is this a calling that passed down through your family?" I said. "Why do you keep it up? The dark fae and their creatures don't bother much with humans these days."

"Not much, but they do, if you know how to look for the aftereffects," Jagger said. "They're vermin. I exterminate them."

The sentiment echoed my own so well I could accept it. But he hadn't answered the first part of my question. He'd tried to speak casually, but a thread of tension in his voice had rung with a deeper familiarity. I looked at the interlocking scars that creased his face.

"Who was it you couldn't save?"

Vermin might kill even an ordinary person if they were pushed into a corner. If they saw that person as a threat.

Jagger's mouth pressed flat. "You didn't come here for my personal story. What you need to be asking is why you're so intent on getting *your* friends killed."

I blinked at him. "What? I'm here to *protect*—"

"The one fellow. I caught that. But what business did you have hauling the other three into it? They're lambs. They haven't got a clue. And you're driving them into the slaughter."

"I didn't want them here," I protested.

"Then why are you still with them?" He glowered at me. "You know what you need to do—what you should have done instead of all this racing around while the shadows ran you ragged. Go straight to that fae. Take the battle to him—just you, no bystanders. You dictate the terms of engagement so they work in your favor, and you take him down with whatever magic you've got. If that's not enough, I'll give you the tools."

I swallowed hard. Maybe he was right. I could have insisted on leaving Keevan, Izzy, and Priya behind so many times, but I hadn't. We needed an end, yes, and it was up to *me* to provide it. But—

"I don't know if I'll have enough to stop him even then," I admitted.

Jagger grunted. "From what I can tell, from that story I know isn't the whole one, you know your enemy better than I could. You figure it out. Or you die. But make it just you."

He jerked his chin toward the gun. "Keep that. And this." He fished a plastic fob out of his pocket and pointed across the dusty ground to a smaller building I hadn't noticed, about a hundred yards behind the one we stood on.

"I've got a van prepped for hunting. Mounted with solar panels and lights. It'll give you a safe haven during the night and a way of blasting the creatures to kingdom come if you time things right. That I'll want you to bring back, if you can."

"Thank you." My fingers closed around the fob. My heart thudded. Was that really all there was to it? I took what I had now and made the best I could out of it?

Did I have much other choice? Coming here had been my only lead.

"If you take this thing down, it'll be an honor to have contributed," Jagger said. "I haven't heard of a dark fae stalking a human like this in my lifetime. Not a trend I'd like to see restarted." He paused. His eyes narrowed as he peered toward the road. "And it looks like you'd better get a move on. Trouble's coming."

I turned to follow his gaze. The edges of the shadows around the crossed trees and Keevan's parked car undulated with a surge of scurrying glooms. My back tensed.

Our time was up.

28

Jagger grabbed another of his sun guns and stalked across the solar panels to the edge of the roof. I followed him, stepping gingerly on the brittle black sheets. The thin shadows of the telephone pole lines along the road were squirming as the dark rabble wriggled and crawled along them, shrinking to avoid the sun.

"They can't make it to the house by daylight," Jagger said. "No matter how long the shadows get. I set up the property and maintain it to ensure that much. But you'll want to be well on your way before dusk sets in."

I glanced at the sky. My stomach clenched, my fingers tightening around the gun I was still holding. "I don't think we've got even that much time."

Jagger frowned. "It'd take more cloud than that little thing to—"

The fluffy white streak I'd spotted drifted in front of the sun, and the beams lighting the ground dimmed slightly. Enough that with a heave and a surge, flits of darkness shot across the open ground between the crossed trees and Jagger's home. They landed, roiling around each other, in the slice of shadow along the eastern wall.

The grizzled man's jaw had gone slack. "Well, hell.

I've never seen them attempt that before."

"It's the mercenary." I hurried across the roof to the east side. "He's sending them extra power. And they're already very keen to get to us—to Darton."

Jagger hesitated a beat before he stalked after me. "Who *are* you?" he demanded.

I'd skipped the whole reincarnation part of the explanation, along with any mention of exactly who Darton and I were connected to, just like I had with Darton's friends. I didn't see how it'd do us any good to get into it now. Instead, I shouldered my gun.

"It's complicated. Show me how this thing works?"

Jagger shook his head at me, but he raised his own weapon. "I've never seen this many swarm together at once either. It'll be like shooting fish in a barrel."

He took aim and pressed the trigger. The seal on the tip flipped up, and a streak of brilliant light cut through the shadow below us. The beam must have hit a gloom, because the edges of the thicker, churning darkness shuddered. The rest of it crept along the edges of the wall as if seeking a crevice to slip in through.

A shiver ran down my back. It was just that wall standing between them and my king.

"Can we only pick them off one at a time?"

"If you try to widen the range, you dilute the light too much to destroy them," Jagger said. "Believe me, you're not the first one to wonder."

"What about that flamethrower you mentioned?"

"Oh, I've got a few tricks up my sleeve if it comes to that."

The forms of the dark rabble squeezed together so tightly I couldn't make out where one creature ended and another began. I aimed haphazardly, figuring I had to hit *some*thing, and pulled the trigger. A puff of shadowy dust dispersed into the air.

Jagger hefted his gun. We fired again and again, but the shadowy mass barely thinned. A thicker cloud grazed the sun, and more shadows raced across the yard to the house. Jagger's hands didn't waver, but his shoulders had gone rigid.

The shade beside the house was swelling with dark vermin now. They swarmed across the wall with a hiss that raised the hairs on my arms. I lowered my weapon. Whatever defenses Jagger had prepared, he'd obviously never imagined facing an onslaught like this.

"I'm sorry," I said. "They're here because of us. We can make a run for it. They'll follow us once they sense we're moving."

Jagger grimaced. "This is a matter of principle now. And they'd smother you before you made it two steps to the van, the way they're coming on. I said I had other tricks, didn't I?"

"I never thought I'd need to use this in the middle of the day," he went on, striding across the roof to a control box protruding beside the hatch. "But it'll take out the lot of them. Give you some breathing space for your escape."

He twisted a knob. A *whoosh* of energy vibrated through the air, and the ground along the border of the building burst into flame. A wave of heat surged over me. I flinched backward with a yelp.

The writhing shadow against the wall burned away with a high-pitched cry that sounded disturbingly like a scream. The shade around the trees and telephone poles frothed as if in sympathy.

I eased back to the edge. The flames crackled in a translucent orange line about two feet tall, all along the base of the building. The sharp smell of burning gas prickled my nose. I let out a shaky chuckle.

"I'm starting to see why you don't have windows."

"If it keeps them away, I'm happy." Jagger came up beside me and studied his handiwork. He smiled. "I've never actually had to put that system to use before. For all my preparations, nothing much ever bothered coming out here for *me*."

I ignored the hint toward his earlier question. "And hopefully they never will. So… how do *we* get past the fire to make a run for it?"

"I wanted to confirm that it'd work. Now you go down and grab that boy of yours and whatever else you brought. The other three kids you can leave here with me. They'll be safe enough if you're right about the dark varmints clearing out once you're gone."

"I—"

He fixed me with a steely look before I was even sure what to say. "You *leave* them. It's bad enough they're here for this."

I shut my mouth. My gut twisted. He was right—of course he was right. I should have been that firm to begin with, instead of putting so many people in danger who'd never needed to be.

"Holler when you're ready to go," Jagger went on. "I'll shut off the flames, give the varmints a chance to get cozy by the house again. Then I'll fry 'em quick while you make a dash for the van. If you run fast enough, you'll get there before they recover."

"Can you keep the fire going long enough for that?"

"It's fed by a county gas line. Unless the supplier runs out, I think we're good."

"Okay." I hustled to the hatch and scrambled down the ladder, ignoring the heavy thump of my heart.

In the kitchen, Priya was still sitting at the table, examining the pale grain of the wood as if she could read stories in it. The others had gotten up. They paused in their puttering around the room when I burst in. Keevan glanced at the gun I was holding. His eyebrows leapt up.

"Now that's what I'd call fighting equipment."

Izzy peered at the empty space around me. "Where's Jagger?"

"Taking care of things so Darton and I can get out of here," I said. My duffel was still sitting behind my chair where I'd put it down. Thank the light I'd brought it in instead of leaving it in the car, even though Jagger hadn't found anything in there useful to his methodology. I heaved it across my back and turned to find four pairs of eyes staring at me.

"You and Darton?" Keevan said. "What about the rest of us?"

"Emma," Priya started.

"They've found us again," I said before she could go on. "The dark rabble. They're going to keep finding us. But it's Darton they're following. I've got... I've got the beginning of a plan. As soon as we're out of here, you three can head back to campus. You should be able to make it there before you even miss Friday's classes."

"That's not the point," Keevan said.

"How are we going to know that you two are okay?" Izzy put in.

We probably won't be. "We have phones. I appreciate

everything you've done to help, but it's only going to get rougher."

Keevan looked to Darton. "You get a say in what happens too."

Darton opened his mouth and hesitated. "I don't even completely understand what we're up against. If Em thinks we're all better off—"

Jagger appeared in the doorway. The way he clutched the frame, his knuckles whitened, made me tense.

"Emma..." he said. "I need you to look at something."

A chill ran down my spine. I grabbed Darton's wrist and gave it a squeeze. "Be ready, by the door." I dropped my duffel there and jogged to follow Jagger to the roof.

Up in the open air, he walked to the front of the building and pointed toward the road. It didn't take long for me to figure out what was worrying him. A little plume of dust shot up from an unnaturally dark splotch amid the shadow beside one of the telephone poles.

"What are they doing there?" he said. "I don't like the look of it."

"They're digging," I said. "Maybe they think they can get at the building from underneath?"

Jagger's stance relaxed. "They'll be disappointed then. This place is standing on solid cement."

Watching the flurry of motion around the hole stirred up a memory. My heart sank. "It might be something else. When they came after us on campus... they dug down to the electrical line and cut it."

"My entire system is internal," Jagger said. "From these panels straight to my private generator."

But it wasn't electricity they wanted to avoid. The

acrid tang of burning still hung in the air. I leaned forward. The flames were sizzling on along the wall.

"You said the gas line is a county one. Hooked up to a supplier somewhere else."

Jagger glanced at me. "Do you really think—"

The line of fire below us sputtered. Jagger's face paled nearly as white as his scars. He swore.

"Go. Go *now!*"

He pushed me toward the hatch, but I was already running. The crackle of the flames fizzled out with a faint *pop* before I'd even made it to the opening. I clambered down the ladder and dashed for the door.

Jagger's footsteps thudded behind me. We froze at a creaking that echoed throughout the entire building.

"What the hell is that?" Keevan's voice carried from the kitchen.

I didn't want to tell him the answer I was almost certain of. A fresh swarm of dark creatures had surged up against the building—and they were pushing on that wall with all their might.

Another creak reverberated through the space, rising to a groan. Jagger laughed, so hollowly my skin turned even colder.

"Oh, no. They're not beating this one," he muttered. He nudged me toward the kitchen and grabbed a bundle of fabric from one of the cabinets as he followed. He thrust it at me. The coarse material settled so heavy in my arms I might have thought it was waterlogged if it hadn't felt completely dry.

"It's no good for any of you to stay in here now," he said to me. "But you know what you have to do once you've got some distance from that horde."

"Jagger," I started. The groaning intensified, and the interior walls trembled. Darton and the others stepped closer to me.

Jagger shook his head at whatever he thought I'd been going to say. "I can get all of you out of here safe. You just have to listen. I'll shout, and then you've got to run. Five seconds, as far as you can make it in that time. Then you throw yourselves down on the ground with that tarp over you. No messing around. Got it?"

"What—"

He grasped my shoulder to cut me off. "I don't know what you're doing, but it must be worth an awful lot if they're that desperate to stop you. Good luck." Then he sprinted off down the hall.

Darton caught my eye. I lifted my shoulder in confusion, my throat tight.

"You heard him. Does everyone have everything they need?"

Keevan gave a jerky nod. Izzy clasped her hands together in front of her. "What's happening out there?"

I was saved from having to answer by Jagger's bellow from somewhere deep within the house.

"Now, get going. And give them hell for me!"

The words from my vision. My pulse stuttered. I shoved open the door and tugged Darton with me. The others spilled out into the sunlight in our wake. I pointed to the building Jagger had said held his van. "That way."

We bolted for it. Priya counted out the seconds with a gasp of a voice.

"Five, four, three, two, one…"

"Down!" I shouted and tossed myself to the ground, dropping my bag beside me. I wrenched and kicked at the thick black material of the "tarp" so it billowed over us. "Everyone get under. Hurry!"

I pulled it over my head. Darton's breath was harsh beside me in the sudden dark. My own hitched. "I just—" Izzy's voice murmured somewhere too my left.

A *boom* thundered through the air. The ground shook beneath us, and Izzy's comment turned into a squeal of pain.

29

Heat seared over the tarp. I cringed beneath the plastic-feeling fabric, my skin aching at the pressure. Then the temperature dipped again, in time with the clatter of objects hitting the ground around us.

Two heartbeats passed before I found the courage to pull back the tarp. I pushed myself upright. The others shifted around me and froze as they took in our surroundings.

The tufts of grass around us were scorched black. Thirty yards away, the building we'd fled spat up smoke from its burning ruin. The walls had collapsed in, the roof burst off in a rainfall of gleaming black fragments. Flames crawled across the interior walls now exposed.

My jaw had dropped. "Jagger?" I shouted, scrambling to my feet. The acrid smell of the smoke filled my lungs, and I coughed. "Jagger!"

No one answered or stirred amid the wreckage. Nothing moved except the warbling flames.

Because the blast had destroyed all of the dark rabble that had been nearby too. Jagger had known it would.

He'd given us our head start by whatever means he could.

I choked up, remembering that last squeeze of my shoulder. *Good luck*, he'd told me. I knew what he'd say now. *Don't stand around dawdling. Get yourself gone.*

He'd sacrificed so much for us. For me. The least I could do in return was make sure that act had been worth it.

"Come on," I said hoarsely. "We don't have a lot of time."

I offered Darton a gloved hand to pull him up. Priya was already standing, peering at the smoking building. Keevan swayed onto his feet.

"My car," he said. My gaze shot to the Toyota beside the crossed trees. Both the trees and the car were blackened now, the Toyota's hood split where a chuck of concrete had hit it. The windshield had shattered in on the front seats. I grimaced.

"We're not going anywhere in that now. But Jagger left us something better."

I jogged the rest of the way to the garage and shoved open the door. The others gathered around me as I eyed the gray van with lumpy fixtures all over its sides and top. Izzy was holding her arm bent against her stomach. Her forearm was blistered red.

"I didn't get all the way under the tarp in time," she said in a thin voice at my startled look. Her eyes gleamed with tears she was trying to blink back.

I swallowed hard. This—her injury, Keevan's ruined car, maybe even the disaster of Jagger's home—was my fault. My fault for letting Darton's friends come this far. My fault for letting them come at all. Jagger had been right.

Whatever little help they'd offered, it didn't justify the danger I'd put them in. It wasn't fair to them when they didn't understand.

"I've got witch hazel in my bag." I shoved my duffel toward Priya. Anyone raised by the light fae should at least be able to recognize that. "Let's get going."

Jagger had given the key and the responsibility to me, so I heaved myself into the driver's seat of the van. Darton climbed in beside me. The other three piled into the back. As Priya rustled through my bag, I stared at the spread of controls on the dashboard, as complicated as the fixtures outside. None of them were labeled. Jagger obviously hadn't imagined he'd been loaning this vehicle out when he'd customized it for his hunting expeditions.

That I'll want you to bring back, if you can. It didn't look as if there were anyone left to bring it back to.

My fingers clenched around the steering wheel. Then I shifted the one stick I did understand and reversed us out into the sunlight.

"Here," Priya murmured behind me. Izzy gasped. My roommate must have slicked some gel over her burn. I turned the car toward the drive, watching for returning glooms or worse.

"When we have a moment to stop, I should be able to at least mostly heal it," I said.

"With magic?" Izzy let out a choked giggle. "No. No, that's okay. I don't want *that.*"

The firmness of the last statement set my nerves on edge. I turned right, away from Peddleton and whatever trail we'd left leading into town. The clouds that had screwed us over not long ago had drifted on, leaving the sky stark blue around the blaze of the sun. Small blessings.

I wished we'd had them earlier.

"Where are we going?" Darton asked quietly.

Yes, it would probably be best to have a more concrete direction than just *away*. I dragged in a breath. Hog's balls, what I wouldn't give to stop and rest my head for a second. But I didn't know how many dark vermin Jagger's last-ditch effort had destroyed or how many others might be homing in on my king right now.

The van cruised by a desolate farm, a gas station-slash-family diner, and a sign announcing we'd entered another county. "Emma?" Priya said.

"I'm thinking." Jagger had said I should go after the mercenary by myself. Confront the dark fae on my own terms. What other choice did I have? Maybe I could summon enough magic to at least stop the mercenary temporarily until I figured out a better plan.

I couldn't confront him until I knew where he was.

I had a sense of the dark fae from my sight-riding last week, from that brief vision when he'd spoken to me. With the right tools, I could figure it out. But a phone app wasn't going to cut it.

"I need a map," I said. "I'm going to track down this mercenary and turn the tables on him."

"Are you sure that's a good idea?" Keevan said. "Can't we, like, call the police or the FBI or something?"

"Do you think the police have any idea how to combat fae magic? I *wish* it were that easy."

"So there isn't any faerie enforcement agency?" His voice was so strained the question didn't even sound like a joke.

"No," I said. "We're on our own."

We rumbled into another town. I veered over to the

sidewalk outside a general store and motioned to Darton. "You come with me. Everyone else, stay here. I shouldn't be more than a minute."

The dusty shop had a rack of maps by the far end of the counter. I grabbed the largest one that covered the territory I needed, and then a couple more in case the mercenary hadn't lingered in his little clump of dead forest after all.

As we stepped out of the store, a shudder of darkness down the road caught my eye. Glooms were slithering along the edge of the sidewalk just a few blocks away. My pulse stuttered.

"Get in, get in!" I pushed Darton toward his door and dashed around to mine. The second I'd dropped into the seat, my foot was on the gas pedal.

I was going to *have* to stop at some point to work the magic I needed. I scanned the passing landscape as we tore out of town. Jagger had the right idea, setting his home apart from everything else that cast a shadow. The light fixtures on the van should help me with that.

I didn't trust the matted, yellowing grass or the uneven sprawls of gravel that allowed too many tiny shadows. And I wanted more distance from the approaching dark rabble too. I pushed the van as fast as I dared go. For several minutes, we roared along the highway.

We passed through another small town. A large hardware store came into view up ahead, with a huge asphalt parking lot beside it. A store-closing sign was draped across the darkened windows, and the lot was empty. And completely flat.

I yanked the wheel and turned off the road. "Uh,

what are we doing *here*?" Keevan said.

"It's the safest spot for avoiding the shadow creatures," Priya said with more assurance than I was comfortable with yet. "No shade for them to creep up on us. As long as the sun stays uncovered."

"Are we going to count on that?" Izzy peered through the window, her brow knitting.

"And are we just going to *sit* here?" Keevan added.

I parked in the middle of the lot. "No," I said shortly. "I'm working on the rest. First, I need to figure out these lights…"

I jabbed at the buttons on the dashboard. Radio—soaring classical music, *so* not what I'd have expected. Air conditioning. Front lamps. Ah, now we were talking. A flood of brilliant light washed away the van's own shadow beyond the hood. Smiling, I pressed the other buttons around that one. Then I stepped out to survey the result.

Light glowed all around the van's sides and across its underbelly. No shadow "varmint" was getting within ten feet of this thing. As long as those panels on top held the sun's power, at least.

I grabbed my duffel from Priya and carried it and the maps to a spot a few feet in front of the van, within the flow of light but enough apart from everything else that I could clear my head. I opened the map that covered the area around the college, spreading it on the ground. Then I dug in my bag for some material to inspire my connection to the mercenary.

Oaks. The trees he'd been living among had been oaks. My hand closed around an appropriate twig.

"What are you doing?" Izzy asked.

"You could call it dowsing," I said. "It sort of is. But

I'm going to need to concentrate, so no more questions, all right?"

I pulled off my glove and drew out the fae knife. The skin on my palm split with just the slightest press of the blade's tip. Bracing against the sting, I dug it a little farther until a few drops of blood pattered onto the map's surface. Closing my eyes, I clutched the oak twig in that hand. My memories of the dark fae and his lair swam up in my mind. I tugged at the energy inside the twig and my own body.

"*On paper as real, bring me to the one I seek,*" I murmured in the old tongue.

My eyelids lifted. The lines on the map were quivering. The twig in my hand shivered with them. Then it twitched in one specific direction. I let my arm follow that pull, repeating my incantation under my breath. A trickle of blood seeped down over the bark. The twig jerked and jerked again, until my hand was poised over a green patch on the map some hundred miles northeast of the college.

The twig rammed downward, so swiftly I almost lost my hold on it. It tapped the paper, smudging it with my blood. My fingers tensed.

Right there. That was where our enemy was lurking. Relief and dread coiled together in my stomach, cool and jittery.

The twig crumbled to dust. I wiped it away, accidentally smearing blood on the hip of my jeans. "Okay," I said, gathering the map. "We'll need to—"

I turned and halted at the expressions on my companions' faces.

Priya looked normal enough. Who knew how much fae magic she'd witnessed before? But Darton and his friends were watching me with wide eyes.

Darton seemed to recover first. "You're still bleeding," he said.

I glanced at my hand. It wasn't a deep cut. Hardly worth expending more energy over. I tugged my glove back on and sheathed the dagger. "I'll be fine."

"The map *moved*," Izzy said. "You *talked* to it."

Well, not exactly, but I didn't see that getting into the finer details of magical practice was going to help anyone.

"Yes," I said. "I do magic. I cast a spell, and now I know exactly where this menace who's after Darton is. But I've got to get to him before his shadows catch up with us again. So—"

"No."

Keevan's voice was so raw my gaze shot to him. He'd crossed his arms over his chest. His eyes flashed when mine met his. "This is enough. I'm done."

30

Keevan's declaration was met with silence. None of us seemed able to speak. "What?" I managed finally. "Why now?"

Keevan flung out his arm in a vague gesture that encompassed my blood-dappled map, the van, and the distant building we'd seen eaten by flames. "I've told you before that I don't understand this. I don't like it. And things just keep getting crazier. That guy—he might be *dead*. My car practically got blown up too. You're cutting yourself up and making maps come to life…"

"I didn't *enjoy* any of that."

"I don't care!" Keevan said. "I just know I'm in way over my head. No regular human being can do the stuff I've seen you do."

"You've lied to us," Izzy said in a low voice. "Haven't you? Or at least there's a lot you've decided not to tell us. What you *have* told us doesn't really add up."

When I opened my mouth to protest—to pile more lies on top of the earlier ones—Keevan held up his hand. "I don't care about that either. If there are things you feel we can't handle, that you've got to keep to yourself, fine.

But I can't keep tagging along like I'm cool with this either. You made it clear you think we're dead weight anyway."

When I'd almost left everyone but Darton behind at Jagger's place. The shock of the explosion had temporarily bound our little group back together, but he was right. I'd already been thinking about where to drop them off on the way to the mercenary's lair. I didn't want to try to explain any more of my history than I already had. I didn't even know how *I* was going to deal with the dark fae, not really, let alone stop him from slaughtering everyone around me.

And yet the idea of them leaving wrenched at my chest.

"We can at least give you a ride back to campus," I said. "Your car—I mean, I'll cover the cost for you to replace it, but in the meantime—"

"Let's not get into that," Keevan said darkly. "I saw a bus terminal in town. I've got my credit card. You paid our way down here; I can manage to get myself back."

Izzy studied me, her pale eyes steady and her chin high. "You don't really want us to stay, do you?"

She stood there so unbending it was hard to believe I'd ever thought she was soft. I found I didn't know what to say. Which was ridiculous, because all I'd wanted from the beginning was for them to take off.

"Right," she said when I didn't answer. Her gaze slid to the man beside me. "Darton…"

"You don't have to go along with this craziness, man," Keevan broke in. "Those things are probably chasing *her*, not you. Let's just get out of here."

Darton reached for my arm, a gesture that warmed and tore at my heart at the same time. A couple days ago, those two had been his closest friends. I'd ripped a chasm between them in just twenty-four hours.

But then, what were the chances he'd survive to miss them all that long?

"I told you before," Darton said. "I trust Emma. I know she's telling the truth. If I went with you, without her—none of us would make it back to campus."

Keevan threw his hands in the air. "Fine. You know my number. If you need bailing out, I'll come. It's her I'm done with, not you."

He stalked off toward town. Izzy's mouth twisted. When Darton glanced away from her, her shoulders stiffened. She turned and hurried after Keevan.

"I'm sorry," I said. "I—"

Darton shook his head. "It's not your fault."

I was pretty sure it was. Whether I could have avoided this situation without getting us into an even worse spot, I didn't know, but I was the one who'd brought us here.

Priya cleared her throat. She'd hung back during the argument, but now she caught my eyes and jerked her head to the side.

"A word, Emmaline?"

I wasn't particularly keen to hear her assessment of our present circumstances, but I followed her a little apart from the van and Darton anyway. The sun beat down on our heads as heat rose in an echo from the asphalt beneath us, roasting us from both directions. The oily smell of the baking pavement turned my stomach.

Priya stopped. "Why have you been so angry at me?" she said abruptly.

My eyebrows twitched upward. "Because… you lied to me the entire time we've been living together? You were spying on me?" How could she ask that?

"You lied to me about an awful lot of things, because you thought I was safer not knowing. How is that different?"

"I didn't know you had any idea the fae even existed!" I burst out. "You knew *exactly* who I was and what I was going through. Of course it was different."

She cocked her head. "What would you have done if I'd told you, even hinted at my association with them? Would you have opened up to me then?"

I tried to imagine it. If I'd seen the armlet with the runes during a casual conversation, if Pri had made an offhand remark about the fae, how would I have reacted?

Panic. I'd have been out of that apartment searching for a new living situation before the dust had settled.

I wasn't angry with her just because she'd lied. I was angry also because I didn't trust the fae, any of them, light or dark, and I would have assumed she'd do more harm than good if she interfered. I still wasn't sure of her motives. But I *was* sure I'd earned the right to that distrust at least a hundred times over.

"No," I said, "but that doesn't make it okay that you were sneaking around, sending back reports or whatever to your enclave. It doesn't matter how important *you* thought keeping an eye on me was. I should have had the choice."

Priya gave me a small smile. "Do you really think I came all this way so I could make a report? Gods, Emmaline, the enclave would have been happy just to know you'd taken the king and all the trouble that surrounds the two of you farther away from them. I knew who you were because they asked me to watch you, but that's not why I agreed to do it."

"Well, why then?" I demanded. "You thought you could 'help' fix a problem *I* haven't been able to in fifteen centuries?"

"Maybe," she said. "And maybe you're right to make fun of that idea. But it wasn't just that either. Do you know what it's like to spend the first eight years of your life with only the fae for company? No, wait, you do. You have to know how it is trying to live in the human world with so many things in your head they'd never believe, so many quirks you never realized were quirky…"

She laughed, a little raggedly. "I've never had any real friends. Any time I started to get close with anyone—as a kid, as a teenager—I'd always accidentally mess it up. By being me. By being weird."

"Yeah," I said quietly. I did know what that was like. It was why I'd stopped really trying to make friends dozens of lives ago.

"I thought it'd be different with you," Priya went on. "Because you were kind of like me. And you know what? It was. You never looked at me like I'd grown a second head or backed off because of some vibe I didn't mean to give off. You were fine with me being me. I was just waiting until I could contribute somehow, until what I knew about the fae might be useful instead of just a secret… We could take them on together, I thought. And neither of us would have to keep going at it alone."

The strain in her voice made my throat close. "Pri…" I said. "It's not that easy. You can't just decide that someone should trust you and then expect that to be all it takes."

She raised her head. "Maybe not. But I don't think it's as hard as you're making it either. I don't know whether it's just that you've gotten so used to only having yourself or that you actually *like* being the only one taking a stand, but you're screwing up, Emmaline. You aren't the only one who cares about him." She pointed to Darton.

"It's not the *same*," I started, but she cut me off.

"You aren't the only one who cares about *you*. But you keep shutting us down, shutting us out. And maybe we haven't been through everything you have, maybe we can't do the same things you can, but I think everyone who was in that van has strength, and you've shut that out too."

My hands clenched at my sides. "It's up to me! It was my spell. It's my duty. He was *my* king."

"But not just yours," she said. "Look, I know you've got a lot of trouble ahead of you. I just needed to say that. Do you think you'll find something for me to do? Or are you going to ditch me the next chance you get, like you tried to back at Jagger's?"

I didn't know what to tell her. "I've always handled things alone. Do you know how to kill a dark fae? Because if you do, you should have spoken up before Jagger blew up his home."

Priya's expression dulled. "Okay. What Keevan said about phones and all that applies to me too. But I don't want to stick around if I'm only going to get in the way."

She set off in the same direction the other two had headed. Keevan and Izzy had already disappeared amid the buildings. I stared after her, my stomach churning.

Good riddance. No more stupid arguments, no more trying to explain the inexplicable. Just my king and me, the way it always had been.

Darton studied me as I marched back to the van, but

he didn't comment on Priya's departure. "What now?" he asked. Ready for whatever I told him.

"We track down that dark fae," I said. "Let's see what we've got to work with." I tugged open the van's back doors and clambered inside.

A restless urge quivered through me. I stalked along the wall, running my fingers over the equipment mounted on it. More sun rifles, set by the windows to absorb power through the glass. A couple of bigger but stumpier contraptions I guessed were flamethrowers, with tanks of gas to refuel them. A hazmat suit of the same tarp material that had protected us from the explosion. Skids of protein bars and shakes—fuel for us.

Nothing that told me I could destroy a dark fae so eager to destroy us first.

I paced back and forth and then sank down at the edge of the floor by the doors. I'd meant to hop out, but the moment my butt hit the worn carpeting, my heart sank with it, and I couldn't move another inch. I rubbed my hand over my face.

"Hey," Darton said. "How can I help? What do you need?"

Nothing, I meant to say. *Just give me a minute to think.* But when I opened my mouth, a swell of anguish choked off the words. I closed my eyes.

I needed my king alive and safe, finally. I needed him to know who I was, completely. I needed not to have to go through this horrible cycle all over again. I needed at least the certainty that if I failed, we *would*.

My first instinct was to swallow those thoughts. That wasn't how I talked to Arthur. I didn't let him see when I was struggling. He was always carrying too much of a burden on his own. I had to be the strong one, the capable one, the one who knew how to get things done and who had unshakable faith we'd see our purpose through. That we could keep going.

But Priya's accusation was still ringing in my head. *You keep shutting us down, shutting us out.* She'd hit the mark better than she'd realized. I shut *everyone* out, even the man who'd stood beside me from the beginning, who'd owned my heart for centuries. I'd thought that was being strong, but it suddenly felt ridiculous.

I'd never been stronger than my king—in some ways, maybe, but overall? Back then, if I'd told him I was worried he'd bend under pressure, he'd have laughed at me.

I couldn't quite bear to look him in the face. When I opened my eyes, I found myself focusing on the whorls of his sweater. My hand trembled, but I reached out and grasped his shirt anyway. My voice came out ragged.

"I need *you*. I need you here, like this, knowing me, believing in me… I don't want to have to start over. I don't want to have to wait another twenty years before I can get just a few days of being with you properly. I—"

The words broke around the fear that was too large to express. My chin wobbled. But before I could even finish panicking over how Darton would respond, his arms came around me. He pulled me into a tight embrace, his thighs pressing against my knees where I sat on the floor of the van, his head tucking next to mine. His earthy scent surrounded me.

"I'm here," he said. "And I'll fight with everything I have to stay here. I know you. I know what you can do. I know what *I* can do, even if I've got a lot more catching up to do. We'll find our way out of this."

Tears burned in my eyes. I blinked them back, tipping my face to his shoulder.

I needed him, and I had him. I should have known that. Whatever the quality or extent of his romantic feelings for me, my prince, and then my king, had always been my greatest friend.

The tender feelings were there too, though. Maybe it was selfish, but I needed that reassurance as well. I lifted my head, my cheek grazing his, and traced my fingers up the line of his jaw. Darton leaned into my kiss.

His mouth brushed against mine with a gentleness I hadn't felt from him before. He kissed me slowly, almost cautiously, as if he weren't sure how I'd respond. As if this were the first time, feeling each other out, rather than the mad rush of the last two times we'd collided.

Those earlier encounters had felt desperate, attempts to squeeze as much contact into a few fleeting seconds as we could. The way he touched me now, the slight shift of his lips—a little closer, a little deeper—the tentative foray of his tongue, gave the impression he was trying to stretch out this moment for as long as it could last.

When a memory swam up through those breathless sensations, I didn't fight it. I let it sweep over me and carry me back to the time when we'd been our best selves— before I realized I wasn't falling into one of the good times after all.

31

The light was wrong. Normally when I woke up, it was streaking across my feet from the narrow window near the foot of my bed. Now it filled the room around me from several directions in a warm glow.

A room that was much larger than mine had ever been. And the mattress beneath me was much softer than I preferred, wafting a faint, familiar-but-not-that-familiar lavender scent from the herbs woven into the stuffing. Because it wasn't my room or my bed.

The weight I'd only just registered against my waist shifted—an arm, wrapped around me. A nose brushed the back of my neck as breath spilled down my back. My own breath caught with the shudder of my nerves.

I was in my king's room. In my king's bed.

I had a fuzzy recollection of stumbling in here late last night after a full day's riding, having followed Arthur out of habit. Of looking around in my exhaustion and not wanting to move another step, but nonetheless saying I should take my leave. And of my king, with a careless yawn and a fatigue-slurred voice, telling me not to be silly. That his bed was big enough for five, so it could surely fit one scrawny wizard as well as himself. That I'd better not snore.

I didn't think I'd snored. More importantly, I wasn't sure how Arthur had come to be pressed against me in this morning embrace when as far as I recalled, we'd fallen asleep at opposite ends of the bed.

Most importantly, as much as I longed to revel in this moment and the tenderness with which he held me, I had no idea how he was going to react when he woke up and realized what he'd done in his sleep.

I lay still. My pulse thudded. Could I slip out from under his arm without disturbing him? Would he be upset if he woke up alone, without understanding why I'd disappeared?

Could I dare to hope he might be pleased to find us in this position?

I'd barely had time to entertain that possibility when Arthur stirred—and flinched away from me. His arm thumped the mattress. I swallowed hard and made a show of stretching as if I'd only just woken too. As if I had no idea what position he'd just removed himself from.

Arthur sat up on the other side of the mattress. "Merlin," he said, "get your lazy body out of my bed. Don't you have your own?"

His usual teasing tone held a sharp note that jabbed at my heart. I scrambled up. "My apologies, sire." I dipped into a bow, watching for my deference to light a spark of mischief in my king's eyes.

They stayed dark. His body—bare except for his underclothes—had tensed. I jerked my gaze away before I was tempted to appreciate his physique.

"We've got a lot to do," he said. "We've returned victorious. I think I'll declare a festival day. You can go make up some effects for the celebration, can't you?"

"A festival?" My stomach lurched. "We defeated one enemy, Arthur, but I don't think you should—"

"I'm really rather tired of hearing what you think I shouldn't do." Arthur shoved himself out of the bed on the opposite side, his *back to me now. His voice had turned all sharp, no teasing. "I think I've proven I can defend myself. Everyone here could use a day to unwind, not least of all me. Off with you. Get on with it. I don't need you hovering."*

"Arthur," I said tentatively, and his head whipped around.

"I said go,*" he snapped.*

I winced and hustled to the door. Down the hall to the staircase, and on into… a van in a parking lot with Darton leaning over me, his breath stuttering against my cheek.

"I'm sorry," he said before I had a chance to center myself in the present. "I'm sorry. Don't go, Merlin. Don't ever, ever go."

My heart flipped over. What memory had *he* come out of? I'd never threatened to leave him, not seriously, but maybe there'd been a time he hadn't known I didn't mean it.

"Arthur," I said, clasping my hands behind his neck. "You idiot, I have stayed with you for fifteen hundred years and never once regretted it. If it's fifteen hundred more, I'll still be there with you on whatever's left of this wretched planet."

His laugh was a tattered sound, and then he was kissing me again, hard now. He pushed forward, and my knees splayed around his thighs until the heat of him burned against me from mouth to groin. A choked sound of encouragement broke from my throat. His tongue swept into my mouth, his hand pushing under my shirt to cup my breast. I arched into him, whimpering as his thumb flicked over the nipple. His other arm tugged me even closer. The feel of him between my legs, so hard, made a giddy shiver race through my core, nearly melting me.

I tangled my fingers in his hair, kissing him with all the passion he'd provoked in me, and he met me with a needy groan. His thumb stroked over my breast again, his other hand trailing down to the waist of my jeans. Gods, yes. We were in the back of a near-stranger's van in an open parking lot, but what did consequences matter when death was only two steps behind us? I wanted him. I wanted *all* of him.

His fingers slipped down to traverse the boundary of my panties—and then stilled.

The pressure of Darton's lips eased back. His body rocked against mine in a faint rhythm that nonetheless electrified me, but he wasn't fully there. Another memory had taken him.

I sighed and scooted back an inch to let the pressure *inside* me dwindle. Then I laid a kiss at the base of his throat just above the collar of his sweater, because I could. Because I wanted one more taste of him before this interruption brought us back to the more urgent business I couldn't afford to ignore.

After a minute, Darton's head drooped. He caught my shoulders to steady himself. A flush spread across his cheeks, but a different sort of eagerness lit his expression.

"I think I know what Ffion was telling me."

I straightened up. "You got back into that memory?"

He nodded. A smile slid across his face, assured and yet with the childlike pleasure of a boy who'd just beaten all his friends at a difficult game. I wanted to kiss it, but I needed to hear what he'd learned.

I nudged him, and he stepped back so I could stand up.

"I don't know exactly how or why I got there," he

said. "I wasn't trying to this time—ah, being focused on other things—but maybe it's because I've been thinking about that memory so much in general?"

"That could have primed you," I said. "But it doesn't really matter. What did you *see*?"

"Lenses," Darton said, as if that explained everything. When I looked at him blankly, he waved his hand. "The pieces of glass Ffion was showing me—they were lenses. Clear sections cut to concentrate the light that passes through them. Like a magnifying glass or, I guess, the crystals Jagger was saying he uses in his guns."

"Lenses," I repeated. My gaze slid across the parking lot and stuck. The shadows beneath the posts and chains that surrounded the lot were squirming. More glooms were creeping along the cracks in the sidewalk to join them. My pulse hitched. Our recent tear across the state hadn't bought us more than half an hour. How long would we be able to stay ahead of them?

I pulled Darton around to the front of the van. "So how were these lenses supposed to help you? What did Ffion expect you to do with them?"

"He was just demonstrating. He said that from what he understood, if you wanted to take on a creature of darkness, you'd need as strong a light as you could gather. And the right lens could concentrate light into something even more powerful than what comes directly from the sun."

That wasn't a strategy I'd given much consideration to, but then, taking down the lesser creatures with a twig and a couple words was less hassle than messing around with a magnifying glass.

"I can concentrate it with my magic too," I said. "Get

in. We can't stay here any longer."

Darton climbed into the passenger seat, but his eyes were still vague. "Sure, but what if you used *both*? You can only put out so much power before you drain yourself, right? But if you pushed yourself to your limit, and we used the right lenses to amplify that effect even further... We could hit this dark fae harder than you could have managed on your own."

He might be right. I looked at my hands as I walked around to the driver's side, trying to picture channeling magic-drawn light through circles of glass.

"Ffion was saying the effect should be even greater with multiple lenses," Darton went on. "If you could hit the dark thing from all sides with concentrated light so it had no way to escape."

An image sprang into my head—a blaze of light bouncing through gleaming shards and striking a center point—one after another, as if forming the spokes of a giant, searing wheel. The power of that idea radiated through me. My father's voice rang up from my memory, with words that no longer felt absurd. *The dark fae can't cope with the unexpected. And we always have chaos on our side.*

I hopped into my seat and fumbled for the key fob. "Okay, but... where are we going to get lenses that do what we want? Dollar store magnifying glasses aren't going to cut it. We'll need the most concentrated light possible. And we're going to need them *soon*." The entire border of the parking lot was jittering with living shadows now. I frowned at the row of switches that would shut off the van's protective lamps. Then I noticed Darton watching me with a funny little grin.

"What?"

He shook his head, the grin staying. "You're so… you. It's always spectacular watching you in the planning zone."

The compliment and the grin were doing something funny to my stomach, but now wasn't the time. "Well, when you're done admiring, maybe you could pitch in with the brainstorming?"

"Lenses…" He rubbed his chin. "High quality ones built for a specific purpose. Maybe some sort of scientific supply store? Except I think I'd need a degree in physics to know exactly what to ask for." He paused, and then started to laugh. "That's it!"

I started the engine. "You're going to complete a B. Sci. in the next two hours?"

"No. Keevan. His sister's in the physics department, remember? I don't know if she's done any optics work herself, but she probably at least knows someone who has or where that kind of equipment would be kept."

I glanced the way Darton's friends had gone, my body tensing. But the clench of my gut I braced for didn't come. Instead, I felt more as if a weight had lifted.

Keevan had wanted to help. He'd wanted to be there for Darton. If we went ahead with this plan, he really could be.

It was a long shot, but what else did we have?

"I know you've been hesitant to let them get involved—" Darton was saying.

"No." The image of the beams of sunlight shooting out in their spokes flashed through my mind again. Chaos was the strength of light's side. And the people who cared about Darton, about me, they were his strength. Our strength. I flicked off the panel of lights and hit the gas in the same movement. "Let's go. We're going to need everyone."

* * *

As we raced out of the parking lot, a clump of glooms hurled themselves at the side of the van. They smacked it hard enough to rock us. I gritted my teeth and pushed the pedal to the floor. We roared onto the street, swerving to get on the right course, and barreled toward the bus terminal.

"I'm sorry," Darton said abruptly.

"For...?"

His mouth twisted. "For not telling you about talking to Ffion and what he told me, back then. I don't know everything that went into that decision, or what might have been going through my mind afterward. But right then when he was telling me... I *really* wanted to come to you with the whole solution worked out. To show you I could fight that battle beside you instead of leaving it in your hands. Maybe I never had the chance to pursue that strategy before..."

Before he'd died. Or nearly, at least. My throat tightened.

"It's all right," I said. "I know you would have. You couldn't have known how it would all play out. They're my kind—more than they are yours, at least. That's why it was my battle. Why it still is. Remember that, okay?"

He nodded, but he didn't look satisfied.

Before I could emphasize the point, our destination came into view up ahead. A bench stood by the curb outside a little ticket office barely wide enough for a door and a window. Izzy and Priya were sitting at opposite ends, and Keevan was pacing on the sidewalk behind them.

I pulled the van over and slammed on the lights, ignoring the stares of a couple passing by. We'd put hardly any distance between us and the dark rabble. I had to make this work, and I had to do it *fast*.

Keevan's head had jerked up. He stopped moving as Darton and I stepped out. Glooms wriggled through the shadows between the buildings and under the awning of the shop next to the ticket office. I held out my hand to keep Darton close to the van.

"You're still here," he said to Keevan.

Keevan smiled crookedly. "The next bus heading in the right direction doesn't come through for another couple of hours."

Priya stood up. "What's going on?"

Izzy stayed on the bench, her back stiff, but she'd turned her head to watch the conversation.

"We have a plan," Darton said. "A good one, I think. And—"

"Darton," Keevan said, sounding fond but deeply exasperated.

A gloom prodded the edge of the van's glow. *Fast.* It wasn't Darton who needed to make amends here. I stepped up beside him. My nerves were skittering, but I made myself speak.

"We can get into the details later. First, I need to apologize. To all of you. For shutting you down when you wanted to help, and for lying. You're right. There's more going on than I've told you. It's only because I didn't want to make things even more confusing for you, but still, that's on me."

Keevan folded his arms over his chest. "And why are you saying this now? Did you figure out something you need us for after all?"

He obviously intended the question to shame me, but I didn't see any point in avoiding that fact. "Actually…" I said. "There is a favor we want to ask from you. And I'm starting to think the key to stopping the dark fae that's after Darton might be all of us working together. If the way I treated you before is a deal breaker, okay. But I am sorry. And this is what you wanted, isn't it? To be there for him?"

"We want to know what's really going on too," Izzy said, fixing me with her cool gaze.

"Not a problem. I can lay it all out for you on the drive up." I motioned to the shadows, which were starting to roil as the dark rabble gathered around us. "We can't get into it here. The things after Darton are already catching up."

Izzy's gaze followed my gesture. She jumped up with a flinch, her face paling. Keevan glanced over too. His eyes widened as he took in the shapes amassing in the shadows around us. He swore under his breath and took a step back.

"I want to get Darton away from here," I said— firmly, to stop my voice from quivering. "I don't want to be standing here with those things so close at all. I'm only taking the risk of talking to you because of how important I think it is that we have you with us."

"I'm in," Priya said. "I'll drive so you can concentrate on the storytelling."

Keevan shifted his weight, his attention still fixed on the dark creatures. "I don't know."

Damn it. "Look, I can't promise you're going to believe me," I said. "It's going to be pretty obvious *why* I didn't want to tell you everything by the time I'm done." Something in me balked, but I'd get over that hesitation. I drew in a breath and let magic seep into my words. "I swear you'll get the whole story. I owe all of you that much."

"Come on, man." Darton clapped him on the arm. "I want you with me for this. If nothing else, it'll be a great adventure."

Keevan's laugh sounded strained, but at least he'd laughed. His shoulders eased down a notch.

"All right. It beats waiting for the bus. But the verdict is out on exactly how much more I'm getting involved until I hear this story."

32

Unsurprisingly, there were a lot of questions when I finished laying out the entire tale. Well, several seconds of bewildered silence that reverberated through the van, and then the questions.

Keevan, sitting at my right in the backseat, pointed at me. "So *you*," he said in an understandably skeptical tone, "were a wizard. *The* wizard—the world-famous Merlin. Pointy hat and robes and all?"

"No pointy hats and robes only on special occasions," I said dryly. Now that the whole story was out there, the tension inside me had dispelled as well. I'd given them everything I could. What they made of it was out of my hands. "And I'm *still* a wizard. I'm still Merlin. I'm just inhabiting a bunch of other people along the way."

"And Darton—" At my left, Izzy's gaze shot to the man in question.

"I was a king of mythic proportions," Darton supplied from the front passenger seat. He'd drooped a little as we'd talked. How much sleep had he managed to get last night? "No one finds that harder to comprehend than I do, believe me."

"You're telling me you've actually *seen* stuff from back then?" Keevan said. "Like, royal pronouncements and jousting and all that?"

Darton's mouth twitched with a hint of a smile. "I haven't gotten to jousting yet, but yeah. I've seen a lot now. I don't believe Em's story just because she said it. I *wouldn't* believe it just because she said it. But it's hard to argue with what's going on in my head."

"What about Lancelot and Guinevere and whoever else? Are we going to run into them too?"

"They never existed," I said. "A lot of embellishments were added to the myths over the years. I recommend forgetting everything you've heard. It wasn't even that exciting a lot of the time. There was a mind-numbing amount of politics, which honestly is mostly people sitting around and talking—or maybe, if you're both lucky and unlucky, shouting—at each other."

"I can support that assessment," Darton put in.

Keevan shook his head. "Well, I don't know. Unless *I* start having visions, it's kind of hard for me to think you're not just pulling my leg."

I looked at him pointedly until he met my eyes. "Yeah. So now you know why I started with the edited version of events."

"It doesn't matter, does it?" Izzy's voice was so low I couldn't tell how much she believed. "Who you were before, I mean. Whatever's going on, those things are after Darton. We know that for sure." When Keevan started to speak, she raised her voice. "We do, Keev. I've thought back to yesterday, when we were running for the car, a lot. You must have seen them too. They were leaping right at *him*—they weren't after Emma."

"I've only known Emmaline for a few months," Priya said from the driver's seat. "So I can only vouch for her that far. But I do know the light fae all talk about the king the Darkest One couldn't quite kill and the fae-blooded one who saved him. That really happened."

"Fine," Keevan said. "Duly noted. Crazy story or not, we need to take down this dark fae thing. I got the impression you have some shiny new plan to accomplish that?"

Darton laid out what he'd seen in his visions of his visit to the alchemist's workshop. He straightened up as he talked, enthusiasm livening his expression. He looked and sounded so sure he'd found the key that my own spirits started to sink.

We were hurtling forward, following the theories of a man who'd never encountered a dark fae. Maybe Arthur hadn't told me about the lenses back then because he'd tried the idea out somehow and found it ineffective, at some later time Darton hadn't recalled yet.

"So will you talk to your sister, Keev?" he said. "All we need are those five lenses. Then we're set."

Izzy hugged her arms tighter around herself. "Is it safe for us to go back onto campus?"

"The dark creatures that came through yesterday morning should have cleared out by now. But Darton and I should keep our distance just in case." I glanced out the window. "If we manage to drive through the night, switching off at the wheel, we'd be almost home by sunrise. We can find somewhere to park and get a little sleep with the solar-powered lights going, then stop by campus and grab what we need. It'll be a couple hours to the forest where the mercenary is staked out. For the plan to work, we'll want to have plenty of daylight left."

"Donielle is going to wonder what the hell I've got going on, you know," Keevan said. "But okay. It's not like I hassle her for favors very often. I'll call her now so she's got time to work things out on her end before we get there." He raised his fist in the air. "Let's do this thing. Let's kill a dark fae!"

He fished out his phone, and I slumped back against the seat. My earlier dread crept up.

Let's kill a dark fae! As if it would be that easy.

We were really going to do this. I was going to drag three uninvolved, ignorant people straight to a dark fae who was eager to spill human blood. How could we possibly surround him without him catching on? What ridiculous part of me had thought the image in my head could become reality?

Jagger's chiding voice ran through my memories. *What business did you have hauling them into it?* I clasped my hands together on my lap, but my pulse thudded on.

Maybe he was right. Maybe attempting this wasn't making up for past mistakes, but the biggest mistake I'd made yet.

* * *

The back of the van didn't make for comfortable sleeping, especially with the dawn glow and the light of the built-in beams seeping through the windows. And even more especially with the memory of what lay beyond that light lingering in my head.

The last time I'd looked out, the shadows had been churning around the van throughout the dirt lot we'd pulled off into. We were driving right back through the mass of them that had been pouring toward us. One wrong move, one failed power cell, and we'd all be dead right now.

My pulse rattled through my veins. Darton and Priya, who was sharing the back with me, had nodded off almost immediately, exhausted from the long drive. Izzy hadn't stirred where she'd nestled on the backseat under one of the wool blankets I'd bought us. And Keevan, who'd tipped back the front passenger seat as far as it would go, was snoring in a faint, whirring rhythm.

I dipped my hand into my duffel and pulled out a stick of incense and a handful of twigs. As quietly as I could, I lay out the twigs, lit the incense, and set it on the floor by my face. I murmured a brief chant under my breath. My body slackened as if I were asleep too. My mind drifted up through the van and out into the open air.

The dark rabble was still gathering, prowling, amid the shadows beyond the beams' reach. I hesitated, weighing the risks. I didn't like leaving Darton here without my direct protection.

But I liked the idea of leading all four of my companions to their deaths even less. I pushed myself up into the air and caught on a swallow flitting past.

The bird couldn't fly as fast as I wanted to travel. I needed to be finished this mission before the alarm went off in the van to wake the others. The swallow's beady eyes spotted a truck on the highway, and I sent it swooping down into the bed. We rode there until the driver made a turn in the wrong direction. I urged the swallow up and onto another vehicle going the right way.

I felt as much as saw when we'd reached my destination. I compelled the swallow into the air again. The haze of the dawn had burned away in the wake of a clear, crisp day. I circled the farms near the edge of the wood. This part of my scheme I didn't enjoy at all, but there wasn't any way around it.

A middle-aged man was leading two horses out to pasture. He walked at a strolling pace that suggested he didn't have anything particularly urgent to do today. That was probably the best option I'd get. He latched the gate, and I sent the swallow diving. I propelled my consciousness out as the bird swerved above the man's head—and then I dropped into him.

Taking up temporary residence in another human being's head felt a lot different from taking over any other sort of animal. Sharper thoughts whispered around my awareness with flickers of images and emotions. I hummed silently into them, willing them quiet, willing them still. Putting the man's mind to sleep.

Then I walked him out of the farmyard and into the woods.

My impressions of this unfamiliar body were muted. I tested my reflexes as I strode along. My limbs moved with only the slightest hesitation. And when I plucked a twig from a bush I passed, I conjured a ball of light from it with a few quiet words.

All right. I had a physical presence. I had my magic. The dark fae mercenary lurked somewhere amid the trees ahead of me. If I could find some way, some weakness, here on my own, I'd make sure he wasn't lurking anymore before I left.

I brushed the man's fingertips over the tree trunks, reaching for the life inside them. So much energy that could be turned into power. How much could I channel into one blast without burning through my own life? It wasn't any good destroying this one enemy if I left my king alone to face all those who would come after.

I had to try. Whatever it took. If the dark rabble took Darton for themselves, at least Arthur's soul would still go free and we'd get another chance. The mercenary might end us completely.

A metallic undertone permeated the air—the smell of the dark fae's lair. The bird chatter faded. The only sound that remained was the rustle of autumn leaves beneath my host's feet.

I stopped when the graying branches of a tree showed through the autumn foliage up ahead. The mercenary was here somewhere. Resting during the day, like a vampire of legend? I wished a stake through the heart would be enough to do the job. I gripped a smaller branch on the sapling next to me and snapped it off.

Maybe a stake *would*. If I could draw enough sunlight through the gaps between the thinning leaves overhead and into this stick, then drove it into his chest…

I took another cautious step—and a chilly voice rang out beside me.

"Ah, the king's would-be protector."

The words seemed to coil in the air like smoke. I jerked around. The lanky, blunt-nosed figure I'd seen in my brief vision smiled at me—a smile that could have cut steel. He stood in the darkest shadows where two pines brushed against each other, his presence congealing the shade even darker.

Okay, not sleeping. I clenched my host's hand around my makeshift stake, fighting for calm against the racing of the man's pulse. I had some advantage. The mercenary hadn't been prepared for me, at least not to kill me on

266

sight. All I needed was a brief opening.

The dark fae looked me up and down. His lip curled in apparent disgust. "This is not the guise I expected. Not only do you commit yourself to those organisms, but you wear their bodies too. I couldn't stand it."

It had been so long since I'd talked to a dark fae that I'd forgotten how insultingly they spoke about people. They saw humans as no different from the deer and the hares that roamed the woods—living beasts with no power and little awareness. They saw humans as *less* than that, really, because at least the other creatures still recognized magic as something real.

I shifted back on one foot, closer to the nearest patch of sunlight. I needed that energy if I was going to make use of any opening I got. "Both sides of my nature have served me well," I said.

"Have they?" The dark fae peered at me, and the tremor of his presence tickled over me. By the light, how young he was—like a sapling, bendable and untested. Stewing with his eagerness to take up this quest for his imprisoned ruler. A ruler he couldn't ever have met. Did he even know who I was, or was he working completely off the vague impressions he'd sensed from her?

A flicker of confidence sparked inside me. "In ways you couldn't understand," I said, just to keep the conversation going.

"Hmm. You've fended off my underlings longer than I anticipated. But I haven't tried all that hard yet. Perhaps tonight I'll come for your king myself."

"You can try." I took another step toward the sunlight. A young soul would be easier to sever from this world than an older one with its roots sunk deep. If I just—

The mercenary whipped his arm at me with a burst of shadow, so abruptly I had only an instant to try to dodge. The dark energy hit my host in the gut. My borrowed body doubled over, a burning ache spreading up through his chest. I forced the man backward, stumbling.

Okay. Not so weak a soul. I had to—

Before I'd even drawn a breath, the dark fae hurled another blast of magic at me. I managed to heave myself sideways, but my mind cringed at the sear of cold. The man's body reeled deeper into the shadows.

No, no. I needed the light.

My host's lungs wheezed as they squeezed air up a suddenly narrow throat. The man I'd borrowed, who I'd sworn I'd return safely, was one blast from dying even if I'd survive.

The dark fae marched forward, and I threw myself with very little grace toward the nearest patch of sun.

My spirit sighed the second daylight hit my face. I would have gasped for joy if I'd had the time to. Instead, I whirled myself around to meet the mercenary's next attack.

"That worthless animal body," he sneered, raising his hand again. I braced myself, pulling the sunlight into me, its rush of energy far too pale before the surge of darkness the mercenary was gathering.

A swallow dove out of the trees, snatching at the dark fae's hair—and he didn't even blink. My swallow? Had some of my purpose rubbed off on it?

But what did he care? It was just one more useless animal to him.

Two thoughts collided in my head: Attempting to kill the dark fae on my own would almost certainly end with me dead and him perky as ever. But he'd just given me the answer I needed to end this for real, if not at this exact moment.

The mercenary slammed a fatal wave of his magic toward the man's body. My fingers tightened around the stick.

"*Light be my steed*," I cried out. The branch crumbled, and sunlight blazed down around me. It swept my borrowed body off its feet, shooting us away from the onslaught and my enemy.

The dark fae let out a wordless shout, and then I was gone. The bolt of light flung the man through the woods and dropped us in a heap at the base of the farm's fence.

I sprawled there for a moment, waiting for my host's heart to settle and confirming no appendages were broken. His tailbone might be bruised, and he'd have a strange burn mark on his belly when he "woke up," but the damage could have been much worse. It *would* have been, if I hadn't gotten us out of there when I had.

I gave his mind a soft pat and pushed myself out of him. The pull of my body dragged me back toward the van—toward the greater trial that still lay before me.

33

I dropped back into my body with a sharp inhale. My eyes burst open. The stick of incense on the floor released only a thread-thin line of smoke from what was now mostly a streak of ash.

A chill had pervaded the van—or maybe I just felt the cool of the morning more deeply after my confrontation with the dark fae. I shrugged my blanket higher over my shoulders.

"Em?" Darton murmured behind me.

I hesitated. Could I avoid a conversation if I pretended I was asleep?

His clothes rustled as he shifted. "You went away somewhere, didn't you? Like before, in the car."

I rolled over to face him. He looked back at me, hair rumpled and eyelids heavy. My heart thumped with pained affection.

If only we could just run. Drive this van to the ends of the earth, always one step ahead of the dark rabble and their masters.

It was impossible. Even if escape had been that

simple, we couldn't sustain a life of driving all night, every night. We'd run ourselves ragged, and then we'd make a mistake, like always. And as soon as the mercenary made good on his threat to come for my king directly, we'd be screwed regardless.

No, if my little trip had convinced me of anything, it was that we needed to stop the dark fae as soon as possible.

"I'm back now," I said softly.

"Is everything okay?"

I shrugged, and he made a face. Easing a little closer to me, he lifted his hand to brush a stray hair from my cheek. The same gesture he'd made the first time we'd touched. Now I didn't have to flinch away. The graze of his fingers sent a fleeting warmth over my skin.

"You won't go off on your own for real, right?" he said. "We'll stick to the plan?"

Guilt pinched my stomach. He couldn't know how "real" the attempt I'd just made had been, but maybe he guessed. Maybe he knew me that well by now. At least I could honestly say, from here forward, "I'm not going anywhere. We're in this together."

Darton inclined his head, touching my waist with a nudge I understood. I rolled over, and he scooted even closer to spoon me. His face tucked against my hair, his arm around my waist. Like that moment long, long ago, except this time, he did it consciously, willingly.

The ache around my heart expanded. I closed my eyes against a sudden burn of tears. Exhaustion washed over me. The last thing I felt before I tumbled into sleep was the brief press of Darton's lips to the back of my neck.

* * *

The shadows along the edges of the wood lay still—for now. I pushed away from the van's window where the others were still peering at the forest. We'd parked on the gravel shoulder of the two-lane highway across from the farm where an undoubtedly now-rather-bewildered man lived.

"We've got an opening," I said, grabbing a canvas bag. "Let's take it while we have it."

Keevan straightened up as much as the van roof allowed. "So it's just the dark fae guy we'll need to watch out for?"

"He sent all the dark rabble he could reach after us, and we left them behind again this morning. But they'll catch up with us fast, so we've got to get moving. There might be a few newcomers in the forest, but they won't bother the rest of you anyway."

"Very comforting," he muttered, but he dropped his phone and watch into the bag when I held them out. Izzy and Priya chucked in their electronic devices too.

They made an odd trio, like members of some sort of new age club, all dressed in similar tunics and trim pants. While Keevan had visited his sister on campus, I'd taken the rest of us shopping at the hippy-dippy place just south of downtown. We were wearing clothes made entirely of natural fibers and dyes.

"Your armlet too," I said to Priya. I'd never sensed any fae energy emanating from the rune-etched leather, but that didn't mean a full fae with sharper sensitivities wouldn't. She shoved up her sleeve to grab it and tossed it in.

Izzy rubbed her arms. "This mercenary—you're sure he won't notice us creeping around?"

"The dark fae—and even the light fae, to some extent—see humans as part of the animal world. And themselves as something higher." My mind darted back to that moment in the woods when the mercenary had ignored the swallow's dive without so much as a twitch. The sneer in his voice when he'd talked about my host's body. My mouth twisted.

"You've got nothing artificial on you now," I went on. "He'll sense there's something living moving around, but you won't seem any more significant to him than if you were a bird or a mouse. Especially when he'll have Darton and me to focus on."

At least, I hoped that was true. I pulled my hair back from my face into its habitual ponytail. "Are you all ready?"

Priya nodded. Keevan clapped his hands with a shake of his shoulders. "Let's get this over with."

"Okay. Stay close to the point I showed you and spread out in a circle around that. Make sure you stop at a spot that's getting some sun through the canopy. With the branches getting barer, that shouldn't be too hard. Then just sit still until I call on you. We'll be about ten minutes behind you to give you time to get settled, but I don't know how long the fae will take to come."

I followed the three of them out of the van and around the side, but I stopped at the edge of the ditch. As soon as I entered the forest, the mercenary would sense my presence.

Even in the early afternoon, the autumn breeze had a cool edge to it. The smell of damp leaves on the verge of rotting filled my nose. Keevan tipped his head, and he and Priya tramped off along the shoulder toward the trees. Izzy hesitated.

"Emma," she said quietly.

"Yeah?" Please, no last-minute doubts. I'd had enough of my own.

She lowered her head, her hands tight by her sides. She looked smaller somehow without her usual flowing skirt and cardigan.

"You and Darton, "she said. "Whatever there is between the two of you, because of whoever you were before... You're more than friends, aren't you?"

Her tone was even, but I heard the thread of underlying tension. My stomach knotted. She cared about him a lot. I couldn't help remembering the jealous twinges I'd felt when I'd thought our situations were reversed.

"The connection between us, because of our history, is pretty intense," I said, which was as close to agreeing as I was comfortable getting.

"You've been trying to save him all this time. You've kept following him, protecting him, *dying* for him, over and over..." She glanced up at me then, peering into my face. "There isn't anything you wouldn't do for him, is there?"

"No," I said honestly. "There's not. But, Izzy—"

She shook her head. "It's okay. We weren't even—I knew there wasn't much chance we'd get back together like that, even before you were in the picture. Maybe it's better being sure that we won't. I can't compete. That's just the way it is. And thank you. For doing all this for him—and for letting me do what I can too."

I groped for an appropriate answer, but I guessed she hadn't expected one. She turned and headed after the others with a brisk, steady stride. I waited until the forest had swallowed her up, and then I climbed back into the van.

Darton was crouched by the seatbacks, examining my runed dagger. Oblivious to the conversation I'd just been having about him, apparently. He raised his head and waggled the dagger as I came over.

"Do you think this will help us at all against the mercenary?"

"It makes dispatching glooms easier, but it's not going to have much effect on a full fae. Anyway, I'm going to need to focus all my attention on channeling the light through the lenses."

"Is it all right if I carry it then? I feel strange being the only one not contributing."

"Giving you a lens wouldn't really add to the effect when you'll be standing right next to me," I said. "But you're contributing in other ways."

"I'm the bait." The words came out a little flat.

"Well, that's one way of putting it." It was probably the most accurate way of putting it, but I didn't have to admit that.

He stood up, stooped beneath the low roof, and cupped my cheek to kiss me. Soft, sweet, and over far too quickly. He was probably trying to avoid getting caught in another memory.

"I would have let you hold on to the knife without any extra persuasion," I said.

He grinned. "I know. The kiss was for me."

Oh, he had no idea how wrong he was.

We clambered out. The sun shone high overhead, beaming strong enough to pierce the gaps in the forest's canopy. That was all I needed to see.

"How much longer do we wait?" Darton asked.

A wild impulse I blamed on desperation flitted through me. "Kiss me again, and then we'll be good to go."

I'd thought he might laugh the request off, but he immediately leaned in. He pressed his lips to mine, hard, nudging me against the side of the van. I lost my breath, lost everything in the sensation of his body against mine. He rested his hand on my waist as the kiss deepened. Then his lips stilled, just for a second. He kissed me again, so thoroughly a whimper worked its way out of my chest.

Our breaths were ragged when he drew back. "You're right," he murmured into the space between us. "The memories do get easier to balance."

"Lucky you." I gave him a playful swat and pushed him toward the forest. We set off side by side. "What did you see this time?"

"Nothing all that revealing. You used to keep twigs in your *hair* sometimes. It really looked absurd. But I appreciated it that time those glooms snuck into my chambers. Assuming that was just the one time."

"There were a few times," I said. "After you talked to that dark fae I warned you about."

"I don't suppose if we asked the dark fae today why they want me so badly, he'd tell us?"

I guffawed. "Ah, no. Anyway, I don't think he *knows*. He's not old enough to have been around back then. He'll never have communicated with the Darkest One directly, not in any coherent way. He's just been able to sense that she still has it in for you after all this time."

On that cheerful note, we treaded into the forest by the stark white trunk of the birch I'd pointed out to the others earlier. I snapped handfuls of twigs off the brushes and saplings we passed and stuffed my sleeves with them.

After several paces, we stopped in a spot where the sun streaked to the forest floor. A bird called overhead. The leaves hissed with the rising of the breeze. Not a rustle from our companions sounded. I had to assume they were waiting as promised.

"I'm here, dark one," I shouted. "And I've brought what you wanted. Are you going to come and get him? Or are you too afraid even when he's right at your doorstep?"

A gloom slunk toward us. I bade it begone with one of my twigs, and the filmy creature blinked out of existence. Darton shifted his weight beside me.

"Really?" I called out again. "You're not even going to come talk to me? I think we've got a few things to hash out. But if you're really going to leave this job to the rabble instead of *earning* the honor you want so much…"

Nothing stirred amid the trees. I swallowed thickly. This plan got us nowhere if I couldn't taunt the dark fae into coming to meet us.

"Isn't there anything else he wants that he'd come for?" Darton asked under his breath. "Other than me dying, I mean."

"Oh, he doesn't want you just dying, not in any old way." That was the one last-ditch trick I was keeping buried deep in my back pocket. If our scheme fell apart, if the dark fae got the upper hand, I'd have to kill Darton before he could. Free my king's soul to follow the cycle onward to its next iteration. The thought nauseated me, but the alternative… "It'll only count as the sort of victory he wants if he wrenches your soul from your body directly."

And possibly ensured it never inhabited another body

again.

Darton's back stiffened. I didn't have time to ask him what about my words had bothered him specifically—I hadn't told *him* just what sort of victory the mercenary was after—because at that moment, a shrouded, pale-faced form stepped between the trees several yards away from us.

The mercenary halted there and peered at us with his silvery eyes. I tensed, ready to throw up a shield if he tried to attack us from afar.

Right now, he was still too far away for *our* attack. I needed him inside our circle, at least twice as close to me as he was now, to be sure.

"What is this game?" he inquired in his icy voice.

"It's not a game," I said. "It's a challenge. One you're apparently too cowardly to meet."

"As if I can't tell you have some ploy you're attempting to engage."

I shrugged. "Apparently you believe I *could* hurt you, or you wouldn't be worried about any 'ploys' I might have prepared."

A couple more glooms glided toward us. I took them down one after the other with my gaze still fixed on the mercenary. My heart beat faster. How much longer did we have before the full force of the dark rabble caught up with us?

"I simply have no need to take the risk," the dark fae replied calmly. "In a few hours, dusk will creep in. And my underlings will have caught up by then, if not earlier. They can spring the trap *and* destroy you and your king. Light always fades, and then darkness remains."

The dark side's favorite refrain. He hadn't moved

even an inch toward us. I fidgeted with the twigs in my sleeve and dipped my other hand into my pocket to close my fingers around the lens. But I had no use for it if I couldn't count on the others to have a direct line of sight to our target. Could I ask them to move to a different position without him catching on? Or—

"I wouldn't be so sure about that," Darton said.

My head jerked around. The dark fae let out a cool chuckle. "And what do you mean by that, Unburied King?"

Darton lifted his chin, the dagger clenched tight in his hand. "I mean I could kill myself right now, and then you'll have no chance at the glory."

I stared at him. "*Darton.*"

He turned, thrusting the dagger toward me. "Do it. Slit my wrist. Deep enough that I could bleed out. I trust you. Let's see how long he hangs back there in the shadows after that."

Every part of me recoiled at the thought. I'd been prepared to kill my king, but not until the last hopeless moment. But as Darton gazed back at me, his jaw set and his expression so determined, I realized he was right. If he were dying, the dark fae would have to act. Have to come forward to finish the job. And then we'd have him.

If I made the cut with enough care, we'd have time. I could heal Darton after. He'd said he trusted me. It could work.

He'd still be bait, but he'd be making a difference in his own way. I knew, looking at him, the echoes of conversations past in my head, how much that meant to him.

Still, I balked. But the mercenary didn't. From the

corner of my eye, I caught the snap of his arm as he whipped a blast of magic toward us.

My fingers clutched a clump of twigs. *"Wood be my wall!"*

A translucent barrier shot up in front of Darton and me, shuddering as the bolt of dark magic crashed into it. The impact reverberated through the air into us. I stumbled, and Darton caught my wrist.

"Em," he said. "Merlin. Let me do this. Now, while it can still matter."

While we still had any chance at all. Sod it. Darkness take them all. I snatched the dagger from his grip. The dark fae was already swinging his hand to hurl another assault.

I gritted my teeth and sliced the blade across Darton's left wrist.

A gasp broke from his throat. Blood spilled down, brilliant against his tan skin, against the green and yellow of the grass and leaves it pattered onto on the ground. I'd forgotten how stark red arterial blood was, all but glowing with oxygenated life. My lungs constricted.

Darton stepped back and sagged against a tree trunk. "Here I am," he said to the dark fae. "Come and get me."

The mercenary had lowered his hands. A sickening hunger shaded his face. Darton's blood streamed on, the coppery scent filling the air. My stomach churned. I slid the lens out of my pocket, hiding it against my palm.

The dark fae took one step forward. Another. His eyes had brightened even as his expression had tensed.

"You really did it," he said, horrified and awed at once. "He'll die."

"Yes," I said, forcing the words from my throat.

"And you'll have no part in that."

A sharp little grin split his face. "Oh, but I still can."

He threw himself forward, balling dark energy in his hand to wallop me when he broke through my shield. Which he would have—if I'd let him get that far.

He was two steps away when I jabbed out my hand with the lens, pointing the curve of it toward him. The dagger fell from my fingers. I thrust my other hand toward the sky, to the gleam of the sun above me.

"*Light of life to me and mine,*" I hollered, and heaved down every fragment of light I could reach, wrenching it into me and out through the lens.

All the twigs still on me disintegrated in a burst of dust. The blaze of sunlight shot through the lens and struck the dark fae square in the chest, just as he shattered my shield.

The mercenary flinched and spun as if to reel away. "Pri!" I yelled, and a figure shot up amid the trees at my left, holding out her own lens. I focused my attention on the beams of sunlight glowing over her and yanked down again. The light condensed into a point that hit the lens and pierced the mercenary in mid-stagger. He lurched in the other direction.

"Keevan!" I cried out. "Izzy!" Another figure standing, then another, and all the light I could summon streamed down toward them to those little circles of glass, until I could barely see anything through the searing haze inside my head.

The dark fae shrieked. The pressure squeezing under my skin made me want to shriek too. But we were hitting him from all sides with ever-expanding daylight, and he had nowhere left to turn.

"I am for my master," he spat out around a groan. "I am for the greatest one!" The power coursing through me started to ebb as my strength sapped away. My vision flickered, but the mercenary's body was spasming. With a choked sound, his shadowy soul broke apart.

The pieces split from his chest and hissed away into the rushing sunlight. His body crumpled.

I swayed. In the moment before I hit the ground, I was aware of nothing but a frantic babble of voices around me.

Keevan reached me a second later. He hauled me up. My head spun, but my gaze narrowed in on the flow of blood coursing over the forest floor.

"Arthur." I threw myself down beside Darton. He tipped his head to the side as I grabbed his wrist.

"I don't even feel that bad," he said in a slightly singsong voice that didn't inspire much confidence. "A little... floaty, maybe, but really—"

"Shut up," I rasped, leaning close to the gouge in his skin. Priya thrust a snapped-off branch into my hand. My fingers closed around it. I pulled at the life within it, every shred I could summon, from the green center into my spell. *"Mend and seal and see him well."*

My anatomy textbooks and studies long ago had etched the layout of arteries, tendons, and layers of skin into my memory. I closed my eyes, seeing them knit back together in Darton's wrist. Darton let out a stuttering sigh of relief.

"Holy fuck," Keevan said.

The effort drained the last of my energy. The branch crumbled through my fingers, and I pitched forward into my king's lap.

34

"Here she comes," Keevan said. I blinked and found myself staring up into Darton's face.

I was still lying partly on his lap, the back of my head resting on his thigh. He looked way too worried about *me* for someone who'd asked me to all but kill him not that long ago.

"How long was I out?" I asked, my voice hoarse.

"A few minutes." Darton smoothed a shaky hand over my hair. "Are you okay?"

I pushed upright, ignoring four noises of protest around me. My head swam with a momentary dizziness and my joints throbbed, but I could live through that.

"I'll bet I shed another year, but I can survive without that. Who needs old age anyway?"

Izzy let out a startled giggle. Keevan looked around. Toward the body of the fallen dark fae. It had shrunk where it lay as if deflated, the pale face already blotchy with rot.

"We did it, right?" he said. "We… we killed it. Him."

"We stopped him from killing Darton," I said with

the proper reframing. "You were great. All of you. We did it." A slight hysterical laugh bubbled up from my chest. "We really *did it*."

"Woohoo!" Priya shouted. Keevan pulled me to my feet. To my surprise, he gathered me into a rib-crushing hug. Then he stepped back and pumped his fist. Darton shifted to get up, and Izzy darted in to help support him. I let her maneuver him to his feet. Her face fell just a little when he waved her off. But watching him stand, straight and mostly steady, she smiled.

"Come on," I said. "Let's get back to the van. We'll have more to worry about if we stick around here much longer." The dark rabble's strength and urgency would have faded with the mercenary's death, but their momentum would keep carrying them this way unless something else diverted them.

We stumbled between the trees and out onto the field beyond them. I fell in step beside Priya.

"Thanks," I said. "For getting me that branch when I was healing Darton. I wasn't thinking clearly enough to grab one myself. And I'd probably have taken two or three years off if I'd worked that magic without it."

She bumped her shoulder gently against mine. "You needed it. I could give it. That's how friendship works, right?"

A little of my previous hesitation prickled through me, but this time, I pushed it aside. "Yeah. So we're still friends?"

She beamed back at me. "Still friends."

We stopped for a moment outside the van. The undiluted sunlight poured over me. I soaked it in, reluctant to leave it for the shelter of the vehicle. In the rabble's normal state, daylight should be more than enough to protect us.

Darton came up behind me and wrapped his arms over mine. He leaned his head against my shoulder.

"You saved me again."

"I do seem to make a habit of it."

I was starting to relax back into him, allowing myself at least one minute to revel in our temporary reprieve before I considered the dangers still ahead of us, when Izzy flinched.

"There's one coming," she said. I followed her gaze. A gloom was rippling along the shadow of the farm's outer fence.

And Izzy had still been able to see it.

I stiffened in Darton's embrace. "What's wrong?" he said quietly.

"She shouldn't be able to see the dark vermin at all now. Not without the extra power the mercenary was sending them." Was it just taking more time than I'd expected for his energy to fade? Or was something more going on? The dark fae's last words, calling out to his master, rang through my head, and my stomach twisted.

He'd sensed her and her desires from across the ocean. There was no reason to assume that was a fluke.

"The Darkest One has been regaining some of *her* power," I said. "More than I realized. If she's getting stronger, all the dark creatures will too."

If she got strong enough, my binding might not be enough to hold her.

"Hey." Darton pulled me closer against him. "We'll get through it. No matter what happens. We've got this."

His touch and his words sent a shiver of memory

through me—an echo of my king's voice as he'd stood before those crowds of lords and peasants alike and addressed them with one of his stirring speeches. The confidence that had come so naturally to him mingled with the strength of Darton's arms around me now. A lump rose in my throat. I tipped my head back against my king, my best friend, my sometimes lover, and opened myself to the sensation rising inside me.

For the first time in a long while, despite the peril I suspected lay ahead of us, I felt a spark of true hope.

ABOUT THE AUTHOR

Eva Chase lives in Canada with her family. She loves stories both swoony and supernatural, and strong women and the men who appreciate them. Along with the Legends Reborn series, she is also the author of the Demons of Fame paranormal romance series, beginning with *Caught in the Glow*. You can visit her online at **www.evachase.com**.